KILLER MATERIAL

KILLER MATERIAL

DAN BARTON

THOMAS DUNNE BOOKS
ST. MARTIN'S MINOTAUR
NEW YORK

THOMAS DUNNE BOOKS
An imprint of St. Martin's Press

Design by Heidi N. R. Eriksen

Library of Congress Cataloging-in-Publication Data

Barton, Dan.
    Killer material / Dan Barton.—1st ed.
        p. cm.
    ISBN: 0-312-25222-6
    1. Comedians—Fiction. I. Title.

PS3552.A76785 K55 2000
813'.6—dc21

                                                        99-462114

First Edition: April 2000

10 9 8 7 6 5 4 3 2 1

To Sam Kinison
for promises kept

Acknowledgments

I'd like to mention the names of some folks directly involved with the publication of this manuscript.

This book was something of a family affair, so thanks to Mom, Dad, Ted, and Jean. Copyediting, proofreading, and related research was done by my father, and I used a great many of his suggestions. Dad, you're hired for the next book.

Edward Zarcoff proofread the final manuscript. He also got me a job at E! Entertainment Television, and there I've found a home and friends for many years.

Darryl Wimberly is a talented novelist, screenwriter, teacher, and loyal friend who stepped in where others had failed and helped me run this one all the way to home plate.

Ruth Cavin, senior editor at St. Martin's Press, bought this manuscript after Darryl Wimberly handed it to her. Her pointed, incisive, and rather funny comments shaped this book into final form and steered me clear of many clichés.

Robert Youdelman is the attorney who helped me negotiate the contract, as I was agentless at the time. I hadn't sold a book in ten years, so he gave me much valuable counsel in closing this deal, and then he got me an agent.

Matt Bialer of the William Morris Agency read this manuscript and signed me up for this book and many others to come. Matt, here's to the future.

Also special thanks to Mitzi Shore of the Comedy Story and Kim Lemore of the Comedy Clinic at the Ice House Annex for keeping me in spots while I wrote this.

Lisa Bradley, thank you for convincing me to pick up this story again and finish it after I'd let it lie fallow. You were there to read every draft over the last ten years and hand it back to me when it wasn't done yet, and when I got the green light from you I knew I had something. You're a woman worth writing a book for.

KILLER MATERIAL

PROLOGUE

This is the place.

Southern California.

Over ten million people live, work, eat, and sleep here.

They grow up, drive cars, get married, raise families, and try to live together. Often they get hurt or hurt each other. Sometimes real bad.

When they need a laugh, they come to me.

My name's Kincaid.

I'm a comedian.

I carry a microphone.

ONE

The police would tell me a few days later that when Art Westcott called me that Saturday midafternoon he had a gun to his head the entire time we talked. He looked up my number, dialed, and spoke to me for two minutes and twenty-three seconds with a .357 Magnum pressed against his left temple. I think about that when I remember answering the phone like a smartass.

"Biff Kincaid," I said, "the comedian that has no Wizard of Oz bit."

"Kincaid, it's Art Westcott."

Art was a tall, weedy character, with a balding Afro and over-sized glasses over a bushy mustache. He slumped around looking like a depressed college professor and was prone to irrational fits of gloom. This wasn't unusual for a stand-up comedian. We're kind of a moody bunch.

"Art!" I said. I knew him from the Comedy Store and a few road gigs. We talked when we ran into each other, always promising a social call but never making it. Maybe this was it. "How are you doing?"

"I'm good," he said, with a gun to his head I couldn't see. "I'm fine. I was wondering if you would do me a favor."

"What is it?" I asked. I never say yes to a favor until I know what it is.

"I need someone to fill in for me tonight down at Chortles' Comedy Club," he said. "You know it?"

"I've been in the place but I've never played there," I said. "Chortles in Hartford Beach, right?"

Hartford Beach is a seaside community only about an hour south of LA in Orange County. Chortles seats close to five hundred people, a good room with a new sound system, but run like a strip club: Push the drinks and fuck the entertainment.

"Right. Richard Moftus is the owner," he said. "He books it himself."

"I think I went down to introduce myself once," I said. "Handed Moftus a tape. Never heard from him."

"Here's your chance to get in good with him then," Art said. "Unless you're busy."

"I'm clear until midnight," I said. "Then I've got a spot at the Comedy Store."

"Good," Art said. "So would you mind calling Richard and telling him we talked this over and you'd be glad to fill in for me?"

"You haven't called him?"

"No."

"You sure you want *me* to tell him?" Bookers hated same-day substitutions almost as much as they hated out-and-out cancellations, and this was a Saturday night show. The comedy grapevine said Richard Moftus was something of a hard case. Not that I minded. Same grapevine said the same thing about me.

"I'm sure," Art said. "You're my first choice."

Art was a very good comedian. He stood in the middle of the stage like a sad sack and barely moved, muttering one line after another into the mike about what miserable luck he had in life

4

and reducing the crowd to hysterics. I went after a crowd with a knife and stone ax. Art made them come to him.

"You have a number for Moftus?" I asked.

"Right here," Art said. "It's area code seven-one-four . . ."

I wrote it down. "You want me to tell him why you're canceling?"

"Something's come up."

"Something personal?"

"You could say that," he said. He was speaking in an odd monotone. Later I realized he must have been trying to signal me. It's a technique POWs used when making forced confessions on tape. "I have to go now, Biff."

"Everything okay, Art?"

There was the briefest of pauses. Perhaps the gun muzzle was dug a little harder into his skull and he had to keep from crying out. "Yeah," he said. "Good luck tonight."

"You, too," I said.

"I always thought you were funny, Kincaid," he said as a permanent farewell, and then there was a click and I was listening to a dial tone.

That was how it all started. I looked back once or twice to that short conversation and wondered if there was anything in our brief talk to indicate what was to follow. I decided, in the aftermath, that there wasn't.

The cops told me that as soon as Art hung up on me the gunman holding him hostage pulled the trigger and Art's head exploded across the phone like a ripe pumpkin.

His body was found with the receiver still in his hand and what was left of his head resting on the cradle of the phone. He knew he was going to die the entire time he was talking to me. He bargained with his executioner for one last phone call so he wouldn't be a no-show at Chortles that night and people would start asking questions.

Once I realized the awful logic that must have led to our last conversation, I used to wonder why Art had chosen to call me and only me. After it was all over, I realized it was because he knew what I would find that night down at Chortles. And out of all the people he could think of in the last minutes of his life, I'd be the one to do something about it without getting myself killed.

Revenge. That's the favor Art was really asking me for, as one comedian to another. He wanted me to find the person who did him in and take them out.

TWO

My next call was to Richard Moftus and I wasn't looking forward to it. He wouldn't like a same-day sub on a Saturday night bill. I checked a paper. Art had been booked Thursday through Saturday. He'd done two shows and was bailing tonight. Uh-oh.

I dialed. A woman's voice answered. "Chortles Comedy Club."

"Richard Moftus, please."

"May I ask what this is regarding?"

"Tonight's show."

"Did you need reservations?" she asked. "Because I can take those for you."

"No," I said. "I'm a comedian. I just heard from Art Westcott. He's canceling. He wants me to fill in for him."

"He's . . . canceling?"

Oh boy, here we go. "That's right," I said.

"Why didn't he call me?"

"He said I should call Richard Moftus," I said.

"Well, who are you?" she demanded.

"Biff Kincaid," I said. "Art called me just—"

"This is ridiculous," she interrupted. "This is unprofessional. If Art . . . Richard's not . . ." She blew out an exasperated sigh. "Hold *on.*"

She put down the phone. I heard her calling "Richard!" as she walked away to go find him. If there's one thing I know how to do, it's make a good first impression with the ladies.

I listened through the phone as a door opened and closed. I heard the woman's voice go up in pitch as well as volume and a low male rumble respond. Steps coming back to the phone.

She picked it up again. "Richard will be right here," she said, exasperated. "Are you still there?"

"Still here." And as popular as ever.

"I can't believe Art canceled," she said. "We're sold out tonight."

"That's good."

"What's your name again?"

"Biff Kincaid," I said.

"And you're a comedian?"

"Yes."

"You ever play here before?"

"At Chortles? No."

"You realize that Art was headlining tonight?"

"I sure do," I said. "That's why he called me. He wanted another headliner."

"Art's funny," she said. "People asked to have him back here."

"Art is very funny," I said. She was upset. I was letting her talk it out. No reason to panic, ma'am. Help's on the way. "I'm not surprised he's made a few fans."

"What about you?" she said. "Are you funny?"

"I'm hilarious," I said. "Ask Art."

"Well, you'd better—here's Richard."

There were some clicking noises as the call was transferred, and then Richard Moftus picked up the line.

"What the hell is this about a comic canceling on me?" *Comic* came out *kawmik*. Richard Moftus's accent had taken the plane in from Brooklyn.

"My name is Biff Kincaid," I said. "Art Westcott asked me to call you and let you know he can't make it tonight. I—"

"No one goddamn cancels on me the same day!" Moftus roared into the phone. I had to hold it away from my head. "No one! You hear me!?"

"I hear you." Marlee Matlin could hear you, buddy.

"Son of a bitch! Kelly! Art Westcott is canceling and this cocktwister says he's supposed to fill in for him."

I heard Kelly's voice respond in dismay. She was the woman who had answered the phone.

"I don't mean to throw your world into chaos," I said. "I'm just doing what Art asked me to do."

"Where the hell is he?"

"I don't know," I said.

"He give you a reason?" Moftus asked. "Not that there's one good enough."

"He said it was something personal."

"Personal, huh? Hope it was personal enough to never play my club again."

"I know you're disappointed," I said. "Kelly told me the club was sold out tonight and Art's a really funny comedian."

"I already know *Art's* funny," Moftus said. "Right now I want to know if *you're* funny."

A mental picture came back to me of the man I was talking to. Moftus was about five feet eight inches tall and heavy to just short of fat. He had thick forearms like Popeye, bushy hair all over his body except on the top of his head, which was as clean

9

as a Colombian landing strip. He had small, piggy eyes and liver-colored lips. He looked like he was made of roast beef sandwiches. And he tawked like dis all da toim.

Me, I'm six feet tall. I don't carry any excess weight. I'm an Irish mutt, so I have a head full of light red hair, freckles, and blue eyes. I do a bit in my act: "I don't tan, I cancer." I'm thirty-three but there's a gym five blocks from my front door and I go there every day. I have to. I like Guinness too much. I am square of jaw but stout of heart. I've got a few dings here and there from some road gigs that got rough. I don't start any trouble, but I don't walk away from it either.

"I'm funny or we wouldn't be talking," I said. "Art called me for a reason."

"Son of a *bitch!*" Moftus yelled into the phone again. "That bastard Art ain't ever playing my club again!"

"So it's five o'clock now," I continued. "Any comic you call in LA has to drive all the way down to Hartford Beach in Orange County to make show time—which is what? Eight? Eighty-thirty?"

"Eight-thirty," Moftus said. He wasn't yelling any longer. He was just fuming.

"Eight-thirty," I said. "Okay, opener does fifteen minutes, the middle thirty, I have to be onstage by nine-fifteen. If you want me there by show time so you don't have any worries, I have to leave within the hour. I'm all set. You either want me or you don't. So let's close this deal or clear the line. I've got teeth to floss."

Moftus chewed on that like a piece of beef jerky still in the wrapper. I think he was used to a little more cowering from a new comedian.

Silence for a full sixty seconds. "Like I said," he began, enunciating his words as though it hurt him to talk, "show starts at eight-thirty. Be there fifteen minutes before show time.

Headliner does forty-five minutes by my watch or he gets middle money. Be a good boy and you get two crispy new Franklins, two free drinks at the bar. Half price on food. You fool around with any of the waitresses, I don't want to hear about it."

"Who else is on the bill?"

"Middle's Kelly Malone."

"Male Kelly or female Kelly?"

"Definitely a female," Moftus said. "She answers the phone here. You talked to her before you talked to me."

"And the opener?"

"Guy's name is Ned Lando. First time here."

"I never heard of him."

"Feeling's mutual, I'm sure," Moftus said. "I'll kill that Art."

"See you tonight."

We hung up.

THREE

I live in the Hollywood Hills, in Beachwood Canyon, below the Hollywood sign. I live on Beachwood Plaza, a little side street that ends in a cul-de-sac. Home when I'm not on the road is an upper two-bedroom apartment at the end of it. There're only a dozen units in my complex, and my place is set back against a clutch of trees and hillside.

I like where I live. It's an oasis in the middle of a big sprawling city that's gotten too big and too mean for anyone's good. I don't hear too many cars at night and no gunshots. There's a market up the hill where I can write a check, and they don't ask for my driver's license because they know my face. I'm going to hang here in the canyon until I make it big. Who knows? Someday I might move into Madonna's house. After I repaint it.

The sun was hanging low in the sky and shadows were slanting across the canyon as I warmed up my Mazda RX-7 and eased out into evening traffic. I quickly left the solace of my canyon estuary and threaded my way onto the 101, heading south at less than thirty miles an hour, then twenty, then ten. That was LA:

People spend their life savings on a car that can go from zero to sixty in less time than it takes to juice an orange so they can sit completely still.

I got there by seven forty-five. Chortles Comedy Club was set inside a minimall along with an Indian restaurant and a video store. Above the entrance was a cartoon caricature outline of a fat man holding a cigar for signage. The cigar smoke spelled out the word CHORTLES, which was also outlined in neon. I think the fat cartoon guy was supposed to be Richard Moftus. That was club owner ego, making yourself into an icon of entertainment. When Hartford Beach thinks comedy, they think Richard Moftus.

I parked in the mostly empty lot and walked inside to find the club devoid of customers. There were two bartenders and half a dozen waitresses. The club was arming itself against the coming crowd. Saturday night. Most comedy clubs made all their money on the weekends. People didn't have to get up and go to work the next day. They wanted to laugh.

I'd been in Chortles only once before. I'd never set foot on its stage, but the quickening pace of the waitresses, the crunch of ice being shoveled into a cooler behind the bar, the empty stool and cold mike onstage in front of a worn, gold curtain, the candles being set out on the tables were all familiar roadmarks to me. I inhaled the residual odors of spilled drinks and sweaty applause. Home.

The wait and bar staff were culled from the local talent pool: much blonde hair, a lot of tan skin carefully unconcealed; all fine examples of Southern California golden youth.

A stunning beauty with teased, sun-streaked hair and bee-stung lips who was far too young for me to do much more than smile at saw me standing in her section. I wondered if this was Kelly but her name tag read BRENDA. "Can I help you?" she asked, in a completely unfriendly tone.

14

"I'm a comic," I said.

Oh, that improved her opinion of me. Her azure eyes did not melt into foam and pulse like the surf at the sound of my glorious occupation. Instead, all power went to the front shields. She took a polite step backward. "Does Richard know you're here?"

"Not yet."

She pointed. "Go up onstage, through the curtain to your left, and through the green room. His office is to the left."

"Thanks," I said to her turning back.

I went up onstage, under the lights. I turned and looked out at the empty club. I could see people were starting to show up outside in twos and fours to claim their tickets before going and grabbing a quick bite somewhere. A line was beginning to form. It was going to be a good night. I'd go up here for forty-five minutes and then hit the Store for a fifteen-minute set. Ba-da-bing, ba-da-bang, ba-da-boom.

I turned left and went into the green room, which was made up of mismatched carpeting and two sagging sofas that had started to sprout gray tape along the seams. None of it was green. There was a rickety wooden table that sported a couple of drink rings as deep and dark as black eyes on a late-show heckler. We comedians are rough on stationary objects. A window unit air conditioner over the rear exit was turned off. Dust had settled onto the vents.

I left the green room via a door that wouldn't quite close all the way, its lock disabled long ago in the aftermath of a bad show. I hung a left and followed the breathing sounds of Richard Moftus.

I knocked lightly on his plywood door and it swung open on the force of my upper knuckles alone. Moftus was sitting on a small wooden stool. His office held a desk that must have been picked up curbside, with drawers sprung open like misshapen teeth. As I watched, he reached up to get a Magic Marker and began to squeak it across his desk calendar, drawing a thick smelly black line through a weekend.

"No, no, no," he said into the phone buried into one fleshy side of his neck. "I don't care how many *Tonight Show*s that cocktwister's done, I ain't letting him headline for no three grand." Moftus turned on his swivel chair and saw me, motioning me inside with a single gesture.

I took another step forward and looked around. There was no place to sit. I stood on some carpet that was suffering serious nap loss.

"Well, fuck him then," Moftus was saying. He had a way of giving his words a menacing spin without raising his voice. "He don't have to play my club. I pay headliners two hundred a show. I don't do special events. What do you think this is—the Ice House? Yeah, yeah. Get back to me and get back in line. But only if he says yes to the money. Far as I'm concerned, he just canceled."

He hung up. He turned to me, jamming the wet chewed end of a stogie back in his maw. "You Kincaid?" he asked, looking me over with his piggy eyes. He was wearing a brown shaded toupee, one that had been hurriedly parked on top of his head. It looked about as natural as a stone garden frog.

"That's me," I said.

"Ah, you're not just on time, you're early. I like that in a headliner." He reached up into one of the mail slots and pulled out a W-9. "Here. Fill this out." He handed me the tax form and tossed me a leaky pen.

I found an uncluttered corner of the desk, bent at the waist, and began to scribble my name and address. Moftus pulled out a box of kitchen matches from a drawer, the kind I used to light the broiler on my stove. He struck two together and put the flame to the end of his cigar, puffing out clouds of blue noxious smoke.

Perhaps this was an incentive to get me to write faster. It was working.

"You get a hold of Art?" I asked.

"I called his number and no answer." Moftus snorted. He sounded like a bull getting ready to mate. "I'm through with him."

I didn't say anything. I concentrated on writing. The cigar smoke was starting to make me feel as if I was standing next to a waste incinerator.

"Don't tell no one," he mumbled when I handed the W-9 back to him.

"Don't tell anyone what?"

He pulled out his cigar. "That I smoked in my own club. Can you believe that? I can't frigging smoke in my own goddamned club anymore."

"Politicians."

"Maybe there's a bit in there somewhere, about how you can't smoke anything anywhere no more."

"I'll get on it right away."

Another reach into another drawer, this time to get a roll of purple movie tickets. He tore two off and initialed each on the back. "Here. The bartenders don't accept these until after the show."

"I don't drink until after the show," I said, taking the tickets.

"Not in my club you don't."

I let it pass. Somewhere down the line, another act must have gone onstage at Chortles shit-faced and walked the crowd. Some guys you tell not to do something and they go ahead and do it just to prove that while you were talking they weren't listening.

The phone rang and he answered it. "Moftus." Pause. "Oh, yeah? Well, you tell that butt-humper there ain't no way in Hell's waiting room that I'm gonna let him . . ."

He was done with me. I retreated into the green room. As I walked in I saw it was no longer deserted. It was inhabited by a lovely redheaded young lady, who had her topless bare back to me. She was wearing a short black skirt, ribbed black tights, and—as far as I could tell—nothing else from the waist up. She had a mane of wavy copper curls cascading down over her shoulders and across the muscles of her back.

"Excuse me," I said, stepping back.

"Oh, hello." She turned around. She was wearing *something* above the waist, a white halter top that skimmed the sides of her breasts so close it exposed curves both smooth and soft. The top was cut like a tuxedo shirt, with a crisp white pointed collar, a bow tie, and small black buttons down the front. Lying on one of the sofas was a smartly styled black jacket. She picked it up and put it on. The curves went out of sight. "You one of the other comedians?"

"Biff Kincaid," I said. "I'm headlining."

"Kelly Malone," she said, extending a hand. "I'm not."

Her hand was warm and soft and smooth and ringless, her nails painted a deep, blood red. She looked like a cross between a magician's assistant and a vampire. Youch.

"Did I talk to you on the phone earlier?" I asked.

She nodded. "I'm the day manager," she said. "What happened to Art?"

"I don't know," I said. "He called me to say something came up."

Kelly winced. "Hope it was important," she said. "Richard hates it when comics do that. No wonder he's in such a bad mood."

"He ever in a good one?"

"When he sells so much booze they run out behind the bar, he is," she said. "Then he gets pissed off if the liquor stores are closed and he can't buy any more to sell."

18

"You're the middle act," I asked, "right?"

Comedy shows are broken up into three standard sets, one for each performer: the opener—who usually emcees the rest of the show—does fifteen minutes, the middle act does half an hour, and the headliner does forty-five minutes. I was the headliner, and I wanted to make sure everyone stuck to their time and didn't go over because I had another spot to make.

"Actually, I prefer the term 'feature entertainer.' "

"That's more politically correct?"

"Yes." She had a quick wit about her. "That or 'comedic American.' "

"I see." I hadn't thought of any really snappy comebacks yet, but give me a minute. Cute I can handle. Funny is also nice. Cute and funny . . . that's kind of the Biff Kincaid combo plate. I was looking at a major distraction here. I was known for my distractions. "Have you seen our opener yet?"

"I don't like the term 'opener,' " Kelly said.

"What do you prefer?"

"Initial humorist."

"That sounds good."

"I haven't seen him yet."

"I wanted to give him my prefatory remarks."

"Your what?"

"My intro."

The intro is what the emcee says about you before he or she brings you on. It usually consists of a listing of TV credits. By calling them "prefatory remarks," I had taken Kelly's own bit and turned it back on her. She liked that. It made her smile.

"Ohhhh . . . ," she said. "And what would your intro be?"

"Some TV shows, some opening gigs, some clubs."

"Sounds impressive."

"If he says it right."

"Have you heard of him before?" Kelly asked. "Our initial humorist?"

"Ned Lando? No. You?"

"No. Must be new."

"If he's opening," I said, "he's new."

"Wasn't too long ago I was opening," Kelly said, tilting her head to peek out at the show curtain. Through it we could hear the sounds of house music, glasses clinking, the chatter of conversation as tables were being seated. "Right on this very stage."

"You local?"

She turned back to me with a quarter smile. "I was born two miles away. I'm as local as they come," she said. "I used to be out there right now"—she nodded toward the showroom—"pushing drinks and shaking my ass for tips."

"You were a waitress?"

She nodded. "That's how I got my start after I'd left my other job last year. I listened to the acts, decided I could do what they do. Then I went to Richard and persuaded him to start an open-mike night here. Then I talked him into making me an emcee. From there I went to opener and started hitting the coffeehouses around here and the clubs in San Diego. Then I finally got my first middle gig. Know when that was?"

"When?"

She struck a pose, cocking one leg and putting her hands on her hips. She was a sexy thing; I'd give her that. She knew it, too. "You're looking at it, baby!"

"Congratulations."

"Thaaaaaaaank you." She turned and peered once again at the show curtain. The crowd noise had risen considerably while we were talking.

"Nervous?" I asked.

"Like a cat in heat."

"Are cats in heat nervous?"

20

"Around a bunch of dogs they are."

"Well, don't rush it," I said. "When you get out there, take your time."

She immediately turned and looked at me. She was looking for advice. I had her full attention. "What else?"

"Nothing else. That's mainly it. Don't rush it. You've got a half hour up there. Open with your second strongest bit. Close with your strongest. Listen to the opener. He might mine the crowd for where-are-you-from, what-do-you-do-for-a-living? Use that. You're local. Does this place draw a lot of locals?"

"Oh, yeah. I used to see their drivers' licenses."

"Use that to your advantage. Do some local stuff."

"Well, if all else fails I can always table dance." "I'm going to say hi to the waitresses and get a drink," she said, and left the green room.

"See you soon," I said to where she'd been standing.

I didn't think about anything else for a while except her: Kelly Malone.

What I'd just met was love, love with capital L, nice legs and red hair. What I didn't know was that in another few minutes, I was going to meet trouble, trouble with a capital T and a tape recorder.

FOUR

I stayed in the green room making friends with the sofa when the curtain parted and in stepped a tall, lanky dude wearing worn jeans and a comedy club T-shirt. Johnny's Comedy Barn in Sacramento. I could have had the same T-shirt, but there are some gigs even I won't play. He had a thin, pinched face and sallow skin, set off by his dishwater brown hair and sharp nose. His eyes were small and slightly slanted, his shoulders stooped, and the thinness of his upper body belied a growing paunch around the waistline. He was an old man at twenty-five.

"Hi," I said.

"Hi."

His voice was a dry mutter. He barely looked at me.

"Are you Ned?"

"Yeah."

"I'm Biff."

I made a show of extending my hand as I stood up. He clasped it briefly and let it go, as if he was moving along a row of hands and testing each one for poultry disease. "Hi."

"Kelly Malone was just here, but she should be back soon."

"Okay."

"You want my intro?"

"Sure."

"Evening at the Improv, Comedy Central, regular at the Comedy Store . . ."

He was looking around the green room, paying attention to everything except what I was saying.

"Got that?" I asked.

"Sure."

"And then what happened?"

"Huh?"

That got his attention, briefly. The old non sequitur callback. Gets 'em every time.

"Something on your mind?" I asked.

"Uh . . ." He did some more looking around the green room.

"What are you looking for?" I asked.

"Nothing," he said. His eyes settled on me, but not for long. They were quick and nervous with large pupils. "How long you going to do?"

"Close to an hour."

His head snapped back toward me. "What?"

"I said, I'm doing close to an hour. Forty-five at least. That's what Moftus wants. He says I do less than that by his watch I get middle money."

"You're *headlining?*" His voice rose to an irritated honk.

"That's what they call it when you close the show."

"Where's Art?"

"Art Westcott? He canceled."

"Why?"

"I don't know," I said. "He called and told me something came up."

"So you spoke to him?"

24

"Yes."

"Anyone else talk to him?"

"Not here."

"Moftus, Kelly . . . ?"

"No," I said. "I had to call them and tell him he wasn't coming."

"When was this?"

"About four-thirty this afternoon."

"Where did he call you from?"

"I don't know."

Ned Lando was staring at me, firing questions like it was the end of an episode of *Perry Mason.*

"I feel like I'm on *Perry Mason,*" I said.

"Who's Perry Mason?"

Kids these days. They don't even have the sense it takes to watch good reruns.

"He's a lawyer on TV," I said. "I don't know why Art canceled exactly—or why you're so interested."

He wasn't going to answer me. The news about Art didn't seem to make him happy. He didn't look like he'd been made happy too many times since he'd gotten that face.

"So," I said, trying to change the subject, "you work the road, huh?"

"What makes you say that?"

I nodded at his chest. "The T-shirt."

He looked down. "Oh"—he looked around—"yeah."

"You work in town?"

"Some."

"Where?" I asked. "The Store? The Improv?"

"I gotta change," he said. "Clothes."

He left.

I didn't tell him that the green room was where you usually *did* change clothes.

I was spending more quality time with my old friend the sofa when Kelly Malone returned carrying a glass of red wine in both hands. A drop had escaped over the side and she scooped it up with her finger, bringing it to her mouth to taste. Steady.

"Have you met Ned Lando yet?" I asked.

"Is he that guy wandering around who looks like he's getting ready to take a shot at the president?" Kelly asked.

"That's him," I said. "When I told him I was filling in for Art Westcott he started drilling me with questions. He seemed to be surprised Art had canceled."

She shrugged and sipped her wine. "Maybe he was surprised."

"But why should he care?"

Another shrug. Kelly looked at her watch. It was getting close to show time. She started getting nervous again.

"You give Ned your intro yet?" I asked.

"No." The intrigue of why Art had canceled had only temporarily distracted her from the anxiety of doing her first middle gig. "He was looking for Pluto."

"Who's . . . did you say 'Pluto?' "

Kelly nodded. "The sound guy."

"Why is he called Pluto?"

" 'Cause he acts like that's where his mind is. On Pluto."

At that moment, Ned Lando stepped back into the green room via the stage entrance. He had changed clothes—sort of. He was wearing a different comedy club T-shirt. This one was for Chortles. Might as well advertise the club you're working.

"Hello there," I said. "Now we're all one big happy family."

"I'm Kelly," Kelly said.

Ned liked her a lot better than he liked me. Most guys would. That didn't make his handshake any slower. "Hi."

"How's the crowd?" she asked.

"Good."

"You find Pluto?" Kelly asked.

"Yeah."

I hoped he proved to be more talkative when he got onstage, Otherwise, we were in trouble.

Richard Moftus kicked open the door to the green room. He had to walk through it sideways. "You grunts ready to start being funny?"

"Absolutely," I said. "I got another spot tonight."

"Where?" Kelly asked, instantly curious.

"Comedy Store."

Her eyebrows lifted. She was impressed. Good.

"Then let's go," Moftus said. He jerked his head at Ned. "It's show time."

The Saturday night show kicked into gear with an offstage intro Richard Moftus had on tape. "Hi. This is Richard Moftus. And welcome to Chortles, Orange County's premiere comedy club . . ." He sounded cute and cuddly, totally unlike the ham-fisted tightwad I'd been dealing with backstage. Maybe there was another side to him I hadn't seen yet.

The crowd's noise simmered down to a respectful murmur as the house lights dimmed and the spotlight shone during the intro, which wrapped up with Moftus saying: ". . . And now, it's show time! Please welcome your master of ceremonies, Ned Lando!"

So he taped it special for every show.

Ned stepped out of the green room as soon as the customary applause started, onto the narrow backstage area and then into the spotlight, vanishing from my sight, awash in audience affection. "Hey, how are you folks doing tonight?" I heard him ask.

Moftus, satisfied, went around front to make sure the bar was selling enough booze. At a ten-dollars-a-head cover charge plus a two-drink minimum, Chortles' three-hundred-plus seats could gross him well over five grand tonight.

Kelly nervously fished her notes out from her thimble-sized purse and went out into the showroom. I was left alone once again.

I cocked an ear toward the stage. Ned was starting his act. He was getting some laughs. Nothing too outrageous. I couldn't hear what he was saying, but he seemed to be doing okay.

I listened more closely, trying to pick out the words.

Wait a minute . . .

Lando was in the middle of a bit, a series of one-liners about the difference between mothers and fathers—specifically, what you do on Mother's Day as opposed to what you do on Father's Day. "On Mother's Day, you stop by the flower shop and get *her* a bouquet. On Father's Day, you stop by the auto shop and get *him* a pair of pliers. Here, Dad."

It was an amusing bit and went on from there, making different contrasts and comparisons.

There was just one problem.

It wasn't his.

It belonged to a comedian named Freddy Tremaine. He was out of Boston. I'd worked with him for a week going from town to town in the Dakotas, both North and South. Every night we'd done a show, he did that bit.

I quickly left the green room and walked around the club to the showroom. I found an empty piece of wall and leaned against it, arms folded, watching.

Lando was up onstage, under the spotlight. He looked a little green around the horns. He wasn't quite used to being the center of attention. There were some earmarks of the amateur I spotted right away. The T-shirt and blue jeans outfit wasn't working. (Not a good idea to underdress your audience.) He looked slightly unconfident, as though he wasn't sure he deserved to be there. He hadn't gotten his stage legs yet.

"Hey, you notice how men and women get ready to go out completely differently?" he said to no one in particular. He'd made no effort to transition between the two bits. It was just turn right, turn left. "Men can get up from a nap and they're like"—he stretched and yawned—"I'm ready."

Laugh.

"Women are like . . ." He posed in front of an imaginary mirror, holding invisible lipstick in hand. "What's your rush? We're only two hours late!" He spoke in an exaggerated lisp. I never understood guys who, when they imitated women, sounded like effeminate men.

That wasn't his bit either. It belonged to Jeff Stella, a comedian out of Georgia. I'd worked with him in Atlanta a few times at the Joke Depot. It wasn't that great a bit when Lando did it, but the way Stella performed it—with his long, lanky frame and a thick southern accent—it brought down the house, even though the wording was the same. It was his—Stella's—and his alone. It wasn't Ned Lando's. Lando had either heard it and stolen it or heard someone else do it and stolen it from them.

Lando let the laughter and applause die down and then he went into a third bit. It was related to the previous bit about the differences between men and women getting ready to go out, but the jump was made too quickly, with no conversational tone. It was as though he was reading from cue cards.

"Hey, this ever happen to you? You're out on a date and you run into someone you used to go out with? And the new woman wants to know who the other woman was? And you have to explain?"

I didn't need to hear the follow-up lines. I knew them. That's because they would have been done—should have been done—by the headliner I was replacing: Art Westcott. It was his bit.

Ned Lando was a thief.

Maybe that was why Art had canceled. Maybe that was why I was here.

As soon as I stepped onstage, Ned Lando would be in the back, watching, listening, and taking notes.

And I was going to have to stop him.

FIVE

As I watched Ned Lando go through his litany of stolen material, I felt a warm body at my side. I looked over and saw Kelly Malone.

"How's he doing?" she asked.

"He's a lifter," I said.

"What?"

She was too new to the game to know what I was talking about. "He's a light-fingers. A thief. A taker. He steals material from other comedians and puts it in his own act." I lifted my chin toward the stage. "At least that's what he's done with his last three bits. I can tell you who wrote and performed them when I saw them first. I can give you their names." I cocked my head and listened some more. "This one I don't know."

Kelly looked at the stage and watched Ned for a full minute, then looked back at me. "Are you sure?"

I nodded. "Positive. Listen to him. That's not his act. These are all separate bits he's culled from other comedians. The connections are awkward. There're no segues. He has no point of view. No ad-libs. He's just working his way from punch line to punch line." I turned to her. "What's your act like? A lot of stuff about being a woman?"

"Yeah, mostly," she said. "That's who I go for, the women in the crowd."

"Good. Then maybe he won't steal from you."

She looked back at the stage as though she was being shown a new species of snake in order to watch it feed. "You think he's here to do that?"

"Sounds like he's been doing that on a lot of his other gigs," I said. "Maybe that's why Art Westcott didn't want to work the same bill with him."

We were talking while leaning against the wall, in whispers, mouth to ear, waiting out the laughs, which were mild but steady. The inchoate assemblage of material wasn't allowing Lando to build any momentum, though. As a result, his setups were quiet, the people watching and waiting to see where he was going to go next. He was going through a preplanned act, and they could tell. Comedy was all about when you lost that layer of presentation, when the crowd suspended their disbelief and it seemed as though you were making it all up for them, right then and there, on the spot. *Well*, I thought, *wait until I get onstage, ladies and gentlemen. Then you'll see how we do it in Hollywood.*

"Then what about you?" Kelly asked. "Aren't you worried he'll steal from you?"

I turned my head from watching Ned Lando and looked at her. It was a look I'd seen Clint Eastwood first give in *A Fistful of Dollars*. There are other people who had seen that look. They don't like to talk about it much.

I said, "I'm not the one who needs to worry."

"I see."

I looked at my watch. "You'd better get ready," I said. "He's almost done."

"Okay," she said. She had her hands clenched in front of her as if in prayer. Nuns didn't normally wear tight, tuxedo-style halter tops and miniskirts with black tights, but if they did I might have gone to church more. "I'm really nervous."

"That's good," I said. "It focuses you."

"Do you get nervous? Still?"

"No."

"I didn't think so."

"Knock 'em dead, Kelly."

She left. I watched her go. She had her head bowed as she rounded the corner out of the showroom to get ready backstage. I imagined she was going to take one last look at her notes. She was going to do fine. It was the overly cocky newcomers who screwed up. I ought to know. I'd been one of them. Certain crowds can be very humbling. Half an hour of stony silence straightened me right out.

I waited out in the showroom while Ned Lando finished his act. I wasn't going to confront him just yet. I'd wait until after the show. I didn't mind if he liked my act, as long as he didn't help himself to any of it. That point was best made after a show. I'd dealt with thieves before. They only understood one thing: fear. Well, that could be supplied.

I watched him wrap it up with a closer he'd stolen from Miami John, a comic from Florida I'd done a couple of cruises with. It was a shlocky routine about going to the dentist. John didn't use it as his closer though. It was more of a middle bit. Miami John used a lot of different character voices to punch it up so it was a lot funnier. Lando didn't have the vocal dexterity to pull it off, so it just kind of lay there.

"Okay," Lando said, when he was done. "So that's my part of the show. Thank you very much."

There was a moderate amount of applause as he put the mike back in the stand. The ice hadn't really been broken with this audience yet. They were still a bunch of different tables. They hadn't been made a *crowd.*

"Our next comedian—hey, when's the last time you saw a girl comic?" Lando said. He shielded his eyes from the lights and scanned the crowd. "Are you ready for a girl? She's a cute girl, that's for sure."

Oh, brother.

"There're a lot of cute ladies here tonight," Lando said. His voice had gotten whiny. There wasn't much inflection to it. "Maybe I'll get lucky later."

No one was laughing. He was just making people uncomfortable.

He dropped his hand from his eyes. "But you're all about to get lucky right now," he said. "She used to work here at Chortles as a waitress—that's how she got her start, but don't worry, you don't need to tip her—so please welcome the very beautiful Kelly Malone."

He stepped away from the mike, clapping. Kelly stepped out. All of her nervousness was gone. She had a shy little smile on her face and a twinkle in her eye. She brushed past Ned and took several quick, dainty steps, bouncing up to the microphone like Bette Midler.

"Hi," she whispered breathily into the microphone, her hands behind her back.

"Hi," several members of the audience called back.

"I don't have much time," she said. "I have to get this outfit back to *The Price Is Right.* " Then she stepped back and posed in front of the curtain like a game show hostess, flashing a brilliant smile.

Laughs. In the middle of the bit she changed poses, like she was showing off a prize behind a curtain.

Some scattered applause and then she reached for the microphone and did a double take. "I'm sorry," she said, "I'm just not used to having something this big in front of my mouth."

She took the mike from the stand to more whoops than laughs. She hefted it in her hand. "Wow, still hard, and I've had it at least two minutes. That's a switch."

Predominately female laughter.

"Want to know how lousy my last boyfriend was at math? Two minutes meant 'all night long.' " Laughs. "I used to ask him, 'Do you think you could possibly have sex with me at least as long as it takes to toast a bagel?' " More female laughter. Women friends were looking at each other, men were looking at the women, amused smiles on their faces. "Not a *frozen* bagel either. Fully defrosted. Let's slice the bagel, put it in the toaster, have sex, and then see if the bagel's done. Is that too much to ask?"

She was off to a good start. I leaned back against the wall and watched her.

Halfway through her act I saw Ned Lando standing in the back of the room.

He was sidling up to a small cutout cubicle nestled in the far corner of the showroom on the other side of the bar. If you put a table there, you wouldn't be able to see the stage. You had to sit on a high stool to see over the bar.

Someone *was* sitting on a high stool, and he looked like he belonged there. He had longish, rock 'n' roll black hair that fell in greasy, thick clumps; a scraggly goatee; large, liquid brown eyes below a lot of forehead; and a slack, open mouth that pointed in whatever direction he was looking at. Occasionally he checked a set of twin bouncing levels of glowing green light bars that dipped and spiked along with Kelly's monologue.

Pluto. The sound guy.

Ned was standing next to him. They weren't speaking. They had already been introduced.

I remembered Ned was looking for Pluto before the show, but he'd had neither music or taped bits in his act. So why did Ned need to see Pluto?

Hmmm . . .

Ned didn't see me watching him. He had his arms folded, his pointy little face completely unsmiling as he locked his gaze onto Kelly, watching her every move. I couldn't tell if it was lust or larceny on his mind. Her material was solid. Was he looking for a bit he could take? One little morsel he could gender switch and use on the next gig? One thing I had learned from running across thieves over the years was that they were a greedy bunch.

As I was watching him, Ned checked his watch and said something to Pluto and Pluto nodded. Ned started to walk backstage.

I checked my timepiece. Kelly had five minutes to go.

Time for me to get ready.

I went to the green room backstage and Ned Lando was standing there. He noticed my entrance with all the interest of watching a toilet tank fill back up.

"I got your intro," he said. "Don't I?"

Which meant he didn't remember it.

"I gave it to you," I said. "You lose it somewhere?"

He didn't get it. He just looked at me. "What do you want me to say about you?" he asked. By intonation, the sentence going up at the end, he let me know that he knew he was asking me to repeat stuff.

"Comedy Central," I repeated. "Evening at the Improv. Regular at the Comedy Store—"

"Oh, yeah, yeah, yeah," Lando said, waving his hand at me.

I nodded toward the stage as I heard a surge of applause and cheers. "Is she getting offstage?"

Lando looked up and saw the curtains part as Kelly stepped through the back curtain. He bolted onstage to take the mike and Kelly stepped into the green room, flushed and happy.

"Well!" she said. "That . . . that was great!"

"Congratulations," I said. I slipped into my best Alec Guinness impression, quoting a line from *Star Wars*. "You've taken your first step toward a whole new world."

She bowed. "Thank you, Obi-Wan Kincaid."

I smiled. I was genuinely happy for her. She'd just middled for the first time. Taking the step from opener to middle is a big one, even bigger than from middle to headliner.

"Did you watch it?" she asked. She was flapping her jacket to cool off. When you step onstage you automatically start to sweat. Her top was clinging to her in certain places so stickily I could see through the fabric. I graciously maintained eye contact.

"Most of it," I said.

"And?" She took her jacket off and started to dab herself with cocktail napkins. Eye contact. Maintain eye contact.

"And you've got it," I said. "You've got the real stuff."

She lifted her top, causing her breasts to bounce. "Of course these are real," she joked. "I'm allergic to silicone."

I laughed. "I meant your material. Sounds like you worked on it quite a while."

She nodded vigorously. "I did. At first I tried this character where I was—"

I held up a finger and she fell silent. I heard Ned Lando's voice starting to list my credits. I looked at Kelly. "I have to go to work," I said. "See you after the show?"

"I hope so." She impulsively hugged me and kissed me on the cheek. "Thank you," she said. "I was so scared."

"You did great."

She winked and I heard Ned Lando say my name and the applause started. I slipped away from her, out of the green room, up on the little backstage platform, and through the curtain, like walking through the looking glass. I left one world and entered another.

37

SIX

Ned Lando stepped aside, and as soon as he was out of my peripheral vision I didn't give him another thought. This was my crowd, this was my night, and it was my show. I took the mike with both hands while still in the stand and—holding it like a dance partner—I launched into my first bit. I wanted to use a laugh break to take the mike out. I wanted there to be no pause in the flow of the show, no chance for these people to think about the pretty, funny girl who had just been up here. Kelly wasn't a dynamite act yet, but she was an interesting image to follow. They had liked her, and they had just spent half an hour in her company. They didn't know me.

"It's great to be here in Hartford Beach because I'm from Hollywood," I said. "The city whose motto is 'I'm going to the ATM . . . cover me.' "

Bull's-eye.

I took the mike from the stand and set the stand aside as the laugh rose and crested around me. Now I was ready to work.

I launched into my next bits, all about being from Southern

California. Earthquakes. Traffic. Tourists. I gave them combinations like a boxer, using my physical language to punctuate. Body, body, head.

I drove my punch lines home, setting my feet on every corner of the stage. I knew comics who just paced and prowled the curtain line, forgetting to even look at the people sitting at the side tables. I'd learned to hose down the crowd with my comedy, let everyone see my face all at the same time. Hit to the outfield. Bounce 'em off the back wall.

I switched from my California stuff to Friday night stuff, which was always a crowd pleaser. "Friday at five isn't just the start of the weekend—it's when we all get to quit our jobs for two days, isn't it? It's all the joy of quitting, but you still have your job Monday. At one minute after five, your boss asks you to do something, you're outta there! Fuck you, I quit!"

Big laugh. I didn't like using the *F* word that much, but it got me into the bit with a big laugh. Then I started in on my workplace stuff, which I was fairly proud of. Not many comedians have bits about copy machines not working and coworkers stealing your staple remover, but I do.

I snuck a look at my watch. I was twenty minutes in. Just about halfway. Right on schedule.

I made a call on the fly. I was going to dump the office stuff and go straight into dating, bridging it with a bit-in-progress about dating someone at the office. That would take me through another ten, and then another ten minutes on family and I'd be home.

I launched into the transition bit. It was based on a personal experience I'd had about five years ago when I was filling in as a temp at an office.

I saw Ned Lando at the back of the room, by the sound booth, watching me.

Taking notes there, Ned? Watch closely. There's a test later.

I leaned into the last half hour of my act as hard as I could, driving every point home, ad-libbing callbacks and throwing in one-liners. I found a man's fortieth birthday party to one side and threw in all my stuff about getting older, which led to my "going to the doctor's office" routine, which ended with a closing bit about annual physicals that took five minutes with all the bells and whistles and left the audience in stitches, the man with the fortieth birthday holding his sides, his wife wiping her eyes with a napkin, and there wasn't any sweeter place on earth right then than right there, on that stage.

The connection you could feel with a crowd that was engaged in your performance could be . . . well, it was better than sex. Better than drugs. Better than anything. Reality paled in comparison. It made addicts out of people. Life was on the stage. The rest was waiting.

That's where I ended up at forty-five minutes by Richard Moftus's watch or anyone else's. I said my good nights and bowed out.

Ned Lando came up to take the mike from me and I handed it over to him. I leaned in close to him as the applause fell around us and said, "We need to talk."

I stepped offstage and into the green room. I went straight to the bathroom and tore off a wad of paper towels, blotting the stage sweat of my face. I took a few seconds just to breathe in and out and calm down. Good show. Good show.

The door to the green room opened and Kelly Malone walked in with another glass of wine in her hand. "Hey there, handsome, that was funny!" she said. Her previous reserve had been nothing more than nervousness and now that was gone.

"Thank you, ma'am," I said.

She walked up to me and impulsively kissed me on the cheek. She drew back her head and left one hand on my neck. "Can I buy you a drink, sailor?"

"Sure," I said. "They have any Guinness?"

"No."

"Stout or ale of any kind?"

"I don't think so," she said. "Well, I know they don't. I pay the bar bills. The closest thing to an import we have is Corona."

"I'll pass."

"How about I sneak a Bass ale in from the restaurant next door?"

"Sold."

She squeezed my neck once before she let go and walked out of the room. I watched her go. She moved like she was auditioning for a ZZ Top video. Ay-yi-yi.

Just as Lando said his last good night, Richard Moftus appeared at the green room door. He had money in his hand and a receipt for me to sign.

"That was all right," Moftus said as he counted out ten crisp twenty-dollar bills. "Not bad, not bad at all. Got the crowd drinking like they were at an Irish funeral. And I imagine with a name like Kincaid you must have been to a few of those."

"A few." I signed the receipt and handed it back to him and got the cash in return. "Thanks." I put the two hundred in my pocket without counting it.

"Call me Monday. Then we'll talk about booking you in headlining for real. And I got a couple of road gigs I can slide you into, if you're interested."

"Always," I said. "Comedy is my business."

"I can tell that." He looked around. "Where's Kelly?"

"She went to get me a drink."

"We got waitresses for that, you know." He worked a fresh cigar out of his breast pocket and skinned it out of its wrapper.

"She offered."

"Don't tell me you got the hots for her, too. Every comic that comes through here does."

42

"She's funny."

"She is." He nodded in agreement. "Proud of that little girl."

I was standing there realizing two things: that Richard Moftus and I were completely out of dialogue to say to one another and that I had not seen Ned Lando since he had said good night. For all I knew he had walked offstage and into the crowd and out the door without me having a chance to read him the comedian's riot act.

"You seen Ned?" I asked Moftus.

"Not yet," he said. "We still got to do business—there he is."

Lando came around the corner from the showroom, a bag slung over his shoulder.

"Let's go into my office," Moftus said. Ned shrugged noncommittally.

They went inside and closed the thin wooden door. I figured I had a few minutes before I had to intercept Ned and confront him about his thieving. In that time, there was one other detail I wanted to check out.

I headed back onstage. The stage lights were dimmed, the house lights were up. The room was empty and the only person still at work was Pluto the sound guy.

I laced my way through the tables and chairs set askew, toward the booth, where he was sitting slumped on his stool, looking like a missing Ramone brother. The Van Halen tape he had been playing to clear out the crowd came to an end and he popped it out. "Pluto, can I talk to you a minute?" I asked.

"Uh, sure," he said. His voice was soft, barely audible. I had no idea why one of the consistent ironies of this business we call show was that audio engineers were always hard to hear.

"There anything I should know about Ned Lando?"

Pluto shook his head. His greasy twists of hair rustled around his forehead like a beaded curtain. "Like what?" he whispered.

"What were you guys doing back here during the show?"

43

Pluto found the lower part of his audio deck suddenly very interesting even though the show was over and the music had been shut off. "Aw, just some stuff."

"If I brought Richard Moftus over here and he asked you, do you think you could remember?"

He straightened up and gave me a pained expression. I could tell it was pained because his mouth opened and closed once before speaking. "Aw, come on, dude . . ."

Self-expression was not one of his strengths.

"You didn't know Ned Lando before this week, but he spent all of his free time back here with you," I said. "Now in my more than a decade of doing stand-up comedy, comedians who spend a lot of time with the sound guy have either taped bits or music in their acts. Ned had neither. That makes me curious. I'll let you in on a little secret. I want to talk to him after the show because his entire act is nothing but stolen bits from other comedians. I'm coming down on him for that."

I'd planted myself right in front of the audio booth, and I was leaning over the board just a little bit. Pluto still wouldn't look at me. "If you know something about that, I suggest you come clean now. Stalling and acting like you don't know anything isn't improving my disposition because you're not very good at either."

He did look up at me, then looked me over. He sized me up like an alley cat and decided he'd be better off if he stood down. Whatever he had set up with Lando, it didn't cover what I could dish out.

"He taped your act," Pluto said.

"He *what?*" I'd heard him. I just didn't want to believe it.

"He taped your act," Pluto repeated. He wasn't used to stringing whole sentences together, and the effort was costing him several healthy red blood cells. "The whole show, in fact. He gave me a hundred dollars to hook up a cassette recorder. Nice

44

little piece of equipment. He didn't care about getting his act on tape too much, but he wanted to make sure that he got your whole show and Kelly's routine, too."

"Did he say why?"

"Why what?"

Idiot. Grow a brain. "Why he was taping our acts?"

"I don't know." Pluto looked down at his board again. "A hundred bucks answered all of my questions."

If Pluto had anything else to say, I didn't hear it because I was out of the showroom and on my way to find Ned Lando with a purpose only the furies have known.

Ned Lando had taped my act. The son of a bitch. He'd taped my *act*.

SEVEN

When I got back into the green room Kelly was waiting for me, a Bass ale in her hand.

"Here you go," she said. "Special delivery."

"Thanks."

"What's wrong?"

I pointed with the bottle neck. "Lando still in there?"

She looked over her shoulder at Moftus's office. "I don't know." She stepped through the green room door and listened. "He's in there with someone and he's not yelling," she said when she came back.

"There another way out of here besides the front?"

"The delivery entrance," she said. She took me by the arm and pulled me out of the green room and pointed. There was a door set in between where Moftus's office was and the green room.

"Where does it lead?"

"Out the back. There's a narrow strip of asphalt that leads to the parking lot."

"Okay," I said. "Go lock the front exit. When Lando comes out, make up some story about setting the alarm and send him out that way." I pointed at the delivery entrance.

"What are you going to do?"

"Head out the delivery entrance and try to intercept Lando on his way to his car," I said.

"What's going on between you two?" she asked. "You barely spoke tonight, from what I saw."

"Remember I said he was a thief?" She nodded. "I checked with Pluto the sound guy. Turns out Lando taped your act and mine."

"He . . . he what?"

"He taped them both our acts," I said. "For his own use or someone else's, I don't know. He paid Pluto a hundred bucks to set up a tape recorder through the audio board." I heard voices behind Moftus's door. Moftus was chuckling about something. "I don't know what's been keeping them in there so long, but when they're done you let me handle Lando."

"Richard's not going to like that," she said. "Pluto taking money from comedians." She looked at the closed office door. "What do you have in mind?"

"I'm going to get back what he's taken from me," I said. "From *us.*"

Two men were going to fight. I think that made her a little excited. "Let me know what happens," she said.

"I'll call you tomorrow," I said.

She pressed a folded slip of paper into my hand. "Tonight," she said.

I didn't have to look at it to know it was her home number. The office door opened, and I heard Ned Lando say good night to Moftus. I turned and left Kelly, noiselessly crossing to the delivery entrance and opening and closing the door to the outside. As I stepped out of the club, the night air was cool and

48

smelled clean, with just a waft of sour garbage odor from the club's Dumpster. I walked along the brick wall of the outside of the club, skirting the fenced enclosure that housed the Dumpster, and ended up just around the corner from the parking lot. I stepped out and looked around. No Ned Lando yet. When he came out, I would have a distance of about twenty-five feet to close between the two of us. I could nail him before he got his car keys out. I just didn't want this to happen in front of any straggling audience members as they made their way out of the parking lot.

I hung back, trying not to be seen. I'd been out there less than two minutes when I heard the same exit door I'd just used open behind me.

I turned to look. I couldn't see who it was because the Dumpster fence was blocking my way. I had a choice. I could either hang back or step out. I waited another second until I heard the person come closer to me, and then I stepped out.

Ned Lando took another step before he stopped and saw me standing in front of him. He was carrying a cell phone and the small shoulder bag I'd seen before, the kind sold in urban outdoor clothing mail catalogs. Lands' End. He was surprised to see me.

"What do you want?" he asked.

"Hand it over," I said.

"Hand what over?"

"The tape you made of my act. Don't play dumb," I said. "It'll give me a headache."

Lando blinked. "I can't do that," he said. He moved to step around me.

I caught him by the arm. Underneath his flaccid exterior was some solid bulk, so I applied my own muscle. "Give it to me," I said. "Now."

He looked down at my hand and then up at me. He didn't want to fight, but he would. "Let go," he said.

"Not until you—"

Then he did the unexpected. He smashed the cell phone into my face and swung the Lands' End bag at my head. Both of them connected solidly and I staggered back, my spine scraping against the brick wall. He sprinted for his car.

I did something unexpected of my own. He still had the Lands' End bag looped over his arm. He was out of reach, but the Lands' End bag wasn't. It was almost dragging on the ground. I reached out and grabbed it, twisting it so the strap closed around his wrist and yanked back.

He slipped backward like he'd stepped on a banana peel. He went down, hitting the concrete alley pavement with a jaw-jarring impact. He blinked hard.

I went for the bag. I thought the tape might be in there. If not, hopefully there was something I could trade for it. Just as I got my hands on the bag, he did a smart thing. Rather than rolling over and trying to get on his feet, he stayed on his back like an overturned crab and waited for me to make my move. When I got my hands on the bag he spun around like a break-dancer and used his legs to sweep my feet out from under me.

I fell backward, using my hands to brace my fall. When I hit the ground, he was on his hands and knees and I was on my back. He jumped on me. I brought a leg up and kicked him in the stomach. He staggered back, dropping the bag. I got to my feet and drove him back against the wall with three punches: two to the face and another to the side. His back hit the bricks and he slumped down to the ground, moaning, his hands going to his stomach.

I turned around and picked up the bag where he'd dropped it. As he lay slumped on the ground I rifled through the bag's pockets. I found an address book, pens, pencils, several blank wrapped cassette tapes and the recorder he'd had Pluto hook up to the sound system. Mixed in there were the keys to a Range Rover. I picked them up and pressed the alarm button. A brand-new tan Range Rover in the parking lot chirped, its lights flashing. It must be his. Interesting. Most opening acts I knew were chronically broke and drove junkers.

I went back to the bag while Lando recovered from our fight. There was a wallet and a checkbook. Miscellaneous receipts. And one cassette tape, neatly labeled: CHORTLES COMEDY CLUB. BIFF KINCAID. KELLY MALONE. Below that was today's date.

I shoved the bag to the side so it landed out of his reach. "You got some fancy equipment and a real nice car for a road hack opener just starting out in the business," I said. I squatted down in front of him, making sure I was out of reach as well. I held the cassette tape up in front of his vision. "What the hell were you going to do with this? You're not going anywhere until you tell me."

He coughed and wheezed. "I already sold it," he said.

"You what?!"

"I sold it to another comedian." He was getting some of his voice back. "To use in his act."

I was mad before. This wasn't calming me down any. I reached forward and grabbed him by the front of his T-shirt, bunching it in my fists. He flinched and turned away from me. I dragged him to his feet. "When did you sell it?" I asked. My voice had dropped to a growl.

"Just now. On the phone."

"For how much?"

"A thousand dollars."

I brought him to his feet, pulling him back away from the wall and slamming him into it again. He wasn't avoiding my questions. I just felt like knocking him around some more. The space between my temples was beginning to feel warm. I had to be careful. I'd lost control in a fight before. It's like stepping into a fever dream. The pain and punishment don't seem real. Blood lust gets the better of you. You don't stop until someone pulls you off, and by then it's no longer a fight; it's become a beating. I'd been on both sides of that argument, and neither of them makes much sense the next morning when you wake up in jail. Or the hospital.

"Who'd you sell it to?"

"Roger," he said. "Roger Fisk. I'm supposed to hand it off tonight."

I let Ned go and he started to slide back down to the pavement, but he caught himself before his butt hit bottom. He looked at me to see if I was going to deliver a parting shot, but I wasn't. I just had one more question.

"Who the hell is Roger Fisk?" I asked.

I saw Ned's eyes flicker just an angstrom off my right shoulder, and as I turned—my body and fists first, head second, ducking to avoid what was already coming—I knew that there was someone behind me who was on Lando's side, not mine, and just about to prove it.

I didn't get to see a face or even a fist. Something hard and solid connected to the back of my head and I went down, knocked out before I hit the pavement.

EIGHT

When I woke up I was looking at Kelly Malone. Not that that's a bad thing. "Where am I?" I said, over the ringing in my ears.

"You're on my couch," she said. She had changed out of her stage outfit. Now she was wearing blue jeans and a denim shirt. The denim shirt was unbuttoned below the sternum and tied at the waist, exposing a nice expanse of her trim abdomen. I noticed, even though my head felt like a watermelon after a Gallagher concert.

She was sitting next to me on a wide, cream-colored couch, and when I tried to get up she gently pushed me back down. I think that was because I closed my eyes and started to weave when the blood rushed out of my head. Weaving while still semi-prone is not a good sign.

"How'd I get here?" I asked. Regaining consciousness makes you ask stupid things.

"I brought you in my car," she said. "Richard helped me put you in the backseat and lug you upstairs."

"Okay," I said. I tried to think of something else I needed to know. I lay still. Her couch was against a wall that was adorned by a framed poster of San Francisco Bay, the Golden Gate shrouded in fog. "How long have I been out?"

"About half an hour," she said. "If you didn't wake up in another five minutes, I was going to call the paramedics."

"No problem," I said. "I've been knocked out in fights before." I started to slowly check each of my major muscle groups. Arms. Legs. Torso. Everything seemed to be working. "Just not from behind."

"Is that what happened?" Kelly said. "Ned Lando knocked you over the head when your back was turned?"

"Not Ned," I said. "I was looking at Ned when I got the sap. Someone else."

"You have any idea who?"

"No." I started to sit up, and this time I made it, although I had to slump over when I finally got upright. "They got away though, didn't they?" Still slumped over, I turned my head sideways to look up at her with one throbbing eye. "Ned and whoever coldcocked me?"

Kelly shrugged with her finely trimmed eyebrows. "I heard tires squealing from inside the club and rushed outside. When I found you, there was a Range Rover speeding away out of the club driveway."

"You didn't get a license number, did you?"

"No," she said. "Do you want me to call the police?"

"And tell them what?" I said. My eyes were squinting shut as large globs of red and purple danced in front of my lightless vision.

"Tell them what happened," she said.

"What happened is that I went out in the alley behind the club with the premeditated intent of assaulting Ned Lando," I said. "Someone came to his aid. End of story. I threw the first punch, if not the last. If the cops came, I wouldn't be surprised if I was the one they cuffed and took off to jail." I reached behind me and touched where I'd been hit and winced. I had a nice little robin's egg growing back there. "Ouch."

"Let me get you some ice," she said, getting up.

I didn't stop her. I wouldn't have stopped her if she was getting me a shot of morphine. Instead, I checked out her apartment. Nice. Big. Your rental dollar went a lot farther down in Orange County than it did in Hollywood. The cream-colored couch matched the cream deep-pile carpeting that stretched across a living room bigger then my entire apartment on Beachwood Plaza. Across from me were three low bookshelves stocked with financial and business self-help best-sellers. On the wall above, framed photographs of Kelly onstage, Kelly with shorter hair in the middle of a bunch of businessmen in a large room filled with computers, and an older man and woman hugging in front of a cabin in the middle of the forest. The man looked fit, and the woman was still a knockout in her fifties. Parents.

To the side were a desk and a computer. "Nice place," I said.

"Thanks." I heard her open the refrigerator door and move items around in the freezer.

"You live alone?"

"No."

"Where's your roommate?"

"He's in the bedroom."

"Oh." I leaned forward. I could see two darkened doorways. One led to a bathroom. The other . . .

I lowered my voice. "Is he asleep?"

"Probably."

"Hope he didn't mind you bringing me here."

She came out of the kitchen with an ice pack wrapped in a dish towel. It looked like a soft, blue plastic brick. "He gets a little jealous when I bring a new guy home," she said, adding in an exaggerated whisper, "but he'll get over it."

I held out my hand for the ice. She held it back. "Lean forward," she said, "and I'll put the ice pack in place and you hold it there. Okay?"

"Okay."

"And let's try not to drip on the nice furniture."

I leaned forward and she gently put the ice pack in place. It hurt for a moment, and then comforting numbness set in. I closed my fingers over hers. She kept them in place for a moment and then gently pulled them away. "Switch hands when it gets too cold," she said.

I heard a sound like a baby yawning from the bedroom doorway. I looked and saw a pair of green eyes hovering about a foot above the floor.

"There he is," Kelly said, in a warmer tone of voice than she'd used with any human. "Come here, handsome."

A piece of the darkness broke away and stepped out onto the carpet. It was a short-haired, black cat, about fifteen pounds. A big boy, looking sleek and fast. His eyes were locked on me like they were about to launch a pair of short-range tactical missiles.

"He heard us talking." Kelly was smiling more than I'd ever seen her before. "It's okay, Shadow. It's Mommy's friend."

Shadow glided across the carpet and leaped into Kelly's lap, purring and offering his head to be scratched. "You allergic?" she asked.

"No."

Shadow moved his head around her fingers, rubbing his nose, ears, and chin against her touch. He flexed his claws. They looked to be about half an inch long, curved and sharp. "You like cats?"

"Some of them," I said.

"That's my handsome boy," she said, like she was talking to a small child. "Did you have a nice nap? We didn't mean to scare you when we came in."

My fingers were getting a little frigid so I switched hands on the ice pack. This sudden action must have startled Shadow. I looked away, and he was gone.

"Didn't mean to scare him," I said.

"It's okay," she said. "He takes a while to get used to strangers."

"Where'd he go?"

"Into the kitchen."

"He's a quick little guy," I said. "I must have just blinked . . ."

Kelly smiled. "Hence the name Shadow."

"I see he's not declawed."

"Oh, no. He goes outside. He needs his claws to climb trees and win fights with the other cats around here. He's scrappy."

"Could have used his help tonight," I said.

Kelly curled her legs underneath her on the sofa. "So what happened?"

I told her about how I'd sneaked out of the back exit to the club and waited for Lando by the Dumpster. "We fought, and then I asked him about where the tape was and he said he'd already sold it."

Kelly's eyes widened slightly. "He sold it?"

"My reaction exactly," I said. "So I knocked him around some more and took it from him."

"Who'd he sell it to?"

"I got a name out of him, but it didn't mean anything to me," I said. "Roger Fisk."

Kelly sat back and blinked. "Roger Fisk."

"Yeah." I switched hands on the ice pack again. "You know him?"

"He's played the club," Kelly said, "like within the last two months. He was opener and emcee, just like Ned Lando was this weekend."

"Do you know how I can get in touch with him?"

"Richard Moftus would," she said.

"I might just try him," I said. "What else do you remember about Roger Fisk?"

"Not too tall," she said. "A really good-looking guy, but a little full of himself. Tan. Said he was from Arizona. Well-built. Wore these tight polo shirts that showed off his muscles. Claimed to have a development deal and that he'd been in Hollywood just a few months. Oh, I remember. He was a weatherman in Flagstaff or Phoenix. I don't know which. One of the cities that begins with an *F* sound. I haven't been to Arizona much."

"I have," I said. There were comedy clubs in both Phoenix and Flagstaff: The Comedy Cabana in Phoenix and Gigglemeisters in Flagstaff. If I wanted to learn more about Roger Fisk on his home turf, I could give them a call. "Any idea why he'd want to buy my act?"

Kelly shrugged. "Like I said, he kept talking about how he had a development deal."

"For what?"

"He said he was producing his own cable special," Kelly said. "This was while I was still waitressing at the club. After the show he hung out at the bar, got drunk, and wouldn't leave. Richard finally had to throw him out."

"A cable special," I said. "That would explain it."

"How?"

"If Roger Fisk is new to comedy," I said, "he wouldn't have the solid half hour to make a cable special."

"What makes you think he's new to comedy?"

"Just a theory," I said. "I haven't heard of him before." I looked at her. "You were there when he went on. How was his act?"

"Terrible," she said. "I thought he belonged on open-mike night, not opening a weekend show."

"Bingo," I said. "If he doesn't have writers or if he's worried about his own performance, it only makes sense that he would pay someone to go around and record other comedians' acts to use on TV."

"Is that what you think happened?" Kelly asked.

"It's the best I have to go on so far," I said. I looked around and felt my own pockets. "You didn't happen to find that tape anywhere near me, did you?"

Kelly shook her head. "What'd it look like?"

I kept looking. "It was a black plastic cassette tape, labeled with our names and the date and the club on it."

"Wasn't there."

"Lando or whoever hit me must have taken it with him," I said. "So I got knocked out for nothing." I pulled the cold pack from the back of my head and handed it to her. "I'll let you know if I find out anything more tomorrow. I have to get to my spot at the Comedy Store." I stood up.

And sat back down. My head began to swivel like it was on a doll in the rear window of a Chevy Impala.

"Whoa, cowboy," Kelly said. "You're not going anywhere."

"Just give me a minute," I said. I stared at the carpet until the rest of the apartment stopped moving. "What time is it?" I asked.

"Almost midnight," Kelly said.

I'd never make it to the Store in time for my spot now, unless they were runing very late. I could call, I could switch with someone going on later . . .

"I already called the Comedy Store and told them you were in an accident," Kelly said.

"No argument there," I said. "I just hate to cancel."

"I don't think you're in any shape to get on the freeway for an hour to go back to Hollywood," Kelly said. "Your car's still at the club." She fluffed a cushion. "I've got some spare sheets and blankets and a toothbrush still in the wrapper. You're welcome to spend the night here."

"I think I might be better in an hour," I said.

"Well, I think I might be asleep in an hour," she said. And yawned. And stretched. I liked the stretching part best. "Better think quick."

I didn't have to think much, and I didn't think I had much choice. "I guess I'll stay," I said. "As long as Shadow won't mind."

"He'll be in the bedroom." Kelly smiled. "He protects me against burglars."

"I never heard of an attack cat."

"Oh, he's been known to be somewhat jealous." She stood. "I once had a date that wouldn't leave, and as he was mauling me on the couch Shadow jumped on his back and started to shred his left ear."

"Is that a warning?"

"Not in your condition," she said, walking into the bedroom. "I don't think you're much of a threat to anybody."

"Not that I was when I was healthy," I said. "Ask Ned Lando."

I heard cupboards open and close in the bedroom. "There were two of them." She came back into the living room carrying sheets, blankets, and a pillow. "And only one of you." She dropped them on the end of the couch I was sitting on. "Pleasant dreams. The couch folds out. You get to make your own bed as well as sleep in it."

NINE

She came to my bed before dawn.

I was asleep, dreaming of long, empty roads and floating circuses; pleasant, long, languorous visions of another world that filled my resting, restless brain. I felt a touch and turned over, reaching out to bring it close. The touch belonged to a hand and the hand belonged to Kelly Malone. I stayed in a state of semiconsciousness, feeling her move into the foldout bed beside me, silky and sheer, to find me ready for her. The only sound in the night was her mouth opening and closing as I moved with her, in slow motion, like we were both made of molten hissing lava. The finale came for both of us when she was astride me, her stomach muscles flexing, her face twisted in a silent shriek. I lost control and lifted her up off the mattress, sitting up to hold her close as we shuddered still.

We fell back asleep together. I woke up second. She was already looking at me through half-closed eyes.

"Well," she said, "I guess I like you more than I thought."

"I grow on people," I said.

"You grow, that's for sure." She shifted under the covers. "How's your head?"

"Which one?"

"The one I'm talking to, dummy."

"Better," I said. "You have the healing touch. Or kiss. Or something."

Shadow jumped on the couch between us, already purring. "Hey, little boy," she said, rubbing his arched back. "Are you hungry? Do you want some breakfast?"

Shadow meowed. He looked at me with feline curiosity, then stepped across the blankets and stuck his nose against mine.

"Is he smelling me?" I said.

"He's saying hello."

"Hello, Shadow," I said. "I promise I didn't hurt your mommy. In fact, I think I made her purr a little bit."

He turned around and showed me his uplifted tail. "Now that's a fine how-do-you-do," I said.

"He's actually paying you a compliment," Kelly said. "He's letting you sniff him."

"How do you know all this?"

"I read a book about cat behavior."

"Why?"

"Because I doubted he'd ever read one about humans," she said. Shadow curled up against her blanketed chest and closed his eyes, purring so loudly his sides rattled. "He kept pooping outside his litter box and I wanted to know how to get him to stop."

"What was the problem?"

"I changed brands of litter on him," she said. "He didn't like it."

"And that's how he let you know?"

"Yep." She smiled, stroking Shadow from his ears to his tail. "Worked, didn't it? The ol' kittygram."

I threw back the covers and stood up. "I'm going to use the litter box myself," I said. "Don't worry. I won't miss."

When I came back out, she was up and making coffee. I was hoping to find her still in bed. I guess the sight of my pale, naked Irish butt, as tan as a scoop of mashed potatoes, broke the romantic spell. As she ground beans and boiled water, I stripped the bed of its sheets and folded it back into a couch. Shadow munched a little dry breakfast, and then Kelly let him out the front door to prowl.

"So what are you up to today?" she asked, while at the stove. She was using one of the sheets as a robe. It was made of blue flannel. A woman of class and taste. I don't think she was in the habit of bringing fellow comedians home. I don't think she was in the habit of bringing anybody home.

"I'm going to try to track down Roger Fisk," I said. "See if I can get that tape back."

Kelly looked puzzled. "What about Ned Lando?"

"I may be done with him," I said. "If Roger Fisk is the guy he sold the tape to, then . . ." I ended the sentence in a shrug. "I'll put out the word about what Lando is up to. Other comics will know to steer clear of him."

"Are you going to want to talk to Richard?"

"If he'll tell me what I want to know," I said.

"And what's that?"

"Mainly what I want is an address," I said. "Where Roger Fisk lives."

The coffee started to drip out of the coffeemaker and into the pot. I could smell it. "Fisk's address would be on his paperwork," she said. "His W-9."

"Uh-huh."

"I have access to those files," she said.

I smiled. "You're willing to spy for me?"

She looked at me with no return smile. "My act's on that tape, too," she said. "I may be green, but I ain't dumb."

"I never thought that." I looked at her. "If you're going to help me get to the bottom of this, I have to warn you that this business we call 'show' can get a little raw."

"I can handle it."

"So far," I said. "It gets too much, you let me know."

She studied me. "You're not like most comedians I've met."

I didn't say anything. I'd heard it before.

She started to smile and then suppressed it. "You done any detective work on me yet?"

"I was just about to start." I looked back toward the living room. "Those pictures on the wall . . ."

"What about them?"

"I'm guessing the older couple are your parents."

"Correct," she said. "They live up in Oregon. Retired."

"And the one of you . . . it looks like you're at some kind of computer place."

"That's on the floor of the Pacific Exchange," she said. "In LA I was a stockbroker. That's how I met Richard. Made him a few thousand dollars."

"Do well at it?"

"Well enough to quit it and enter the extremely high-paying and secure world of stand-up comedy. Richard had me as a guest at Chortles, and I was hooked. Started going up at open mikes and then Richard offered me a few waitress shifts and then the day manager job for about a tenth of what I made as a broker. Luckily, I followed my own advice. My own investments have me set up for a while."

"From stockbroker to stand-up," I said. "You ever do any material about the stock market?"

"I tried," she said. "Most people don't have a sense of humor about their investments. It would depend on the day. If the market was up, everyone thought it was great. If it was down, they were too miserable to laugh." She poured coffee. "I thought I'd just wear tight tops instead." She passed me a cup.

"You don't need to do that to work with audiences," I said.

"No, but it sure worked with club owners," she said. "Think I got hired at Chortles as a waitress because I knew so much about initial public offerings and price earnings ratios?"

I laughed. "No," I said. "I guess not." I sipped from my stoneware mug. She made great coffee.

There in the kitchen, we drank coffee and looked at each other through miniature pools of steam. The business of pouring the coffee had slipped the sheet from around her neck to down by her shoulders. Her tousled hair and lack of makeup made me think of last night, now lost somewhere in the breaking of the dawn, an hourless time when she'd wrapped her limbs around me, luring me deeper into her.

"What are you thinking about now?" she said.

"Nothing."

She looked downward, below my waist. "Looks like something's on your mind."

I followed her gaze. "This is why Scotsmen wear kilts," I said.

She set her coffee aside and stepped forward, letting the sheet fall from around her. Within two steps she was in my arms, warm and smooth. I set my coffee aside and we kissed deeply. I could taste the bitter brew on her tongue.

When we parted she took her hands from around my neck and slid them across my chest, lowered them to where I was pointing like a divining rod. "My, oh, my," she said. "You are a natural redhead, aren't you?"

I looked down at her. "And you're not."

She looked back up at me and smiled, her hands working me into pure steel. "Secret's out."

TEN

According to his W-9 form, Roger Fisk lived at 6530 Sunset Boulevard, #1463.

"That's a mail drop," I said.

"How do you know?" Kelly asked.

"I live in Hollywood," I said. "There aren't many apartments on that part of Sunset Boulevard. Mainly motels. But there're lots of places that will give you an address for ten bucks a month." It was just before noon on that same Sunday morning. Kelly and I had driven over to Chortles, and she had let us into the club using her set of keys. "Copy shops. Shipping places. They rent out boxes all the time."

"Would they know where to find Roger Fisk?"

I shrugged. "You pay cash for a mailbox and no one asks any questions."

"Sounds like something you've done," she said.

"Look at my paperwork," I said. "I still do it. Think I want anyone tracking me down? Let's check Ned Lando."

She went back to the files. "His paperwork's missing."

"Who took it?"

"Richard's the only one who has the key to this cabinet," she said, "besides me."

"That you know of."

She hadn't thought of that. "True."

Kelly put Fisk's paperwork back in the folder and put the folder back in the file drawer and slid the file drawer shut. We were in Richard Moftus's office. As Kelly had warned me before we entered it, if Moftus found us in there rummaging through his papers he'd fire us both. Before we dug out Fisk's paperwork, I'd checked the older Chortles schedules. Roger Fisk had opened there six weeks before. The headliner had been Joey Mosh.

Back in another set of files were comedians' headshots and résumés. I found Fisk's. The headshot backed up Kelly's description. Full wavy hair, tan good looks, square jaw, light eyes. He looked like an infomercial host, not a comic. His résumé listed a few clubs in Arizona, leading with the Comedy Cabana in Phoenix. A casino up in the mountains north of Phoenix. An acting teacher. A degree in broadcasting from Arizona State. A brief paragraph told of his history as a weatherman in Flagstaff for the last three years. Hosted "Fisky Business," a segment devoted to "the wackier side of northern Arizona." Now there's some comedy. No agent. No manager. I found the office photocopier and made copies of both the headshot and résumé.

I gave the original back to Kelly, and she closed and locked both file cabinets with a key she carried around with the ones to her car and apartment.

"Know of anyone else Richard Moftus might have given a key to those file cabinets to?" I asked Kelly. "Specifically anyone who wanted to steal Ned Lando's tax paperwork?"

"No."

"He married?"

"Who?" Kelly asked. "Lando? Or Richard?"

"Richard."

"Divorced."

"Girlfriend?"

"Never says anything about one," she said rather lightly. There was more she could have said than that, but I don't think it had anything to do with Ned Lando.

"Who gives these forms to comedians to be filled out?" I asked.

"Me or Richard," Kelly said. "Me if they come in during the day; Richard if they wait until show time."

"Any difference in doing your paperwork during the day as opposed to night?"

"It seems to take a lot longer during the day," she said ruefully.

"Some of them hard to get out of the office?" I asked.

"Or away from the bar," she said.

"Did Fisk talk to anyone while he was here?" I asked.

Kelly made a face. "He wasted a lot of time trying to pick up all the women in the place," she said. "Me included."

"Was there anyone he might have had contact with who would know how to get in touch with him?" I asked.

Kelly shook her head. "I can't think of anyone."

"I can," I said. "And I need you to take me to him."

Pluto's real name was Kurt Anderson, but everyone called him Pluto. I was surprised his name didn't read that way on his mailbox. He lived inland from Hartford Beach in an area called Hartford Heights, in a cheap one-room apartment that he shared with another rock 'n' roll wannabe. I hated to wake these guys up at noon on a Sunday just to tell them heavy metal was dead, but it had to be done.

Pluto answered his own door, his eyes narrow with sleep. He was shirtless. He had a chest so pale you could see veins through his skin. One of his rose-colored nipples had a silver ring through it. He wore black jeans over his unnaturally skinny waist. His lanky black hair hung around his head like the roots of an upturned tree. The goatee was no further along. On one shoulder he had a tattoo of Pluto. Not the planet. Mickey Mouse's dog.

Kelly told him why we were there. He invited us inside. He waved to his roommate's prone sprawled body, asleep on the kitchen floor. "That's Mark," Pluto said. "He's a drummer." Well, that explained everything.

Kelly and I sat gingerly on the edge of a futon Pluto had been using as a bed. Apparently he'd won the toss last night. The room smelled slightly dank. Pluto sat in a chair that looked like he'd picked it up off the street. He rubbed an arm, warming his feet on the worn carpet.

He looked at me. "You okay, man?"

He meant the knot on the back of my head.

"I'm good," I said. "Thanks for asking."

"No problem," he said. "I got beaned after a show once. Some death rocker thought I was after his chick when she was really screwing his own keyboarder."

I nodded. Ah, to be young again. "I wanted to ask you about Roger Fisk," I said.

"Who?"

"Roger Fisk," I repeated. "He's a comedian. He played here about a month and a half ago. Kelly remembers him rather well." I turned to her for a description.

"He's under five ten," Kelly said. "With brown hair and brown eyes. Tan. Good-looking, like a catalog model. Square jaw. Wore polo shirts and khaki pants. Kind of the yuppie golfer look."

"Oh yeah, man, that guy sucked," Pluto said. He bent over to look for something he had stored between the bottom of the chair and the carpet.

"So you do remember Roger Fisk?" I asked.

"Yeah . . ." Pluto found what he was looking for: a circular metal beer tray littered with seeds and stems and an open pack of Zig-Zag cigarette papers. Time for his morning coffee. He pulled the tray up onto his lap and began to roll a joint. "What do you want to know about him?"

"I want to know if you had any contact with him," I said.

Pluto lit up and inhaled. "Fisk wanted me to videotape his act," Pluto said, holding his breath. "This was on Friday. Asked me if I could rent a video camera for Saturday and run the audio through my board and get performance-quality sound while shooting on Betacam SP. I said yeah and I priced the job at five hundred. He said for that he would buy his own camera and do it himself. I said go ahead. So he did."

"I remember that now," Kelly said. "He did bring in a video camera."

Pluto took another hit off the joint. I could smell it. Some major green. Now I knew where all his money went. Not to mention his spare brain cells. He proffered the joint to both me and Kelly. We waved it off. He shrugged and kept toking. "But he didn't buy a Betacam," Pluto continued. "Those things are expensive. He brought in a Super VHS. And he brought someone to run it, too," Pluto said. "Some bruiser. A bodyguard. Sets it up at the back of the room and still wants me to run the sound through my board. I said no way. You don't use me; you don't use my board. I mean, since then Moftus sprung for a soundboard but I was using my own that time. I told him no way."

"And what happened?" I asked.

"Fisk's bodyguard comes over to me and squares his shoulders and says in this deep voice, 'Mr. Fisk really wants you to cooperate. I suggest you do.' I mean, this guy isn't that big but he's built, you know? Solid." Pluto squeezed a bicep to illustrate his point. The pot's effects were kicking in. Pluto was feeling expressive. He leaned forward, reliving his story, not just telling it. "And I said, 'You tell Mr. Fisk he can stick it up his ass.' Well, I didn't really say that, but . . . I let 'em. For fifty bucks."

I turned to Kelly. "Do you remember this bodyguard?"

She shook her head. "No. My station was near the front of the stage."

I turned back to Pluto. "So what was this bodyguard's name?"

"George. I overheard Roger call him that." Pluto coughed out a laugh. "I thought that was funny. Such a tough guy with kind of a nerdy-sounding name."

"What'd he look like?"

"Black hair, tied back in a slicked-back ponytail." Pluto ran his fingers over his own downy growth. "Had a goatee. Wore a white suit, like he thought he was a Miami coke dealer or something. Deep voice. And he didn't know how to operate the camera. I could tell. Roger let me know he had just bought it that day. George was thumbing through the manual trying to get it to work."

"Did they get Roger's act on tape?" I asked.

"They tried," Pluto said. "I don't know if it stuck to the tape or not." He shrugged. "You get what you pay for. He sucked, anyway. Roger."

"You watch all the acts, right?" I asked.

"I have to, man," Pluto said. "It's my job."

"What was Roger's like?"

"Just bad. Some old jokes. He didn't have enough to even open."

"Joey Mosh was headlining that night," I said. "He kill?"

Pluto thought. "Yeah. He saved the show."

"What happened after the show?" I asked.

"Joey got in his car and split. Roger went to the bar with George," Pluto said. "I packed up and went home."

I turned to Kelly. "And it was there at the bar . . ."

She nodded. "He started to chat me up."

"What'd he say?" Pluto asked.

"Just talk about how he had a development deal; he was going to produce his own cable special . . ." Her turn to shrug. "The usual showbiz bullshit."

"Comedians," I said. "You can never trust 'em."

Pluto laughed. "Hey, man, that's funny. 'Cause, you know, you're a comedian. You're funny, too. I didn't get a chance to tell you, but you got a good act. You too, Kelly. You're coming along."

I stood up. "Thanks, Pluto," I said. I heard his roommate get up in the kitchen, blow his nose without a hankie, and spit into the sink. Time for us to go.

Pluto stubbed out his joint on the tray and set it down. "So what are you guys after Fisk for? You think he might have kicked your ass?"

"I don't know if that was him," I said, opening the door and letting in sunlight and fresh air. "And I got sucker punched from behind. Face-to-face, I don't go down so easy."

"No, I bet you don't. Well, let me know what happens," Pluto said.

"I will," I said. I let Kelly escape through the front door first. "Thanks for the information."

"Hey, why didn't you just talk to the guy that canceled?" Pluto asked as he stood in the doorway.

I stopped. "Do you mean Art Westcott?"

"Yeah. He asked a lot of the same questions you did."

"When?"

"After Thursday night's show. I told him pretty much what I told you. Maybe he's found out something else by now."

"What did he say about Art?" Kelly asked, once we were back in my car. We'd picked up my RX-7 when we were first at Chortles.

"That he asked the same questions I did," I said. "So he knew who Roger Fisk was. Maybe he had already made a connection between him and Ned Lando."

"So why did he cancel at the last minute?" Kelly asked. She put a hand on my leg. "Not that I'm sorry he did."

I put my hand on top of her hand. "Me neither." I took my hand away to steer. "I don't know why he canceled. But if he was on the trail of Ned Lando and Roger Fisk the same way I am, then it all might fit together somehow." I had to try to call Art as soon as I got near a phone.

She looked at me. "So what now?"

"Now?" I said. "Now I'd like to talk to Richard Moftus again."

"He'll be in the office Monday."

"That's tomorrow," I said. "I don't want to wait until tomorrow."

"He's not available today," Kelly said. "He likes to spend his Sundays alone."

"You said that a little too quickly," I said, "which makes me think you know where he is, and you don't want me to find out because he'll know that you told me."

She was silent.

"It's your act on that tape, too," I said. "For all I know, Roger Fisk has listened to it and has already made plans for either himself or someone else to do your bits—maybe on national TV."

"I know where Richard is," she said, "but it's not that I'm not supposed to tell, I'm not even supposed to know. Understand?"

"Here's what I think," I said. "I think that Roger Fisk has no development deal—just money of his own. Enough to throw around and hire bodyguards and buy video cameras and make himself look and act like a big shot. I think he's come here from

Arizona trying to break into Hollywood. Who knows? Maybe he's a big hit back home, and he thought he'd be a big star out here by the end of the year. He got the videotape made to show someone else, maybe a manager or some network people or folks at a production company. Guess what? They didn't like it. They thought he stank. They told him to work on his act. Go back on the road. See you next pilot season.

"But what little I know of Roger Fisk, he doesn't sound like a particularly patient sort. He wants what he wants, and he wants it now. How to solve the quandary of having no act but wanting to be a comedy star as quickly as possible? While trying to solve this problem, or maybe even before, he meets Ned Lando. He sees what Ned Lando's specialty is and asks how he'd like to cater to Fisk's needs on a private consulting basis. In other words, steal for him. You with me so far?"

"Sure," Kelly said.

"Well, that's as far as I've gotten."

"And you think Richard Moftus knows the rest?" she asked.

"I think he definitely knows the answer to one question," I said.

"What's that?"

"Why Ned Lando worked his club for free."

ELEVEN

Richard Moftus spent his Sundays on a sailboat he kept in the Hartford Marina. Kelly had me drop her off at her place before she gave me the slip number. I guess I'd pressed her a little too hard on giving up Moftus's location; she didn't kiss me good-bye. I told her I'd call her. It sounded phony. It wasn't, but it sounded that way. Like a new bit I hadn't worked out all the way to the punch line.

I drove out to the marina in the Sunday late afternoon traffic, shielding my eyes from the slanting sun and rolling down the windows as the air got cooler and cleaner the nearer I got to the water. When I get rich, I'm moving to the beach.

I parked blocks from the marina and walked the rest of the way after doing a drive-by of the place. The Hartford Marina has valet parking that charges six bucks. Welcome to Southern California. Land of unnecessary luxury.

Moftus didn't see me coming. I walked past rows of empty powercraft, yachts, and houseboats resting in the water. I found his sailboat, floating in the setting sun. It was a sloop, about thirty-five feet long, built for comfort as well as speed. It was where he played Sunday Popeye.

Moftus was sitting on a cushion in the cockpit of his sailboat, drinking amber liquid out of a highball glass. He was wearing a white golf shirt that was stretched tight over his enormous abdomen and he had a small white captain's hat on his head instead of a toupee. The effect was more fitting than comic, not because of the weekend sailor's outfit, but because Moftus himself looked more comfortable and relaxed.

He heard my footsteps and ignored them until he realized somene was coming his way. He turned in his seat and fixed me with one eye. "Kincaid," he said, "you're just in time for happy hour." He raised his glass. His voice was softer, less of a growl. The Brooklyn accent was still anchored on every word.

I stopped at the edge of the slip. "Permission to come aboard, Captain?"

He didn't get up, but gave a nod of approval. "Granted."

He watched me make the transfer from land to boat.

"Not much of a sailor, are you?" he said. He pronounced it "sailah."

"I've played cruise ships," I said, sitting on a cushion. "Don't think I've ever been on a sailboat before, much less steered one around." I looked around. The deck was freshly washed. The sails were neatly furled. The wood was polished. Everything was shipshape.

"Too bad," Moftus said. "Kelly sails." He reached in a plastic pouch next to his cushion and drew out a cigar. He set his drink in a holder on a table that folded out from the helm and set about the process of cutting and lighting the cigar. It was a ritual and he took his time. "You don't smoke these either, do you?"

"No."

He lit up, puffing with pleasure. "You drink?"

"That I do."

"Yeah, me asking an Irishman if he drinks. What do you drink?"

"Guinness."

"I got a can of Murphy's Irish Stout down below," he said. "I was keeping it for a buddy of mine across the bay, but . . ."

"Sold."

Moftus gestured vaguely. He was fine where he was. So was his drink. I went below. The cabin was kept as neatly as the rest of the boat. The galley was polished to a shine. The dining table was set for two. Beyond a closed door was a bedroom, presumably. It smelled like Moftus had just taken a shower.

I found the Murphy's in the galley and in the bar an imperial pint glass, just my size. One thing you could say about Moftus, his boat was his castle and he received visitors well.

I poured the Murphy's and was heading back up when Moftus called down to me. "Hey, punch the CD player on, will you?"

I scouted around, found the player, and turned it on. Green letters and symbols glowed but nothing happened. "Nothing's happening," I called out.

"It's automatic," he said.

I took that to mean I hadn't done anything wrong and my part of the job was done. I went up and joined him on the deck, sitting on a cushion across from him. There was a light breeze. I caught a whiff of fresh cologne. "You expecting someone?" I asked.

He looked at his watch. "In about thirty minutes."

"Nice boat you got here."

"Thanks."

"What's her name?"

"The *Trifecta*."

"Like at the race track?"

Moftus nodded. "I used to gamble. You?"

"A little. When I play Vegas."

"This was more than a little. I'm thinking of changing her name."

"Why?"

" 'Cause I quit gambling."

"Oh." I raised the Murphy's. "Here's to her, whatever she's called."

He nodded slightly and took a drink. The music came on. Big band. Hip and hopping.

"Who's this?" I asked, nodding to a speaker.

"Count Basie."

"I like it."

"Yeah," Moftus said, "I can't stand that rock and roll crap. None of them junkies can sing anymore."

He didn't seem to be in any particular hurry to do or say much. His eyes were resting on the horizon. He was gazing out at the water, drinking some booze and smoking his cigar and waiting for the next thirty minutes to pass.

"I suppose you wonder why I'm here," I said.

"No."

I must have looked puzzled. He sighed. I was bending his mood, if not breaking it. "Let me guess," he said. "It has to do with Ned Lando."

"Why do you say that?"

"I was the one helped Kelly carry you to her car."

I nodded. "Thanks for that."

He shrugged. "Like I ain't lost a few rounds myself in a back alley."

"There were two of them," I said.

"At least. Lando don't look so tough, and you Micks is a hard-headed bunch."

"We're not known for our diplomacy."

Waves slapped against the hull.

"Kelly must have told you where to find me," he said.

"She didn't want to. Don't be mad at her."

"I could never be mad at Kelly," he said.

I let that pass. There was something else there. Like when Kelly said Moftus didn't have a girlfriend.

He turned his massive head. "You, on the other hand, are a comic. And comics I get mad at all the time." He drank again. "Monday through Saturday. You caught me on my day off."

"I don't know if you heard this part," I said. "Lando made a tape of the show last night. His act, Kelly's, and mine."

"How do you know that?"

"Because Pluto told me." I left out the part about the hundred bucks. "Lando gave him the recorder."

"And he just plugged it into his soundboard out of the kindness of his heart?"

"All I wanted to know about was what he and Lando were talking about before the show," I said. "I didn't ask him for any other details. But as soon as he told me about the taping, I went outside to stop Lando on his way to his car. Then I got clobbered from behind." I indicated the knot on the back of my head.

Moftus nodded. "You see who hit you?"

"No," I said. "But before I went out, I found the tape in Lando's bag. He didn't want to give it to me because he had sold it—to another comedian who also played your club just a few weeks ago."

Moftus nodded. "Roger Fisk."

My turn to be surprised. "How'd you know?"

He drained his glass and started to crunch the ice. " 'Cause it was Fisk that booked Lando into my club."

"But . . . Fisk . . . I heard he wasn't such a good comedian," I said.

"He stinks," Moftus said. "So does Lando."

"So why did you book them?" I said.

"I didn't," Moftus said. "They booked me."

I shook my head. "I still don't get it."

"You like this boat, Kincaid?" Moftus said. He waved his cigar around. It had gone out. "You like the *Trifecta?*"

I nodded.

"It's all I got," Moftus said. "I live in a one-bedroom apartment. I drive a ten-year-old car. All I own, all that's really mine, we're sitting on right here."

"What about the club?" I asked.

"I got a mortgage on it," Moftus said. "I own the tables and chairs and the bottles of booze behind the bar. That's about it. I finish paying off the club next year. I got a buyer lined up. He'll probably turn it into a blues club. Blues is hot right now. Comedy's cooling down."

"Then what are you going to do?" I said.

"Set sail," he said. "For parts unknown." He smiled. "I'm done with LA, with showbiz, with busting my hump to make rent. I never owned a house or a new car. This is the third business I ran, and the first to turn a profit. How old do you think I am?" He parked his burning cigar in his mouth and struck a pose.

I took off ten years. "Forty-five."

Moftus laughed and took off his sailor's cap to show his bald head. He was missing his toupee. He had a fringe of dyed hair around his ears. "I'm fifty-six," he said. "But for thinking I'm forty-five, I'll book you back."

"Thanks," I said. "What's all this got to do with——"

"Ned Lando and Roger Fisk?" Moftus asked. He put his cap back on. "Simple. I need money. And they paid me to book 'em."

I had never heard of anything like this before. "They paid you?"

"That's right."

"But I saw a W-9 for Fisk in the office," I said, and immediately wished I hadn't.

"Aw, going through my files at the office, too, huh?" Moftus said. He grinned, but it was forced. He was talking around his cigar and he took it out to make his point. "Take a look at that W-9. I never turned in the government's copy. I wanted to fire him the first night. That's all these guys are getting, is opening spots. You can't pay me enough to book a shitty middle or headliner."

"But why?" I said. "Why pay you?"

" 'Cause I wouldn't book 'em normal," Moftus said. He laughed. He was out of booze and ice. "Great idea, huh? Wish I'd thought of it sooner."

I wanted him to keep talking. I took the empty glass from his hand. "Another?"

"Sure." He pitched the cigar butt into a bucket. "Scotch and water."

I went down below and made him a fresh drink with some Glenfiddich. I don't drink hard booze but I know the good stuff. I came back above and handed it to him with another question. "So take me through this," I said. "You booked Fisk six weeks ago as an emcee."

"Right." Moftus nodded as he drank.

"And he stinks."

"Yep."

"And you want to fire him."

"No," Moftus said. "I did fire him."

"You *did* fire him?"

Moftus nodded. "Told him I'd get someone else to open. That Saturday might have been Kelly's first time opening, but I never got a chance to offer it to her."

"Why?" I asked. "Fisk offer you cash on the spot?"

"No, his *manager* calls me Saturday afternoon," Moftus said.

"His manager?" I said. "He's got a manager?"

"Yep."

That information wasn't on Fisk's headshot. Roger Fisk had no agent or manager listed. "Who's that?"

"David Kelton," Moftus said.

"Kelton?" I said. "I heard of a booker named David Kelton a long time ago . . ."

"Same guy," Moftus said. "He started out booking rooms and now he manages comics. At least he manages Roger Fisk."

"So Kelton calls you . . ."

"And he says how he heard about what happened and how about giving Roger another chance. Naturally, I laugh in his face. He starts to argue with me and I hang up on him. He calls me back. Fisk'll work for nothing, Kelton says. No money involved. Roger's got no comedy tape on him, he needs tape to look at himself, some very important people in the entertainment industry want to look at him, he's got a development deal in the works . . . the usual bullshit."

"Right," I said.

"So I says no way. But this time I say good-bye before I hang up on him. Then he calls back one last time and says, 'How about you keep Roger Fisk in as opener and I pay you a hundred dollars.' I say, 'What?' I think I'm not hearing him right, you know? He says, 'A hundred fifty.' I said, 'You're gonna pay me a hundred fifty to book in some shit act so he can get some tape on him?' Kelton says, 'Two hundred.' Don't take me long to figure out that playing dumb is making me rich. I say, 'I don't know . . .' " He sipped his drink. "By the time I got off the phone with David Kelton, Roger Fisk is booked back into my club and he's paying me five hundred dollars."

"Jesus," I said. My pint glass was empty. Foam was sticking to the side of the glass. The Basie disc had changed. Now we were listening to some solo piano. "I never heard of such a thing. Why?"

"I got debts," Moftus said, "to some very impatient people in the world of sports betting."

"No, I mean why did Kelton feel the need to pay you?"

Moftus shrugged. "He wasn't paying me five hundred dollars to ask questions."

"Who paid you?" I said.

"Fisk did."

"Cash, check . . ."

"Cash. Night of the performance. Then he proceeded to go up on stage and eat the big beefsteak of death." He shook his head. "I went backstage and counted my money as he stank up the place. Lucky I had Joey Mosh headlining or I would have had to give refunds."

"Yeah," I said vaguely. "Mosh is funny." I leaned in toward Moftus. The sun was starting to set. I was getting a chill. "How did you hear about Ned Lando in the first place?"

"Kelton calls me back two weeks later. Says he got another hot comic. I says as far as I'm concerned he ain't got one. Kelton says this guy's better. This guy's different. Wants me to book him as opener and emcee. By then I'm using Kelly as opener and house emcee, you know? This last weekend was her first time as a middle."

"She did great," I said.

"Yeah, I thought she would." Half the new drink was gone. "She's a great gal, Kelly. Too bad I'm old enough to be her freakin' dad."

I nodded.

"I mean, she looks great, you know," Moftus said. "Just a knockout." He tapped the side of his head. "But smart, too. Business smart."

"Don't find that in too many comedians," I said.

"Don't find that in too many *people*," Moftus snorted. "She used to be a broker. Paid for this boat with some of the money she made me in the stock market. The rest I lost at the track and betting college ball." He shook his head in self-disgust.

"Ned Lando," I said.

"Oh. Yeah." He looked at his drink and probably decided that he was talking too much about things that were better left unsaid. He put the glass in a holder and folded his hands. "So I just hang on the line while Kelton realizes I ain't booking Lando without a little . . ." He rubbed his fingers and thumb together. "You know."

"Yeah."

"And we go back and forth and finally we settle on another five hundred bucks. So I book him and then Art Westcott cancels on me yesterday afternoon and that's how you and me become acquainted."

"I take it Lando paid you."

"Cash," Moftus said. "In the office while you were talking to Pluto. But I'm done with pay-for-play. Jesus, both those assholes sucked."

"That's all you know?" I said.

Moftus shrugged. "That's it. In nine months, the club is going on the block, and I am out of here."

I looked around. Dusk was settling in at the marina. I heard a dog bark. There was no traffic noise. It was a nice place to be. I breathed deeply. The sea air filled my lungs, clean and cleansing. "That'll be nice," I said. "Even if you don't go anywhere."

"Yeah," Moftus said. He picked up his drink and glanced at his watch. "Now if you'll excuse me I am expecting someone . . ."

I stood up. "My apologies to your friend."

Moftus stayed seated but he blinked. "Who?"

"The one whose Murphy's I drank." I waggled my empty glass.

"Oh. He'll get over it."

I ran my drinking glass back downstairs, rinsed it out, and left it in the sink. I came back up.

"What are you gonna do now?" Moftus asked.

"I got a spot at the Store tonight," I said.

"I meant about getting beaned on the back of the head."

"Find Roger Fisk," I said. "Maybe David Kelton. Or Ned Lando. See how all of this is connected. Get the tape of my act back."

"Call Kelton," Moftus said. "Maybe he'll pony up a few hundred for your trouble."

"You mean so I'll forget about it?" I said. "And go away?"

Moftus shrugged. "Worth a try."

I shook my head and smiled. "I'm not ready to set sail around the world just yet."

"Just trying to save you another bop on the head," Moftus said. "My experience is they serves as warnings."

"That's been my experience, too," I said. "One of these days I'll learn to pay attention to them."

"You chase this down and get your head caved in, that's your business," Moftus said. "But do me a favor."

"What's that?" I said.

"Leave Kelly Malone out of it," Moftus said.

"I will," I said. "You think I want you on my ass, too?"

He grinned, showing cigar stains on his teeth. I made a minor show of stepping from his boat back to dry land. I turned and saluted him and walked away in the settling night.

I found his visitor in the parking lot. She was parking a compact car with the valet service and staring at her ticket, thinking six bucks? She was the same height, the same hair color, the same build as someone else both Moftus and I knew.

"Kelly?" I said.

She turned and looked at me. It wasn't her. In the face you

could see the difference. The eyes were made green by contact lenses. The makeup was applied a little too heavily. The set of the mouth came from years trading something else besides stocks and bonds.

"Who are you?" she said.

"A friend of your client's," I said. "You're looking for Richard Moftus, right?"

"Slip 148-A," she said. She wiggled her parking ticket. "I can't believe they went up on this again. It used to be four-fifty."

Her voice was different, too. Higher pitched. Her enunciation was a little sloppy.

"I parked three streets down," I said. I tilted my head back toward Moftus's boat. "He's waiting for you." I turned to go.

"Hey," she said.

I stopped.

"Who's Kelly?" she said.

"You are," I said. "For tonight."

She didn't smile. "I've been Kelly for six months now, every Sunday night. He makes me dinner, drinks too much, then tells me about his rotten childhood and starts crying. Or sometimes we sit and listen to that old-timey music of his."

"That's all?" I said.

"He can't do anything else," she said. "I leave when he falls asleep." She cocked her head and her hip. In the fading light the resemblance was distinct. No wonder she arrived after the sun went down. "You telling me there's a real Kelly?"

"Yes."

"And who is she?"

"The woman he loves," I said. "Take care of him." I left.

"Hey," she called after. "What's your number? You're cute. Maybe sometime you'd want me to be Kelly, too?"

TWELVE

After leaving Richard Moftus's boat I headed back up to LA. I had a 10:15 spot at the Store, so I hit the Laugh Factory and the Improv beforehand, chatting up whomever I could find, looking for Roger Fisk. He'd been seen at the sign-up nights at the Factory. Same at the Improv. At the Store, I found his name on the schedule as part of Potluck Night. I checked with the emcee. Fisk had tried to get a showcase in order to become a regular, but no luck yet. He'd gotten a three-minute spot at 7:17 and had barely said hello when he'd gotten "the light"—a blue neon star set stage left that was the signal to get off. The emcee said Fisk had slipped him some coupons to the strip club where he was hosting an amateur night. He showed me one. Paradise Isle. He gave it to me.

After my spot, I drove back down the Strip toward Paradise Isle. It was on the east end of Sunset, past Vine. Not an establishment I'd patronize on a regular basis, but I used to have a storage space on that end of Sunset so I knew where it was. Strip clubs aren't that hard to find. Paradise Isle had the signs out front reading LIVE NUDE GIRLS. David Brenner used to do a bit about signs that read "Live Nude Girls." Like who would pay to see dead ones? Maybe in New York.

I parked. It was Sunday night on Sunset, so spaces weren't plentiful, but they were free. I could have used the lot in front of Paradise Isle, but I wasn't looking to make any friends that night and I didn't want to have to go back for my wheels. I left my car near my old storage company and walked a block back.

I used the coupon to get in. My ticket was taken by a thick-faced bouncer with a buzz cut and too much beer weight on him. No goatee, no ponytail. Definitely not George. A sign posted above the entrance read: NO GUNS. The fun never stopped here at Paradise Isle.

I walked in to the blare of music I would never listen to by choice: pulsing techno mixed with rap samplings. Kids these days and their music. Ach! Nothing but a bunch of noise, I tell you.

Paradise Isle had low ceilings, spinning multicolored lights, and tonight a lot of empty tables and chairs. On stage, a pneumatically enhanced Latina woman was twirling on a pole, her breasts bare, her bikini bottom still in place (so the club could still serve booze), and an expression on her face like she was thinking about what she had forgotten to pick up at the store earlier that day. Sitting ringside were half a dozen day laborers, two with dates.

I found a table near the back and sat down. A waitress in scanty lingerie was on me like a fly, and I bought a beer for five bucks, tipping her two. No Guinness Pub Draft. No Murphy's Irish Stout. No Sierra Nevada Pale Ale. No Anchor Steam. Not even Samuel Adams. They had the same beer in bottles that they had on tap. It tasted like spiked soda pop.

I sat and waited for the dancer to end her routine. As a comedian, I'd played one strip club in my entire career. It's a little hard to set up a bit about airline food when a table full of drunk guys are heckling you with "Show us your tits!"

The dancer ground to a halt and reached down and put her modified sweatshirt back on as the spectators applauded by placing dollar bills on the edge of the stage. She bent down to pick them up, bestowing quick thank-you kisses. An emcee stepped out behind her with a microphone. A guy. Wavy brown hair. Light hazel eyes. Muscles underneath a tight T-shirt. Tan. Good-looking, like a TV weatherman.

Roger Fisk.

"Angie!" Roger yelled into the overamped mike. "Let's hear it for Angie!"

I did my best to applaud. It didn't make any difference. The deejay cut out the music, and I realized I would be the only one clapping and the last thing I wanted to do was to draw attention to myself. There was dead silence over the PA, a lull in the show. That didn't stop Roger though. Angie left via the shimmering curtain in the background, and Roger was alone onstage for a minute to work his special magic.

"Our next dancer is a blonde. Now I don't want to say that blondes are dumb, but did you hear about the blonde who went to the doctor and the doctor says, 'You're pregnant,' and the blonde says, 'Oh, is it mine?' "

Roger waited. Nothing. Maybe a moan.

"So the doctor says, 'Haven't you been using your diaphragm?' The blonde says, 'No.' " He was using a high, whispery voice for the blonde's dialogue. "The doctor says, 'Why not?' She says, 'Well, it's really hard to swallow.' " He stroked his throat, acting out the joke.

Some patient smiles, but that was it. Jesus Christ, this guy was awful.

"Wake up, people," he admonished. "It's comedy."

He just let that hang out there, while an uncomfortable silence stretched out.

"All right," he said, "you assholes don't deserve her, but here's Dolores!"

The music kicked back in. Roger swept an arm up and Dolores came bouncing out. She was indeed a blonde, wearing a stewardess outfit that she quickly doffed as she slithered up and down the metal pole that stood center stage. I was sorry I couldn't watch Dolores any longer. She looked like she had some promise.

I watched the sides of the stage for Roger Fisk. He didn't appear. He must have been lingering back in the dressing room, hitting on the other dancers. As Dolores shimmied out of her sequined bra—I told you she had talent—Roger made a lazy entrance out of a side exit. He walked along the bar, got a fresh drink, and sauntered to a raised area by a second dance stage that was now dark. He plunked down at a table, joining some bruiser in a coat and tie with a black goatee and a black ponytail, thick eyebrows over a very serious expression. George. Roger's bodyguard.

Hmmm. . . .

That made two of them. With the bouncer in the front, more like two and a half. I couldn't take two and a half guys by myself. I would have to think this thing through. George and Roger quit talking to watch Dolores go through her moves. George especially. I had an idea.

The waitress came by and I got another beer. This time I tipped her three bucks and asked, "How about I get a table dance?"

"Oh, I don't dance," she said. "You'd have to ask one of the girls."

Five bucks found its way onto her cocktail tray. "How about Dolores?" I said. "Could you send her over when she's offstage?"

She batted her false eyelashes at me. "Sure."

"Have her meet me by the front."

I picked up my beer and moved to a midway point against the wall out of sight of both George and the doorman. Dolores had two numbers, the fast one she opened with and the slow one she followed it with. I watched her. She was no amateur. She was a professional looking for a job. She worked the rim of the stage, whipping her head back and forth in time to the music, sinking to her knees to gyrate with a flexibility that would have made a yoga instructor proud, her face slack and eyes closed with overwhelming desire. She took stray dollar bills and stuffed them into her panties, using them to heighten her pleasure. And I thought I had a great closing bit.

She was just what I needed. She got offstage to genuine applause, Roger got back on, and the music was cut again.

"Dolores!" Roger said, getting another round of applause. "Man, have I got something to think about when I get home tonight!"

I snuck a look around the corner. George was applauding, a leering smile peering through his goatee.

Roger launched into another lame joke. "A plane goes down in the Atlantic Ocean, and all who are left alive in the same life raft are a priest, a preacher, and a rabbi . . ."

Dolores was at my side. "Hi, honey," she said, smiling big. "What can I do for you?"

She was pretty up close and in person. A lot of makeup, but she took care of herself. She had her top back on, but that didn't hide much. "It's not what you can do for me," I said. I peered around the corner and pointed out George. "It's my buddy's birthday over there and I wanted to give him something special."

"Like me?"

"For a few minutes."

"Twenty bucks," she said.

I gave her the folded green. "He liked your act," I said. "His name is George."

She looked over at George again. "He really your buddy?"

"No."

"It really his birthday?"

"No."

"What's the real deal?"

Among her other attributes, she wasn't dumb. "I'm going to have a word with his boss," I said. "George bodyguards the emcee."

"You guys gonna fight?"

"I hope not," I said.

"What's this about?"

"An international banking matter," I said. "Now I need a distraction as soon as Roger gets offstage. I need George looking at something else besides the man he's supposed to be guarding."

"One distraction coming right up," she said. "Roger tried to put his hand up my ass." She looked me over. "Too bad George didn't send me over to take care of you. I like blue eyes."

I smiled back. "Too bad."

She left. Roger wrapped up his joke onstage. ". . . and the rabbi says, 'Beats the hell out of pork, doesn't it!' "

Nothing.

"OK, let me tell you people something," Roger said. He'd had a few drinks by now. He was feeling a little bold. "When I'm a big star, you're gonna wish you'd laughed." He wasn't joking. This wasn't a bit or a put-down. He was serious. "You're not gonna be able to afford to get in to see me. You'll still be down here sucking up this shitty cheap booze, while I'm starring in my own sitcom. And the Comedy Store and the Improv and the Laugh Factory and all those assholes can just kiss my ass." At that he bent over and slapped his butt.

The audience members lightly chuckled at that. They thought

he was trying to be funny or just tripping. Either way, they found it amusing.

The inappropriate laughter seemed to mollify him, and he straightened up with a smile on his face. "Now that's better," he said. "Our next performer is—fuck, I forgot. Candy, who is it?"

"Wanda," said a female voice over the PA. I took it that was Candy.

"Okay, please welcome the very beautiful . . . Wanda!"

Wanda came prancing out and Roger stepped offstage. I looked over at Dolores. She was already at George's table, bending over to whisper to him, her body blocking the bar exit where Roger had come out last time.

I made my move.

I headed for the bar while the audience was watching Wanda and George was watching Dolores. I put my beer on the bar and took a stool. Within thirty seconds, Roger Fisk came out of the exit and stopped by for a refill five feet away from me.

"Hey, Mike," Roger said. "Another Seven and Seven."

Mike the bartender looked like he'd had his fill of drunken emcees. He was shorter than Roger but stockier. "How about just a 7UP, Rog?"

"Come on, man . . ."

"Candy says you're cut off, Rog," Mike said. "No more drinking on duty."

Roger reached in his pocket for a wad of hundreds. "How 'bout a bottle then?" Roger said. He peeled off a C-note. "Let me take the bottle, I'll go in the back, and nobody'll know the difference."

"Rog—"

I got up off my stool. "You Roger Fisk?"

Roger looked up. "Huh?"

"Are you Roger Fisk?" I repeated.

"What about it?"

"Ned Lando says he sold you my act."

That stopped conversation. The music was loud where we were standing and so I wasn't surprised when Roger said, "You talking to me, motherfucker?"

His headshot had not been airbrushed or retouched. Up close, Fisk was as handsome as a soap opera actor, and maybe that's what he should have been instead of a comedian. His jaw was wide and angular, his tan skin brown and smooth with no wrinkles. His hair was thick and curly, and he had let it grow a little long over his collar and ears. He had deep-set hazel eyes and a pouty mouth that was now twisted in a fierce snarl. I placed him at twenty-five, maybe twenty-seven. He was in premium condition, with muscles that roamed beneath his skintight white T-shirt. Young and full of booze and fury.

I stepped in closer and raised my voice. "Ned Lando says he sold you my act. I'm here to cancel the deal."

Mike put a glass of straight soda in front of Roger. Roger stared at it numbly and pocketed his wad of hundreds. He stood up straight, appraising me. "And who the hell are you?"

"My name's Biff Kincaid," I said. "I'm a comedian. Ned Lando taped my act last night. When I told him I wanted that tape back, he said he'd sold it to you. I'm here to get the recording back and to tell you you're not to use any of my material in any way, shape, or form."

Roger looked at me. We were now less than three feet apart. Wanda was working her magic onstage. Dolores was entertaining George. Mike had found something interesting to do at the other end of the bar. Roger took a half step away from the bar and caught himself. He was drunk.

"You understand me?" I said. "Give me that tape."

Roger reached out for his glass of soda. "Fuck off, asshole," he said, and threw the carbonated sugary water at my face.

I ducked underneath quick enough so that only a splash

caught my shoulder, and I grabbed Roger's arm. Staying low, I pulled him over my shoulder and rolled him onto the floor. I picked him up by a handful of hair. "I am not kidding around with you," I said. "I want that tape back. Now. Tonight."

"George!" Roger yelled.

"Your hired muscle can't hear you," I said, "and he can't see you either." I shook his head back and forth by the hair until he winced in pain. The couples sitting ringside started to look over at the ruckus. "Listen to me. I'm going to let you up and you're going to go get that tape and hand it over. Understand?"

His eyes were closed. "Yes."

I let him go. His head fell back and hit the floor. His eyes popped open and he got up slowly.

I stepped back to let him rise. He staggered to one side, then another, so badly I reached out to steady him.

My mistake.

When I stepped in to help him stay on his feet, Fisk straightened up with all his strength behind an uppercut that connected so well I felt it through my face, down my spine, and between my shoulder blades.

I went back, taking down an empty table and all four chairs.

Now I was lying on the floor, wondering if it was better to get up or to lie still. The knot on the back of my head was pulsing like an open wound.

George had seen through my clever ruse and discarded Dolores's distraction. He rushed over, but his first concern was making sure Roger was still standing.

"I'm all right, George," Fisk said, looking down at me. "You can help the paramedics carry out this dirtbag here—when I'm done with him."

George looked at me with the kind of compassion coyotes have for housecats. He hadn't seen me when I walked in the door, but he remembered me now.

On his feet, George was big: six one or six two, and wide like a fullback. He was muscle by the pound. Up close I could see his hair was jet black, slicked back into a ponytail held by a strip of bandanna, and his goatee was neatly trimmed. His eyes were so brown as to be black, his face slightly rounded with a thin, sharp nose. Across his neck was a smattering of acne. Steroids. Another bodybuilder on the juice.

"Hey," George said, "this is the asshole from the club who got in a fight with Ned Lando."

"He don't learn so quick," Roger said. "Let's teach him a lesson he won't forget. Anytime he looks in the mirror."

George held out his hand to Roger while he looked at me, the fingers flat and long, and Roger swiped his palm against George's and suddenly Roger was carrying a butterfly knife. Roger flipped it open expertly, the steel blade dancing wickedly until it locked. Knife in hand, Roger stepped toward where I was lying on the floor, little birdies singing in my head.

Onstage, one of the naked girls—Wanda?—started to yell. The music cut off. I heard chairs scraping as the customers turned around to watch Fisk cut me up like a bad credit card. Suddenly, amateur night had gotten a lot more interesting.

Fisk twisted his fist in my shirtfront and tried lifting me up by my buttons. I let him. I had to wait until the time was right to turn the tide. His handsome, tanned face was twisted by blood lust. He wanted to watch me ooze the red stuff.

He took the knife and held it against my throat and spit in my face. "Fuck you," he said, "and your jokes," and lifted the blade up.

He was strong and he had a knife, but he didn't know anything about bar fighting. When you've squared off against loggers in Montana cowboy bars, you've learned a few tricks.

I'd kept one knee down as he stepped over me and now I brought it up like a teeter-totter board, right between his legs.

His head went back, his eyes squeezed shut, and he dropped the knife. I got my footing, stepped back, and kicked him in the stomach, and as he folded forward I leaned in with a right cross that knocked him back on his ass.

I bent down and picked up the knife just as George decided to come over and show how tough he was. I turned to him, the blade pinched between my thumb and forefinger, ready to throw. He stopped in his tracks. He looked me up and down and his right hand twitched toward a bulge in his suit jacket.

"You're not quick enough," I said. "You throw down on me here, and I'll plant this right in your neck."

His hand relaxed. I spun the knife closed, just to let him know I knew how to do it, and slipped it into my pocket as a souvenir. The floor manager came over, a Eurasian bleached blonde. She wore a silk teddy that deliberately didn't quite cover the tops of her siliconed breasts, stuffed so full with implants they didn't even bounce when she walked. Her face was rouged and mascaraed like a drag queen's, and she looked like every sailor's fantasy after three weeks out of port. I found her to be one of the least attractive women I'd seen that night. Then again, I've never had a thing for strippers.

"What the hell is going on?" she asked. She had a squawky voice. It explained why she'd never made it to the Broadway stage. She turned to George. "George?"

"Candy, this punk was hassling Roger," George said. His lips didn't move much when he talked, but he spit his words out clearly and his voice rumbled like a diesel engine. He sounded like Charles Bronson. He had a knife scar across one lip. I think the goatee was meant to hide it.

Roger moaned as he rolled over on his hands and knees and tried to stand. George went to help him get up.

Candy looked at me. "You a comedian?"

"Yes, ma'am."

"You're the first one who's gotten the best of Roger," she said. George had Roger in a chair and had run to the bar to get him some ice. "And there've been several who've come here looking for him."

"How many have there been?" I asked.

"Two," Candy said, "maybe three."

"And what happened?"

"Usually they're the ones George is helping to get up," Candy said, "and Roger is telling me what happened." She looked me up and down. "I ask him why they come gunning for him, and Roger always says it's over a girl." To her, this seemed to be a stupid reason. "Is that it?"

"No."

"What, then? Money?"

"Another comedian taped my act," I said, "and sold it to him. I want it back."

This she hadn't heard before. "For that you came in here and put my emcee on the floor?"

"Don't look that tough, do I?" I asked.

"Well, you're a redhead," she said.

"Irish," I said. "We pick a good fight."

Sirens. Candy turned and looked over her shoulder. "Dammit," she said softly, "one of the tryouts must have gotten excited and called the police."

"Normally they don't come that quick," I said.

"Honey, you'd be surprised how fast a cop can come," Candy said, with a little smile. "Especially in here."

I let that pass. "I'd better get out of here," I said. I pulled two twenties out of my wallet. "That's for the damage."

She took it and snapped a garter belt over the money. "I'll put the cops off your tail," she said. "Say it looked like a fair fight to me."

"It wasn't," I said, "but I won it anyway."

The sirens got closer. "You tell Roger your name?"

"Sure."

"You want to tell me?"

"Biff Kincaid."

She turned and pointed. "Go through the stage curtains and into the kitchen," she said. "Between the stove and the fridge is a fire exit. It leads to the alley. You can jog left and squeeze between two buildings and be on Sunset or Fountain in thirty seconds."

"Thanks," I said, and left the way she told me to.

THIRTEEN

Within the hour I was home, sipping a pint of Guinness to ease the pain in two parts of my head: the knot on the back of my skull from Saturday and now a punch to the jaw on Sunday. I was getting knocked around a bit. I'd had two pints of stout cooling in the fridge and the second one I held against my face. Internal and external application was definitely killing the pain.

Earlier that night I'd found my car where I'd left it on Sunset and managed to get back to Beachwood Canyon without running afoul of John Law. When I walked through the door I had a message from Kelly Malone that I didn't return. She wanted to know what Richard Moftus had had to say. Now it was after midnight and my head hurt even more when I thought about how I hadn't learned anything besides how hard Roger Fisk could hit. I had to take a different approach.

I drained the first pint and opened the second. I had Fisk's résumé, and I had the name of his manager, David Kelton, an ex-booker I'd barely heard of and I thought I knew them all. Ned Lando was still on the loose somewhere, for all I knew still taping acts and sending them to Fisk. Fisk himself was a no-talent who was beating his head against the Hollywood sign. He couldn't even get showcases at the Store.

Despite the late hour I tried Art Westcott's number. No answer. Not even a machine. Hm. I wondered how else to get in touch with him. Maybe he could clear this up a little bit.

It didn't make a lot of sense to me, and show business, as crazy as it was, did operate on one principle of logic and that involved cash flow. There had to be money being made somewhere, but who was making it? Not Roger Fisk. He seemed to be handing it out—to Lando, to George the bodyguard, and to who knows who else. Maybe he had slipped Candy a couple of bucks for the stage time.

I thought about all of this while I polished off the second pint and listened to some late-night blues on the lower end of the FM dial. Then I turned off the lights and sat in the silent dark for a while and realized that when it came right down to it, nobody knew much of anything, not even when the next earthquake was coming to bring the whole city down around our ears.

I got up Monday morning and hit the gym to try to heal myself with some weights and cardio. I soothed my aching head with a steam bath and a good shower. My jaw was red and purple in patches, too tender to shave. I decided to let my beard grow out for a few days, but shave it off after the end of the week. A face full of red hair tends to make me look like a lumberjack.

I went by Art Westcott's apartment at eleven o'clock that morning. I had tried his phone number once again before leaving and gotten the same response as I had last night: The line rang endlessly without being answered by anything, human or machine.

Art lived in Ocean Park, a seaside community between Venice

and Santa Monica that had attained cityhood just last year. His apartment was on the upper floor of a boxy, four-unit, sandstone duplex on Fourth Street between cross streets named Anchor and Sail, four blocks from the beach. Ocean breezes greeted me as I cruised by to case the joint.

I parked on the street and checked his mailbox first. It had a day's worth of envelopes in it, maybe two. I went to his front door and knocked. Apartment 3. No answer.

I checked the windows. Nothing. Blinds drawn.

No one else seemed to be home. It wasn't even the lunch hour yet, and on Monday most people would be at work. I circled around the building to the alley in the back. There I saw a way in. Art had left his bathroom window half open. If it wasn't nailed or painted in that position, I might be able to force it upward and crawl in. My only problem was how to reach it.

I pulled my car around to the back and parked in the middle of the alley. Standing on the roof, I was able to hook my fingers inside the bathroom window and pull myself up, grunting and straining as my running shoes found purchase on the peeling paint of the back wall. I clung with one arm while I shoved the window up with the other. It gave readily.

Up, over, and through. The window opened next to the shower. I clambered in, one foot landing in the tub, the other in a wicker wastebasket. I straightened up and looked around outside. I didn't think anybody had seen me. Yet.

The first thing I noticed was the smell, like someone had left meat out or a rat had crawled into a wall and died.

I turned around, checking the bathroom. Nothing there. Soap and shampoo. That was it.

The bathroom opened up into a short hallway, and the smell was even stronger there. To one side was a bedroom and an unmade bed. I looked around for any signs of packing, to see if he had hit the road after talking to me. His hanging bag was in the closet. I rummaged around and found a boxful of dirty magazines. Just like my house.

I went out of the bedroom and into the living room. I stood in the middle of the empty apartment and looked around. No dishes in the sink. No notes left for anyone taking in mail. Nothing. The blinds were drawn. Sunlight streamed in from a crack in the kitchen window shade, sending a golden shaft through the stillness. Dust motes twirled slowly in the air.

The smell was like a dry, dirty cloth on my face. I couldn't say for sure what it was, but I knew what I didn't want it to be. The light was blinking on his answering machine, right next to a cordless phone, still in the cradle. One message. I played it. His mother, calling from Florida. Just wanted to say hello. That was it.

I reset the answering machine and looked around the living room some more, breathing through my mouth. Art had an office area set up by the kitchen, and I leafed through his papers to see if there was anything telling. Just bills. A subscription renewal notice.

In the kitchen were a few dirty paper plates and a cold cup of coffee. At the other end of the kitchen was a door that led to a laundry room or a screened-in porch or maybe a second bedroom. Some of these older apartments were built a little quirky that way. The smell was coming from there.

I looked around for spoiled food, even checking under the sink to see if I could find a garbage bag with beef ribs or a ham that had been left out in the sun to rot. Please, God, let me find something like that.

The garbage had been removed.

Then I saw there was a second phone outlet in the kitchen, with a line plugged into it. My eyes followed the line to where it disappeared under the door on the far side of the kitchen. The door was closed. On the kitchen counter next to the door was an open box of detergent and a bottle of bleach, as well as a basket of dirty clothes. Why Art had needed a phone in the laundry room, I couldn't say.

I slowly stepped up to the side door in the kitchen that led to the laundry room. I knocked twice, then turned the knob slowly to the right. As I opened the door I could hear a faint humming that turned into a buzz, and as the door opened all the way I saw the buzz was coming from dozens, no, hundreds of flies that filled the room, flies born of the maggots that were now crawling out of what was left of Art Westcott's skull, most of it having been blown away as messily and completely as if a planet had struck an asteroid, scattering debris among the cosmos.

In one hand he still had the receiver. His hand was on the cradle. What was left of his head lay in between. So that was why there had been no reply, why the line had just rung through. Call waiting.

I concluded this right before I went to the sink to throw up. After I'd finished heaving from the sights and the smells and the sounds from three feet away I staggered back into the bedroom. I tried to use the cordless to call the police, but it was useless unless I wanted to go into the laundry room, pry the phone out of Art's dead fingers sticky with brain matter and hang it up. With that thought I went into the bathroom and threw up again.

I was in a small, windowless interrogation room paneled with white tiles at the Ocean Park Police Headquarters. The white tiles had holes in them. That was to absorb sound. Maybe I was expected to scream at some point.

When I was first escorted in by a police officer, I'd looked for a two-way mirror. There was none. I guess that had gone out with the nightstick and the telephone book. Instead, up in one corner was a video camera that watched me patiently with its single glass eye. I held up a hand and waggled my fingers.

I was sitting by myself at a scarred, wooden table on a plastic chair anchored to the floor. I tried to shift the table away from me and found it was anchored, too. I still had my belt and shoelaces. I could hang myself if need be. Coppahs, you'll nevah take me alive.

The police had arrived at the scene in Art Westcott's apartment less than five minutes after I walked out Art's front door and called from a pay phone on the corner. I had gone back inside to await their arrival, puking a third time for good measure. A squad car came with two uniforms, who sealed off the apartment and took me outside so I could get some fresh air. Vomiting is exhausting business.

One of them stood watch while the other one called in for more help. I sat on some grass by the sidewalk and let the ocean breeze ruffle my hair and clothes. The taste of bile burned in the back of my mouth. I could have used a mint.

More police cars came. The cops talked among themselves until two detectives arrived, one short and thin, one tall and heavy. The shorter one was Latino. His name was Chavez. The taller one was Caucasian. His name was Hirsch. Chavez was better dressed, with a pressed, white dress shirt and a silk tie and charcoal pants and black shoes. His hair was in a modified buzz cut and glistened black in the sun. He called to people by their last names and walked fast. He was a young guy. Maybe thirty.

Hirsch lumbered around at a slower pace, muttering underneath a combed walrus mustache. He had a shock of graying, unruly hair over eyes as big and dark as a Saint Bernard's. He looked like a fortyish Kurt Vonnegut. His shirt was wrinkled. His tie was askew. His khaki pants were well-worn and bagged at the ankles. He called people by their first names and smiled shyly when they called him "Detective."

They made their separate ways toward me. It was Chavez who looked me over and said, "Let's take him in," as if I couldn't hear him.

"Am I under arrest?" I asked.

Hirsch shook his head. "Just for questioning. You don't have to go if you don't want to."

Chavez stuck a wad of gum in his mouth and looked at his watch. "Well, we gotta talk to him somewhere."

"You got another stick of gum?" I asked.

"Not here," Chavez said. "At the station house."

"I'll go," I said.

So I rode in with them and they turned me over to a uniformed officer who showed me into the interrogation room, and now I was waiting for Mutt and Jeff to show up again.

Chavez was the first to enter. He took a seat opposite me on the other side of the table. His chair wasn't bolted down. He had a computer printout in his hand and he read that instead of looking at me.

"You wanted to ask me some questions . . . ?" I queried.

"Wait for my partner," he said.

"You got that other stick of gum?"

He reached in his pocket and flipped it at me. I caught it and unwrapped it. Spearmint. It tasted a lot better than what was already in my mouth.

Hirsch came through the door carrying two cups of water. "Sorry I'm late," he said. He set a cup in front of me. I drank it. I was feeling slightly dehydrated. Hirsch watched me gulp it. He set the second cup in front of me and I sipped that more slowly.

"All right, Kincaid," Chavez said, turning to the video camera and making a circling motion with his finger as if to signal an observer to roll tape. "Let's start from the top."

I told them everything.

"Wait a minute," Chavez said, fifteen minutes later when I was done. He held a hand up in the air as if trying to stop an annoying parrot from chattering. "You're telling me that this is all because of some stolen jokes?"

"I don't know if that's why Art Westcott is dead," I said. "I'm saying that's what led me to find him that way."

"Uh-huh."

"Biff," Hirsch said, "I know it must have been hard for you to see your friend's body like that."

"Worse for him," I said.

"But can you think for a moment why anyone would want to kill him?" Hirsch asked.

"No."

"Think," Chavez said.

"I am thinking," I said. "I have been thinking. Thinking is one of the things I do best."

"I got a hard time buying this is just over someone's comedy act," Chavez said to Hirsch.

"Maybe it isn't," Hirsch said to Chavez.

They looked at me and then left the room to talk between themselves. I waited for them. Twenty minutes.

"We checked out your story," Chavez said to me. "LAPD Hollywood Station didn't get a call to Paradise Isle Sunday night."

I shrugged. "I heard sirens," I said. "Maybe they stopped somewhere else."

"This Kelly Malone," Hirsch said. "Can she account for your whereabouts Saturday night?"

"Sure," I said. I looked from Chavez's impassive mug to Hirsch's sympathetic features. "You guys think maybe it was me?"

"You who what?" Chavez said.

"Me who shot Art Westcott in the head."

"Biff, we have to eliminate all suspicion," Hirsch said.

"How'd you know he was shot in the head?" Chavez asked.

"His brains were blown out all over the laundry room floor," I said. "That was a slight clue."

"Biff, we checked telephone records," Hirsch said. "It looks as though Art was killed not too long after he talked to you."

"Yeah, like maybe you were the last person to speak to him while he was alive," Chavez said.

"Anyone speak to him after he was dead?" I asked.

"You got a smart mouth on you, pal," Chavez said.

"I got a license for it," I said.

"Comedy," Hirsch said. "That must be a tough racket."

"Ask Art," I said. "He'll tell you."

"Unless, of course, you held a gun to Art's head and made him call your machine," Chavez said.

"I didn't think of that," I said.

"Phone records still show a toll call, even if he didn't talk to a live person."

"And here I thought I had an airtight alibi."

"Where can we find this Roger Fisk?" Hirsch asked. "He doesn't seem to have a permanent address."

I shrugged. "I been looking for him myself."

"What have you been looking for him for?" Chavez asked.

"Originally to get the tape of my act back."

"What if he don't want to give it to you?"

"Doesn't mean I won't get it back," I said. "And while I was at it, I thought I might ask him where he was Saturday afternoon while Art was getting his eggs scrambled."

"Get yourself off the hook, huh?" Chavez asked.

"Art Westcott was my friend, and he was a better comedian than Roger Fisk will ever be," I said, not being funny and not trying to be. "And I don't like it when bad things happen to good comics. It's not something I can just let go."

"Biff, I spoke to Ned Lando," Hirsch said.

"Yeah?"

"He doesn't know anything about a tape," Hirsch said. "He says there was no fight between the two of you, and he never heard of a Roger Fisk."

Silence. I stopped chewing my gum.

I looked from Hirsch to Chavez back to Hirsch again.

They waited.

"Am I supposed to confess?" I said.

"It's good for the soul," Chavez said.

"You can tell us anything you want, Biff," Hirsch said.

Silence. Again.

"What happens now?" I said.

"Tell us again," Hirsch said, "about how Art Westcott died."

"Sure," I said. "But first . . ."

Chavez straightened in his chair.

"Can I have another stick of gum?"

FOURTEEN

They let me go around three in the afternoon. I don't know if Hirsch or Chavez believed my story. They both had mastered the art of being inscrutable. I wasn't under arrest, so either my story held up or they didn't have enough proof to keep me on ice.

I drove home, letting the jumble of Art Westcott, Roger Fisk, and Ned Lando toss and turn around inside my brain like the unresolved premise for a new bit. I had more reason than ever to find out exactly what was going on. I seemed to be at the center of it, and it all seemed to be connected by lines I couldn't see. I thought over everything I'd learned. I was on my way back to Hollywood, but what was I going to do when I got there? Who was I going to talk to?

I got back to my place and started making calls.

It was still Monday. The only club that I remembered Roger Fisk listing on his résumé was the Comedy Cabana in Phoenix. My first phone call was to the talent booker there. His name was Everett Foster. We'd known each other for a couple of years, as he'd brought me in from an open miker to feature to headliner. I played there twice a year now and always did well.

The Cabana was in a shopping mall. Nothing set it apart from the other two hundred clubs out on the road, except it was just an hour from LA by plane. It didn't have any sister clubs. It was five years old. One day it would go out of business and become a dry cleaner's or a drugstore. All that would be left would be a pile of headshots and some T-shirts.

The only thing working in the office that Monday morning was the answering machine. I left a message for Everett to call me back. I checked my calendar. I was booked back in about three months. I could tell him I was just doing my calendar and wanted to reconfirm. And by the way . . . about this guy Roger Fisk . . .

I checked the phone book for the number of David Kelton. There were a few listings, but none belonged to David Kelton Management. I got in my car and drove to the Samuel French bookstore on Sunset and checked the listing book they had for personal managers. No David Kelton.

I went back home and called Kelly Malone. She wasn't home. I tried Chortles. Kelly answered the line. "I was wondering when you were going to get back to me," she said.

"When did you call?" I asked.

"Last night about eight," she said.

"I didn't get in until after midnight," I said.

"What were you doing?" she said.

"Getting beat up," I said.

"You seem to have a talent for that," she said. By her playful tone I could tell the police hadn't called her yet about Art's murder. "What happened?"

I told her about last night, starting with my visit to Richard Moftus. I left out the part about his look-alike visitor.

"You're serious," she said. "You got in another fight just last night?"

"With Roger Fisk."

"He didn't say anything to you?" she said. "He just hit you?"

"I think he called me a motherfucker."

"Wow," she said. "Makes him an honorary Irishman."

I would have laughed, but there was more she needed to know. "The police haven't called you yet, have they?"

"Which police?" she asked. "About what?"

"Kelly," I said, "Art Westcott's dead."

She didn't know how to take that. She hung on the line, silent for a while, trying to think of something to say.

I filled the gap with details. "I couldn't get him on the phone so I went by his apartment," I said. "I found his body inside, and then I called the cops. They just let me go."

"How?" she asked.

"How did the police question me, or . . . ?"

"I mean, how did he die? Art. How did Art die?" She was confused. I understood. Death was a confusing business. A lot of times the reaction was disbelief. Who? Dead? But I was just talking to them. They can't be dead.

"Someone shot him," I answered.

"So he was murdered."

"Yes," I said. "I mean, I'm not a police officer or a crime lab technician, but yeah, it looks like he was murdered."

"Do the police have any suspects?" she said.

"Yeah," I said. "Me."

"Biff, they don't seriously think you murdered Art Westcott, do they?"

"I don't know for sure, and I don't think I'm supposed to," I said. "I got the good-cop, bad-cop routine all afternoon."

"But what are they doing?" she asked. "Are they talking to people, are they taking fingerprints . . . what? How are they going to find out who killed Art?"

"We'll know they have a serious suspect when they arrest one.

In the meantime, they're proceeding with their investigation," I said. "The detectives who questioned me said they might call you. I'm glad I beat them to it."

"So am I," she said. "Biff, this is terrible."

"I know."

"Art was such a nice guy . . ."

"Funny," I said. "Funny guy."

"Oh, he was hysterical." She sniffed. She was crying. "I saw one show here where I thought he was going to get a standing ovation."

"I saw one where he did."

"I'll miss him."

"Me, too."

Silence.

"I want to see you," Kelly said.

"I'd like to do more than just see you," I said.

"Likewise." She sighed. "So what are you doing?"

"I'm trying to find Roger Fisk's manager," I said, "David Kelton. I want to talk to him about his star client."

"Still?" she asked. "You don't think Roger Fisk stealing your act is related to Art getting murdered, do you?"

"Now did I say that?" I said. I tapped the phone with my finger. "Is this thing on?"

"There some way I can help with this?"

"There is if I can get you to give me David Kelton's phone number," I said. "I think Moftus might have it."

"I can check Richard's office," she said.

"Is he in yet?"

"No, he's always late on Mondays," she said.

And you don't want to know why, I thought. "Okay," I said. "I'll hold."

"Why don't I look for it and get back to you," she said.

"Call me when you've got it," I said. "I'll carry my pager." I gave her the number.

"When am I going to see you again?" she asked.

"I don't know," I said. "Let's set something up later."

"Okay," she said. "Bye."

"Bye."

I hung up. She had sounded unsatisfied. Maybe she had wanted more from me in this troubled time. Perhaps she would have preferred I drop everything and rush to her side: I have to see you. I have to touch you. I have to smell you. I can't live without you.

I used to do things like that. I don't anymore. It's been a matter of years.

I didn't have anything else to do while I waited for Kelly to get me David Kelton's phone number so I got in my car and drove back onto Sunset and found the place where Roger Fisk kept a mailing address. I tried to get the Korean clerk behind the counter to tell me something about who rented box 1463, but ten dollars a month buys you silence, if nothing else. I left after he told me I go now or he call cops. Okay, okay. I go now.

When I got back home I had a message from Kelly: "Boy, you don't stay in one place long, do you? I have a number for you. David Kelton is at 818-367-4836. And you already know how to reach me."

She hung up.

I was about to call Kelton when the phone rang. I picked it up. It was Everett Foster at the Comedy Cabana. Normally, he was a bouncy, lively guy; about five five; a little paunchy; a wannabe comic who could never make it work onstage except as an emcee on the open-mike nights. So I was surprised by his subdued tone—not to mention what he said.

"Biff, I've been meaning to call you," he said.

"Same here," I said. "I just wanted to reconfirm my dates three months from now . . ."

"Um. Yeah. About that." I stopped talking. I heard paper shuffling, and then Everett started hitting computer keys. "We've had a change of ownership."

"When?"

"Last month," Everett said. "And we're handling bookings a little differently now."

"Uh-huh."

"I can tell you more when the schedule comes up on my computer screen."

Computer screen? Last time I was at the Cabana they'd used a notebook and a dull pencil. I didn't like the way this sounded. I'd heard this speech before, but never from Everett. Something had happened.

I decided to cut to the chase. "I'm out, aren't I, Everett?"

"We have a new policy regarding bookings," Everett said. "I can't just do them myself. They have to be approved by the new management."

"Everett, don't bullshit me," I said. "What's going on?"

Silence. "You're off the schedule."

"Fine. That's three months' notice. I can fill that time somewhere else," I said. "That's no problem."

"I'm glad, Biff, because I don't enjoy telling you this."

"It's no money out of my pocket," I said. "Not yet, anyway."

"Good."

"But can I ask why?" I said.

"The new ownership change," Everett said.

"Does this apply to all comedians," I said, "or just me?"

"All repeat bookings have to be approved by the new management," Everett said. He sounded like an operator for an

HMO. He'd had to say these phrases before. They'd been written for him and approved by a committee.

"And who are the new owners?" I asked.

"There's just one," Everett said. "He's a comedian. His name is Roger Fisk."

"Roger Fisk is now the owner of the Comedy Cabana?" I asked.

"That's right," Everett said.

"What happened to Steve Parker?" Steve Parker had been the owner of the Comedy Cabana the last time I'd played Phoenix.

"He got an offer he couldn't refuse," Everett said. "By that I don't mean a horse's head in the bed. I mean he got offered a lot of money for this place."

"The last time I played the Cabana nobody in Phoenix had probably heard of Roger Fisk," I said.

"Not true," Everett said, "we'd had some contact."

"Everett," I said, "can you tell me what happened?"

He sighed. "I may have to get off the phone if someone else comes in," Everett said.

"Understood."

"But I can tell you what I've been able to find out," he said.

"Okay." I was going to hold off on telling him everything that had happened here.

"Fisk's dad was a real estate developer up in northern Arizona," Everett said. "I don't know if you're familiar with the area . . ."

"Not really."

"Most people think Arizona is just flat desert, but up in the north there're mountains," Everett said. "There's been a real estate boom that's been going on up there for the last ten years. Some developers have been trying to turn it into the next Santa Fe. Developers like Carter Fisk."

"Who's Carter Fisk?" I said.

"Roger Fisk's father," Everett said. "Roger's grandfather was a rancher. Carter inherited a lot of land and started to turn it into retirement villages. He started doing this is the seventies, when Roger was born. He'd go to Texas, New Mexico, Phoenix, even Arizona, and market to the recently and soon-to-be retired."

"I take it he did well at it," I said.

"More than well. He got rich. To let you know how rich, five years ago Carter Fisk launched a gubernatorial campaign that went nowhere but resulted in lots of TV and print ads," Everett said. "He decided he was going to spend so much money for his campaign that it would actually be cheaper to buy a TV station in Flagstaff and make his ads out of there to be distributed across the state."

"Wow," I said. "So Roger grew up getting anything he wanted."

"Carter had two daughters but only one son," Everett said, "Roger. Roger wasn't interested in the family business. He wasn't interested in much of any kind of business, except for . . ."

We said the last two words together: "*Show* business."

"You got it," Everett said.

"And so Dad decided to help his boy out a little bit?" I said.

"Dad wanted him to get it out of his blood," Everett said. "He thought Roger was just sowing a few wild oats, which Roger had been doing since he was about fourteen. Carter got him hired as a weatherman at the TV station he owned in Flagstaff while he— Carter—flew around the country in his private plane trying to mount another political campaign."

"He was serious about this governor business?" I said.

"He wasn't going to run for governor again," Everett said. "He was going to run for president of the United States."

"You're kidding," I said.

"This man was rich, Kincaid," Everett said. "We're not talking movie star rich. We're talking real estate rich, stock market rich. Genuine wealth. Carter Fisk was going to Washington and buying power lunches for any junior senator that would let him in the door. He bought a radio station up in Show Low, Arizona, just so he could air his political reports and commentaries from Washington. He caught Potomac Fever bad.

"Then on a trip home, his plane ran into a storm in the mountains and went down. Carter Fisk, his wife, and one of his daughters were all killed. This was less than a year ago," Everett said.

"And Roger inherited his father's fortune," I said.

"Right," Everett said. "His dad thought that responsiblity would straighten Roger out. But he's not the only child left alive. He has an older sister, one who's trying to keep the family business together and doesn't want Roger pissing it all away. Funny thing is, she's contesting the will while she keeps working for the business her younger brother now owns. Technically, she works for him. But Roger cashed in a few million and headed for Hollywood."

"What about the TV station job?"

"Well, this was kind of funny," Everett said. "Right before Roger inherited the station himself, he'd gotten booted off the air by the station manager. Seems that Roger couldn't stay sober long enough to do the ten o'clock report and would go on the air and say things like 'we've got a big fucking storm heading in and it's gonna rain like shit, so get inside or you assholes are going to be wetter than a Vegas whore on New Year's Eve.' "

"The mind of a comedian at work," I said.

"Oh, he's not ashamed of that at all," Everett said. "He's got tapes of himself—on the air, drunk as a lord, cussing away. What's really funny is when they cut back to the news anchors and they try to cover for him. 'Uh . . . thank you for that . . . Roger . . .' "

I chuckled. "Does sound funny."

"He's trying to get it on some of those blooper shows, but no one's bit so far," Everett said.

"I don't think anyone's biting on his comedy act out here," I said.

"What act?" Everett said. "Oops. Oh. Good. Lucky no one's here."

"Exactly what I wanted to talk to you about," I said. "I was working this last weekend—"

"Wait a minute," Everett said. "Someone *is* here. Kincaid, I'll call you back."

He hung up.

Dammit. I put the phone back in the cradle and thumbed through my book. I had an old home number for Everett, so I tried that and got an answering machine. Everett's voice was still on it. I didn't leave a message. If he forgot to call me back at least I had a way to get in touch with him.

I called David Kelton's office, out in the Valley. A female voice answered.

"Production office," she said.

"I'm trying to reach David Kelton," I said.

"He's not here right now."

"Should I try back later?"

"After four o'clock," she said. It was now almost three-thirty.

"What's this the production office for?" I asked.

"Who is this?" she asked.

"I'm Steve Floundercatch," I said, "with AFTRA. I'm calling regarding an overtime complaint." AFTRA was the television and radio performers union.

"You'd have to talk to David," she said. "He's the line producer."

"He told me to call him at his office," I said. "Is that the same as the production office?"

"You'd have to talk to David."

To see if his office is the same as the production office? "I'll call back after four," I said.

I hung up. People in show business loved to play cloak and dagger. What were they making out there—chemical weapons?

I wasn't getting anywhere. There was one other person I could call who just might be able to give me some information.

I dialed a number. It was not yet four but there was always the happy-hour crowd.

"Paradise Isle." This was a man's voice. Not George's. I heard music in the background.

"May I speak to Candy, please?" I said. "I'm calling to confirm a nail appointment." Last night when I'd met Candy I hadn't noticed her nails, but I'm sure they were as obvious in their appeal as the rest of her.

"She's onstage right now," the voice said. "Call back in half an hour."

No one in the world wanted to talk to me. "All right." I hung up and headed out the door. By the time I was supposed to call her back, I'd already be there.

FIFTEEN

It was twenty minutes later when I walked into Paradise Isle on Sunset. There are no windows in a strip club. It's like a casino: If you didn't want it to be daytime, it didn't have to be. It was any time you wanted it to be, sugar. The beer was flat, the drinks watered, and the women weren't nearly as good-looking in the bright light of day.

There were about ten men just off the early shift crowded around a horseshoe-shaped stage where a young slip of a girl—she couldn't have been more than twenty—gyrated to old eighties metal hits, her breasts cartoonishly enhanced so they hung on her chest like so much ballast.

Behind the audience members was a hot hors d'ouvres buffet. I could smell the steam tables from the entrance, the cafeteria odor of fried chunks of potato and pork from the leftover lunch. The sign outside had read TRY OUR FREE HAPPY HOUR BUFFET AND ALL YOU CAN EAT LUNCH, and I had the feeling everything on the buffet worked the whole eight-hour shift. Below that was the outline of a busty young lady with stars for nipples. If that didn't say down-home cookin', I don't know what did.

Once inside, I looked around first for George and Roger, then Candy. No one from last night was here. I got a diet soda from the bartender and told him I was here to see Candy, gave him my name, and got a plate of food.

It was early in the happy hour or late in the lunch trade, so the food was as mangled as if a Turkish horde had run through it on horseback. The chicken was stewed, I didn't even want to look at the beef Stroganoff anymore, and the pork carnitas were glued to the bottom of the pan. I found some sandwich makings at the end of the bar and put some turkey next to some whole wheat bread. I took a seat at one of the many empty tables with a wide view of the room and a clear shot at the door. Yep, I was the new marshal in town.

I made short work of the food, and just as a half-naked waitress took my plate I saw Candy come out of the office door behind the bar. She was wearing a short, wraparound skirt and a loose, cut-off top, clothes that could be easily doffed if one of the dancers missed her shift. She had her bleached blonde hair up and had yet to glop on her makeup to its full density. This was her business look.

Her eyes scanned the crowd. She saw me and motioned me back behind the bar. I joined her and she held the door for me as I stepped through. There was a purple light illuminating a flight of carpeted stairs and we went up, out of range of the music volume that made any conversation other than shouted drink orders impossible. Candy was wearing a perfume that could have been used to fumigate foxholes. It was mixed in with a cigarette smell. She was a smoker. Darn. And I was going to propose.

We went up to her office at the top of the stairs. The door was already open. Red carpet on the floor, worn and taped together. Posters on the wall of her glory days, which must have been all of five years ago. She used to headline at the Seventh Veil. Photos of her topless with drunk entertainment and sports celebrities. The battered metal desk was neat. It held a glowing PC. A phone. Files. A board that marked all of the dancers', waitresses', bartenders', and bouncers' shifts.

Candy sat behind her desk and reached for a pack of cigarettes and a lighter. I took a visitor's chair that must have matched a couch and loveseat that were still at Goodwill. She brought an ashtray out of a drawer. "You get home okay last night?" she asked.

"Yes," I said. "Thanks for the getaway directions."

"No problem."

"What happened to Roger?" I asked.

"After a few scotches at the bar he was fine," she said. She lit up a cigarette. A menthol. "He was going to sue everybody in sight, but once he got drunker the world looked to be a much better place."

"It usually does," I said. "George take him home?"

She shook her head. "I took Roger home with me. He wanted to go find you, but I got his mind onto other things." She smiled with a tired lasciviousness.

I nodded, my face remaining expressionless. "Thanks, I guess."

"No charge," she said. "It wasn't that big a sacrifice. He's young, he's darn cute, and he's in great shape. Even when he's drunk he can still keep up with me. I appreciate stamina. What can I do for you today?"

"Last night, before I had to leave so suddenly, you said that there had been other comedians who had come and gotten into fights with Roger," I said.

"That's right," Candy said, blowing out a stream of smoke. "You're the first to win."

"Who were these other comedians?"

"I don't know," she said. "There were only two or three of them."

"One of them named Art Westcott?"

"I didn't know their names."

"Taller than me. Skinny. Glasses. Bushy mustache. Dresses like a college professor."

She shrugged. "By the time I saw these guys they had at least one eye swollen shut, their glasses broken, and their mustaches bloodied."

"Can you remember when this happened?" I asked.

"All in the last two weeks." Candy tapped the ash on her cigarette. "Roger's only been here that long."

"How'd you book him?" I asked.

"What's your interest?" she asked.

"Like I told you last night, Roger bought a tape of my act. He might be buying tapes of other comedians' acts as well. I want my act back." I paused. "And I want to know why he's stealing material."

"Is the big problem that he didn't pay you?" she asked.

If she was sleeping with Roger, she was going to be talking to him. I wanted that to work in my favor. "The big problem is that he did it at all," I said. "He paid someone else to steal it for him."

She nodded. "And how much are you looking to get?"

"For my act?"

She nodded again.

"It's not for sale," I said. "I did some checking up on him today. I know he's got money and he's throwing it around like a man with three arms. He's a rich kid from Arizona whose only gig before was as a weatherman on a TV station his dad used to own in Flagstaff. He's out here in Hollywood, thinking he can buy his way into the comedy world. It doesn't work like that."

"I don't know that much about comedy," Candy said.

"Could a bad dancer buy her way onto your stage?"

Candy smiled. "A dancer, no."

"How about a comedian who wanted some stage time?" I said.

Her smile faded. "You want to know if I'm paying Roger Fisk?" she asked.

"No," I said. "I want to know if he's paying you."

Her face didn't change. "It's been a slow month."

I waited. One cigarette had to burn out and she had to light another before she spoke again.

"He came in here as a customer," she said. "I don't dance anymore, except like earlier today when one of the other girls didn't show up. I manage the floor and I emcee. When I got offstage one night Roger sent me a bottle of champagne. Onstage I'd said it was my birthday, but that's part of the act. He knew the drill: We sell that same bottle three times a night. We all take turns having birthdays five nights a week. The champagne bottle goes back behind the bar while the girl drinks ginger ale. When I went over to say thank you, he slipped me twenty bucks for five minutes. I thought he meant a table dance. He meant onstage, himself, under the lights, telling jokes. I hesitated and he made it fifty bucks. At a hundred I thought, *What the hell?* At the next break I announced we had a special guest comedian and brought him on."

"How'd he do?" I asked.

Her smile peeked out again. "You ever play a strip club?"

"Once or twice," I said, "on the road. A long time ago."

"That crowd come to see comedy?"

"No," I said. "But I got them laughing."

"Well, you must be some comedian then."

"I do my job," I said. "What about Roger?"

"They wanted the girls back."

"Imagine that."

"I told him from then on to do his comedy up front and then just a little bit in between as emcee," Candy said. "He comes in about three times a week for that, and he pays me two hundred an appearance."

"How is he onstage when he's not been drinking?"

"Awful." Candy stubbed out her cigarette. "This morning as I was getting dressed I told him I can't have any more of these fights and put him on permanent vacation."

I lifted my eyebrows. "He's fired?"

She dropped her head once in a half-nod. "Let's just say he's more trouble than he's worth."

"I imagine he didn't like that," I said.

"I'm going to like it even less if I have to let some dancers go because I'm not getting the extra six bills a week from him. Roger was too hungover to do anything about it," she said. "He was too hungover to even let me make it up to him." The lascivious smile again. "I had to pour him into a cab to send him home."

"Where can I find him besides here?" I asked. "Where does he live?"

"I don't know," Candy said. "He's been here less than a dozen times."

"You ever heard of David Kelton?"

"No," she said. "Who's that?"

"Roger's manager."

"I might know him if I saw him," Candy said. "Roger's had some people in. He said he was showcasing for them."

"He ever mention a TV deal of any kind to you?" I asked. "Any development or casting deal with a network or production company?"

She shook her head. "We didn't talk a lot. He said maybe two dozen sentences to me after I hired him. One of them was, 'I like your tits.' "

I didn't say anything.

"What do you want from him anyway?" Candy asked.

"I want my act back," I said. "I want that tape he bought of it back in my hands. And I'll drag him off your stage or any other and pound him like a nail again and again until he gets it through that handsome mug of his."

"He's got a bodyguard," she said. "George."

"George was no good to him last night," I said. "There's something else, too. Since last night."

"What's that?"

"That comedian with the glasses and mustache I mentioned? Art Westcott?"

"I told you I couldn't remem—"

"He's dead."

Long silence. "How?"

"Someone shot him in the head."

"I assume the police know about this?"

"Absolutely."

"Do they have a suspect?"

"As far as I know, it's me," I said. "But Art was my friend, and I think he knew Roger Fisk was stealing material, too. I'm having a hard time convincing the cops that someone would kill to be funny, so I thought I'd keep asking questions on my own."

Candy stayed seated, but lifted her legs up off the floor and put them on her desk, letting the leather skirt slide back just three-quarters of an inch. Her legs were not long but well muscled and tan. I didn't look. I knew what she was trying to do. I was being a tough guy, and she liked to take tough guys and soften them up. It was a business move.

"You're not like most other comedians I've met," she said. "And running this place, I've met a few."

"That makes me feel so special."

She angled herself in her chair so that her blouse fell open and I could see she wasn't wearing a bra. She didn't need one.

Her silicone sisters would survive earthquakes and hurricanes.

She was flashing me. She didn't mean anything by it. She was used to being the one in control, and she was used to dealing with guys like Roger, and this was how she got control. Nothing personal. She just wanted to see my reaction.

I said, "I've got to go," and stood up. That was my reaction.

She looked a little pouty. "You're not leaving me, are you?"

"You've got a club to run," I said. "I've got to find Roger Fisk and tell more people I didn't kill Art Westcott."

She made a move to get out of her chair and acted like she was stuck. She put out her cigarette and meekly held up a hand. She wanted me to help her to her feet.

I took her hand and pulled. She stood up, pressing herself against me, smelling like cigarettes. Up close, she looked like a dime-store makeup counter. "Thank you," she breathed.

"You're welcome," I said.

She didn't let go of my hand. "Will you come back and see me some time?"

"Sure," I said. "I'll buy you a bottle of champagne for your birthday."

The veneer cracked and I saw what lived under her surface, what she'd been before she bleached her hair and went under the knife. She was a businesswoman now, running a club and calling the shots, keeping the cops and the crooks at bay, but something had twisted her way back. Maybe Daddy had left early or Mommy hadn't held her enough, but it had left a hole and she was trying to fill it up. The only time she felt hollow again was when she met someone totally, completely unavailable. Like me.

"No . . . ," she said. Her false eyelashes fluttered and she touched her face with her press-on nails. "I . . . I'd like to see your comedy routine sometime."

"I'm at the Store most weekends," I said. "I'll let you know."

"Please." She turned around and handed me a business card

after writing something on the back. "You can call me here." She turned it over to show me the handwritten number. "Or there."

The other number was home or a cell phone or voice mail. I nodded and pocketed the card. "Okay."

There wasn't anything else for me to say and nothing more I wanted to hear. I turned and walked downstairs back toward the loud music, the bad food, the thin crowd, and the bored, lonely, naked women, who were using all their strength and cunning to charm a dollar out of a wallet from some guy who was hoping to spend it on another beer.

SIXTEEN

"Production office."

"Is David Kelton in?"

I had left Paradise Isle and come back home. No messages on my answering machine. It was after four. I thought I'd try Roger Fisk's manager again.

"No, he isn't," the same female voice I'd talked to before said. "May I take a message?"

"I'll try back later."

I hung up. I waited five minutes, cleared my throat three times in a row, lowered my voice, and added a southern accent. Then I called back on my cordless phone while standing on the street in front of my apartment complex. There's not much traffic at the end of a cul-de-sac, but the distance made it sound like I was on a cellular phone.

"Production office."

"I got a d'livery here for a Donald Kelton," I said in my new voice. "And I thank I got the wrong address."

"It's David."

"Pardon me?"

"This is David Kelton's office." It was the same woman I'd talked to twice that day. "That's who you've reached."

"David Kelton . . . ," I repeated.

"And what address do you have?"

"One-two-two-five-six Ventura Boulevard." I turned the last word into boul-e-vard. "The cross street is Tujunga."

"No, no, we're at one-six-four-eight-two *Riverside* Drive," she said. "The cross street is Wormer."

"Huh," I said. "Wonder how I got the wrong address then."

"I don't know, sir." She didn't like her job. She was meant to be a star. Her agent hadn't called her in three weeks. That was all in the way she said, "I don't know, sir."

"Okay, kin ah just come through the front, or . . . ?"

"Glass doors in front," she said. "We're in Suite C."

"Okay," I said. "See ya soon."

She hung up, not knowing how unwittingly she had played into my clever scheme.

I drove out to the Valley, cruising back and forth in front of the address a few times until I was sure I had the right place.

Then I parked around the corner, found a cappuccino and sandwich place within line-of-sight distance, and settled in with an *LA Weekly* to watch the comings and goings at 16482 Riverside Drive.

I was there for two hours, all of it in the thick of rush hour. I had two lattes, a sun-dried tomato and feta cheese sandwich on focaccia that was a hell of a lot better than what I'd eaten at Paradise Isle, and a bottle of mineral water. I'd spent more than ten bucks and seen a trickle of undistinguished visitors come in and out of the building. There was a driveway that led to a lot in the back. Some people parked in the back and used a rear entrance, so I didn't see them. There were metered spaces in front, and they didn't sit empty for long. I watched as a blue

Toyota edged out of the space closest to the rear alley while a tan Range Rover waited patiently for it to leave.

A tan Range Rover.

I set the *Weekly* down and stared as the Toyota took off, the Range Rover angled into the space, and Ned Lando got out to deposit coins in the meter.

He wore dark sunglasses, perhaps to hide some of the bruises I'd planted on his face when we'd tangled in the alleyway behind Chortles Saturday night. He still had the same pinched, sallow face; the lanky, dirty, dishwater brown hair; and the huge, baggy, black T-shirt and baggy jeans as when he'd stolen my act. He was carrying a briefcase of some kind.

He put a single coin in the meter and then walked inside.

I settled up my bill at the cappuccino place and got in my car, edging it around the corner to a metered space of my own, less than half a block away, on the opposite side of Riverside. I shut off the engine and sat waiting.

I didn't have to wait long. Ned Lando came back out in less than five minutes, still carrying the briefcase, still sporting the sunglasses. He got in the Range Rover and took off east down Riverside.

I gunned my RX-7 to life and followed him. He turned south off Riverside and east again on Ventura Boulevard. Studio City. This was where a lot of the TV situation comedies were shot, up at the Radford CBS Studio Center. Lando changed lanes and I thought he was going to turn in, but he kept going.

The Range Rover began to curve as the main drag of Ventura Boulevard rounded the Hollywood Hills and became Cahuenga. He started to pick up speed, but I caught him at the lights near Universal City. With the Hollywood Hills on the right and the Hollywood Freeway on the left, I hung back long enough to see if he was going to get on the freeway. He was headed into Hollywood.

The summer sun was still over the hills as I followed him down the Cahuenga Pass to Sunset. He took a quick right onto Vine and parked in front of the marquee of a television studio that had been home to a famous daytime syndicated talk show program in the seventies. I couldn't remember the host's name off the top of my head, but it was in the Merv Griffin/Mike Douglas/Dinah Shore era. Since then, as far as I knew, the theater had stood empty amid the noise and squalor of downtown Hollywood except for occasional location shoots, things like that. I drove by it a lot and sometimes there were trucks outside.

Lando had taken the last metered space on the block in front of the theater so I slid into one of the paid lots and agreed to the dollar-fifty-every-twenty-minutes rate they had posted. The limit was like eight bucks. Lost ticket pays maximum. Welcome to the entertainment capital of the world.

I parked in the back of the lot and walked out wearing a baseball cap and dark sunglasses, the hat low and snug across my eyes and ears. I have to hide the red hair when I'm on stakeout. It's a dead giveaway.

I skulked around at a newsstand across the street from the TV theater, while keeping an eye on Ned Lando's snazzy new sport utility vehicle, copying down the license number for safekeeping on a magazine I proceeded to buy.

Again, I didn't have to wait long. Ned Lando came storming out, his sunglasses off so I could see in his eyes that something was wrong. He stalked to his car, jerked open his door, and threw his briefcase in. A security guard the size of a small moose casually appeared in the doorway and held the door open to watch Lando leave. Lando couldn't resist the easy target. He rolled down the passenger side window and yelled something at the security guard. I couldn't hear it all, but I could hear the word "jackass."

Then he started his car, raced the engine, and took off with a screech of rubber.

Something had happened. I could either jump in my car and follow Lando, or I could see what was going on inside that TV studio. By the time I could reach my car, pay for parking, and get into traffic, Lando could easily be on the freeway, lost in a sea of cars. I stayed put. Lando could wait.

Something had upset him inside the TV theater. A meeting hadn't gone the way he had planned. I had the feeling Roger Fisk or David Kelton had something to do with it. Roger might still be too hungover from last night, fighting with me and frolicking with Candy.

That would narrow it down to David Kelton. He hadn't been out at his production office all day. Was he holding down the fort here? What was he up to? I wanted to get inside and find out.

TV studio. Security guards. There was an unpleasant scene waiting for me inside if I was discovered. I wondered how I could make myself invisible. The wafting odor of pizza from the hole-in-the-wall eatery next to the newsstand gave me an idea.

I went inside the pizzeria—named Guiseppe's but staffed entirely by non-Italians, unless they had Italians in Korea—and ordered a large cheese to go. I ordered a separate slice while waiting for the pie to bake and keeping an eye on the front door of the theater. No one else came in or out. Maybe they were all using the rear entrance.

The slice wasn't bad. Not as good as Prizzi's or Palermo's, but not bad. Come to Hollywood, California. Home of not-bad pizza.

While I was waiting, someone came out the front: a well-dressed man in his early thirties; slight of build; blond, thinning hair; square jaw; and a handsome face that looked somewhat ravaged beyond its years. David Kelton?

I watched him walk around the theater. Two minutes later a Lexus pulled out into the traffic on Vine, Kelton at the wheel. How come everyone working with Roger Fisk drove great cars? He headed north on Vine, toward the freeway and the Valley.

When the pizza came out of the oven, I paid ten bucks for it and scribbled the theater's address on it. I walked across the street, the sunglasses and hat still on. A hot pizza is like a cute dog. Strangers will talk to you just to touch it. Especially at dinnertime.

By the time I got across the street, all four sets of glass doors were relocked, including the one I had seen the security guard use. I gently knocked on a door with my foot and peered inside through the tinted surface. I saw the same security guard who had chased off Ned Lando get up from behind a card table set up in the middle of the theater lobby and amble toward the door.

I stepped back as he opened it. He was about six feet six inches tall, with a white shirt, a black tie, black pants, and a blue blazer. On one sleeve of the blue blazer it read ACTON SECURITY. On a pin over his breast pocket was a plastic photo ID. His first name was Otis. He had a shaved head, no mustache, small eyes, and heavy jowls. He looked to be about twenty-five years old and 275 pounds. He could send me sailing out the door and into the gutter with one punch. He held the door open with a paw the size of a turkey loaf.

He looked at the pizza and then at me. Bingo.

"Can I help you?" he asked. He had a high, soft voice, made all the more menacing by his size.

"Delivery," I said, gesturing with the pizza.

"Come on in," he said, stepping back. Big guys get hungry a lot. He'd hate to see me walk away.

Inside, the theater had yet to be restored to its former luster. I'd say it had been twenty years since anyone had painted its walls, and a good five since the carpet had been cleaned. I guessed it was a movie theater in its heyday, perhaps one of the old movie palaces still built with vaudeville stages that used to dot Los Angeles in the twenties and thirties. That made it older than I thought. Even in this condition, not a cheap place to rent. Someone was spending some major bucks.

I stopped at the card table. On it was a sign-in sheet on a clipboard. There were a dozen names written on it under today's date. The last one was Ned Lando. The only company I saw represented was someone from Audiences Unlimited. They did extra casting. I wondered what they needed to see Roger Fisk or David Kelton about.

From inside the theater I could hear voices echoing in the cavernous surroundings. A heavy object rolled across the stage on little wheels. One voice changed location as it walked from the stage toward the entrance, where I was. He said something about being right back. He'd left something upstairs, he yelled over his shoulder as he ran up the aisle. Then to my far right one of the theater doors opened up into the lobby and a guy my age with a headset on ran up a curved set of carpeted stairs right next to the bathrooms. Offices.

Something was going on.

Otis locked the doors behind me and reseated himself behind the card table. "What's the name on the delivery?"

I pretended to look at the delivery slip as I set the pizza down. "Kelton."

Otis frowned. "David Kelton?"

I faked another look at the slip. "It just says Kelton."

"He just went out to dinner," Otis said.

He must have been the man I'd seen go out the front. "Hm," I said. "Maybe it was somebody else then."

The headset guy came running back down the stairs, holding tools in each hand. "Hey, Phil," Otis said. Phil hit the ground walking and came over to the desk. He had glasses and a beard and curly hair, and he wore a flannel shirt and blue jeans. "You know anyone ordered a pizza?"

Phil shook his head. "No, but we sure could use one on set."

"I meant anyone upstairs," Otis said.

"There's no one upstairs," Phil said. "David just went to dinner."

"He go to dinner with Roger?" Otis asked.

"No, I think he went to dinner to pick *up* Roger," Phil said, smiling sardonically. "Off the floor. Roger ain't been in all day."

"I gotcha." Otis turned to me. "Sorry, but nobody here ordered a pizza."

Phil wanted to head inside, but he hesitated. "I'm serious," he said. "How much is it?"

"Ten bucks," I said.

Phil put down the tools and reached for his wallet. "Sold."

I tore off the delivery slip and handed it to him.

"Otis, you want some?" Phil asked.

Otis reached in his pocket. "Yeah, put me in for a couple slices."

"Naw, keep your money; you've had a busy day," Phil said. "You don't get paid enough to toss comedians out of the building."

"Tell me about it," said Otis.

"What happened anyway?" Phil was making conversation as he thumbed through the flat money in his wallet.

Otis shrugged. "He got hired; he got fired. Same as happens to all of us."

Phil pressed a ten and two singles into my hand. "Thank you, my good man," he said.

"Thank you," I said. Wow. A tip.

"Where's this come from?" Phil asked.

"Guiseppe's," I said. I leaned over and pointed. "Right across the street."

"Great," Phil said. I had set the pizza box on the card table. Phil spun it around and opened it in front of Otis. "Otis?"

Otis reached in. Two slices easily fit into his hand. "We need some napkins," he said.

"Want me to get some?" I said.

"We got some in the theater left over from lunch," Phil said. He looked at the two heavy tools in his hands—one a kind of wrench and the other some sort of meter—and then at the pizza and then at me. "As a matter of fact, would you mind carrying this in?" He tilted his head toward the pizza.

Bingo. I was in. "Not at all," I said.

I closed the pizza box, picked it up, and waited patiently beside Phil, who asked, "Otis, can you get the door . . . ?"

Otis opened the door with one hand while balancing his pizza slices in the other.

I followed Phil through the door.

The theater was a thousand-seater, the size I'd played throughout the country while I was opening up for some bigger acts. This one had three sections with no balcony. It smelled of dust and disuse and better days. The ceiling was molded in fine detail, with a chandelier over the front of the stage. The velvet on the seats was worn, but still in one piece.

Onstage were half a dozen stagehands, who were ambling about in front of a backdrop that was a mockup of the Hollywood sign: crooked white letters set in a mountainside. But the "Holly" had been replaced by other letters so that it read ROGERWOOD in letters eight feet high.

ROGERWOOD. What the hell?

Roger Fisk was building himself a TV studio. But for what? A talk show? I'd have to scan the trades and see if he was in production and with what network or cable outfit.

Phil had been walking ahead of me at almost racing speed. He reached the stage before I was even halfway there and yelled

"Pizza!" All work stopped immediately as the men clustered around. Phil turned around and motioned impatiently for me to hurry up. I was busy gawking. "Come on, fella, quit rubbernecking and get the food here!" Always one to come right to the point, that Phil.

I trotted up to the stage and turned over the pizza box to the crew, who descended on it like wolves on a wounded deer. In thirty seconds I was looking at an empty box.

"Cokes," one man said. He was in a T-shirt, his belly bulging over his belt buckle. He hadn't shaved since he'd last paid his rent. "We need some Cokes."

"Got some upstairs," Phil said.

"What are you guys building here?" I asked.

Phil glanced at me. He'd thought I'd left. "A set," he said.

More silence. They wanted me to go. All I heard was chewing.

"For a TV show?" I asked.

They looked at each other. They didn't like questions. Or they had been told not to answer them.

"Something like that," Phil said.

"Well, enjoy the pizza," I said, and turned to go.

I saw Otis. He was already through the door and rolling down the aisle toward me with his big man's gait. "All done?" he asked.

"Sure," I said, wondering, *Why all the security?* What was so hush-hush?

Otis let me pass him and raised a hand still greasy from pizza at Phil to let him know everything was under control.

I doubted Otis would be a great source of information, but once we got to the lobby I decided to try him anyway. "They going to film something in there?" I said.

"I don't know." Otis kept walking toward the front door, keys in one hand, the other hand guiding me without touching me, steering me toward the outside.

"What's 'Rogerwood'? "

"Got me." He unlocked the door and held it for me. "Have a nice day."

"See you later," I said as cheerfully as I could. I walked away from him back toward Guiseppe's, just in case he was watching. I kept the hat and sunglasses on. Didn't want to blow my cover.

I was standing at the corner of Hollywood and Vine just as my pager went off, vibrating against my hip. Someone was calling me from an 818 area code. Out in the Valley. The number was vaguely familiar. I'd seen it before, but I couldn't remember where.

I found a pay phone on the Boulevard and returned the call.

A male voice answered with my name. "Kincaid?"

"Yeah," I said over the traffic noise behind me. "Who's this?"

"Ned Lando," the voice said. "I want to talk to you."

SEVENTEEN

"Why'd you lie to the Ocean Park cops about me?" I asked. "Aren't you afraid to lose your best source of material?"

"I don't have your act anymore," Lando said.

"I know," I said. "You taped it and sold it to Roger Fisk without my consent."

"That's what I wanted to talk to you about," Lando said. "Where are you?"

"At a pay phone."

"Where are you going to be later?" he asked.

"The Comedy Store," I said. "Tonight. I got a spot at nine-thirty."

"See you then," he said.

"Don't walk in with the tape recorder or you won't walk out," I said.

"Kincaid, you don't know—"

I hung up on him.

There was no point to any more tough talk. I wanted to know what had happened between him and Fisk, but I'd be glad to wait for him to tell me. Of course, he might be letting me think he wanted to turn state's evidence on his old boss just to get next to me again. If he was setting me up, there wasn't anything I could do about it. If George and his three ugly brothers came at me in the parking lot behind the Comedy Store, I'd yell for help from the doorman and reach for the nearest heavy object and start swinging until Ireland was free again.

I went back on stakeout at the theater on Vine for the next half hour. I went from a coffee shop to the newsstand to a sandwich place, burning dollars along the way. No one came back in. At seven o'clock, Phil and his crew left. A half an hour later Otis locked up the front, put on his coat, and went home. The place was left dark. What had happened to David Kelton and Roger Fisk was anyone's guess. Maybe they were back at the office on Riverside. Maybe Kelton couldn't get his client out of bed.

I got my car out of hock from parking—eight bucks maximum—and drove the five minutes back from the Boulevard to Beachwood Canyon. When I got home there was a message from Kelly Malone. She'd called while she had been manning the desk at Chortles Comedy Club. She was hosting the open-mike show tonight and wanted to know if I'd like to come down to Hartford Beach and do a guest spot.

I called her back. "What time?" I said.

"We go to midnight," she said.

"Traffic should be clear," I said. "I could make it by then."

"You playing somewhere else?"

"The Store," I said. "Ned Lando paged me. He wants a meeting."

"About what?"

"I don't know," I said. "Maybe to tell me what's going on with him and Roger Fisk. Maybe to beat my head in."

"Don't get your head beaten in," she said.

"Hasn't happened yet," I said. "Not for lack of trying."

"Can I see you later?" she said.

"Sure."

"I'm sorry about Art."

"Me, too."

"I want you to tell me everything," she said.

"I will," I said. "More than you want to know." I told her to keep a twenty-minute spot open and ready for me and I'd be there later that night. I hung up and started getting ready to go out.

An hour later I began to hit the clubs. I had dinner at the Improv, splitting my second pizza of the day with Johnny Lancaster, a comedian I'd worked the road with a few years back. We bullshitted about the business in general, and as other comedians drifted to and from our table I managed to drop the names Roger Fisk and Ned Lando around the room as bait and no one took it. Both men, it seemed, operated under a veil of secrecy, cloaked from comedy gossip.

I even asked about the theater up on Vine near the Boulevard.

"The Doug Stone Theater?" Tom Connelly asked. He was a tall, skinny, piano-playing comedian from Seattle who affected a grunge rocker look.

"Is that what it is?"

"Yeah." Connelly reached for more pizza and signaled for a refill on his iced tea. "You remember Doug Stone. Had a daytime talk show, like Merv Griffin and Mike Douglas."

"Barely," I said. Two younger comedians sitting at the table looked at each other and shrugged.

"I do. Had a lot of comedians on back in the seventies," Johnny Lancaster said. "Leno, Letterman." Lancaster turned to me. "On right after Dinah Shore."

"Lasted five years," Connelly said. "I remember the show, but the theater's empty now, isn't it?"

"I thought I saw some production going on there today," I said. "Equipment vans."

"Where are you talking about?" Lancaster asked.

I told him.

"There's a theater there?"

That was the best information I got all night. The Doug Stone Theater.

The hour was early and all the nightbirds weren't out yet, much less ready to sing. If I wanted to, I knew I could make the circuit more than once: Improv, Laugh Factory, and the Comedy Store. But with Lando waiting for me, I headed up to the Store early and watched the doorman seat people. I checked out the schedule. Lando wasn't on it. I chatted up the doorman and the cute girl working the booth. They had never heard of Ned Lando.

I hung out on the patio in front of the Original Room, looking out onto Sunset Boulevard, watching the cars go by. I was particularly interested in tan Range Rovers. I spotted one, but it kept going. There was a woman at the wheel with a dog at her side.

Show time. I was up sixth. I watched the acts scheduled before me. No Ned Lando by the time I took the stage, but I didn't care. The house was filling up and I was ready to rock them. The comic before me had done a little of the where-are-you-from-what-do-you-do-for-a-living routine that only Jimmy Brogan could pull off well (maybe because he'd invented it), but I'd learned there was a busload of conventioneers from the hotel next door visiting from New York. There'd been a good laugh when the comedian onstage had asked, "How's New York?" and one of the visitors had answered, "Cold!"

I had an old routine about weather that I'd written on the road when I was touring in the middle of winter. "Don't be fooled by Southern California, folks," I said, after I'd done my opening lines. "The rest of America is cold." I then did the typical Southern Californian confronting snow for the first time and possibly trying to snort some. A cheap laugh, but it worked. I used that to go into earthquakes and mudslide stuff.

The fifteen minutes went by quickly and by the end of it I was getting solid laughs at the end of every line and just rode out my regular material all the way to the light. I ended with a flying routine that was old and smelled of road hackdom, but if Lando was there I wasn't going to burn any of my new stuff he didn't already have on tape.

I did good, brought up the next comic, and I left to healthy applause. Thank you, good night.

I made my way through the dark to the back of the room, down the stairs, and into the rear hallway that led to the back parking lot. I stood out by the sign to the Belly Room, nodding and saying hello to the other regulars.

"Kincaid."

I turned. I didn't see where the voice came from right away. Somewhere in the darkness in between the parked cars.

"Over here."

In the back of the parking lot stood a tall, thin shadow. Ned Lando.

I shoved myself away from the Belly Room sign and walked toward him. There was space behind the kitchen, and he could have someone hiding there, but there was only one way to find out.

As I got closer, I could see Lando's pinched, sallow features. He was wearing a long, black coat. I tilted my chin at his hands in his pockets. "What are you packing?"

Lando snorted. "Kincaid, are you crazy? You think I'd bring a gun to the Comedy Store?"

"I'm not talking about a gun," I said. "I'm talking about a slightly used tape recorder."

He lifted the flaps of the coat. We were standing in deep night shadows behind several stationary automobiles against a concrete embankment butted up against a hillside. "Naw, I ain't wired. Man, you don't trust other comics too much, do you?"

"You're not a comic to me," I said.

"Hope you're this much of a hardass when you meet up with Fisk," he said.

"I already met up with Fisk," I said. "And I'm being much nicer to you than I was to him."

"How so?"

"You're still standing, aren't you?" I said. "I put him down like a bad heckler."

"You're the one who beaned him at the strip club he was working?" Lando smirked. "He said it was the jealous biker boyfriend of one of the dancers he was plowin'."

"It wasn't," I said.

"What about his bodyguard, George? Didn't he make a move to protect his boss?"

"Is that what George is supposed to do?" I said. "I wondered what his function was."

"George was the one who knocked you out the night you and I got into it at the back of Chortles," Lando said. "Sapped you right on the back of your head."

"George has not posed a problem for me yet, face-to-face," I said.

"He did for Art Westcott."

I stepped closer, instantly more attentive. "What do you mean by that?"

Lando stepped back. "Ease up, Kincaid. I know you and Art are buddies."

"*Were*," I said. "*Were* buddies." He didn't know. Time to tell him. "Art's dead."

Lando did a convincing double take. "What? Dead!"

I nodded. "I'm the one who found him in his apartment today,

with half his head blown away." I paused another few seconds
to let it sink in. "The cops called you yet?"

Lando was wiping his face with both hands. The game had
changed on him, suddenly and without warning. He looked
around, as if the cars in the parking lot might start closing in.
"No," he whispered. "Why would the cops call me?"

"Because I gave them your name, asshole."

"Oh, thanks, Kincaid," he said angrily. "I owe you one now."

"Detectives grilled me for two hours this afternoon. They think
I might have done it."

"You don't seem too scared."

"Don't have a guilty conscience," I said. "And cops don't
scare me any."

"When's the last time you saw Art?" Lando asked. "I mean
. . . before . . ."

"He called me Saturday afternoon to get me to fill in at Chortles."

"Makes sense," Lando said. "George wondered if you were
that guy. He said, 'Is that the guy Westcott called?' "

I felt my palms chill. "When did George ever meet up with
Art?"

"That's what I asked him Saturday night after I gave him the
tape," Lando said. "After he put you down, he hustled me into
my Range Rover and sped us both back up to LA. 'Where's Art?'
I asked."

"And what did he say?"

"He said for me to shut the hell up; said I asked too many
goddamn questions."

I was going to have to find George and let the cops know where
he was.

Lando continued: "George has done some other shit for Roger
that I don't know about and I don't want to. Sometimes George
will come into a club or Kelton's office—you know, with that

153

ponytail, goatee, and earring he looks like a friggin' pirate—and Roger will ask him something like 'Did you take care of that problem we talked about?' And George will just nod once. Roger likes to act tough, but with George it's not an act." Lando shrugged deeper into the folds of his coat. "I got a bad feeling about him."

"Think George already has a record with the police?" I asked.

"You could say that," Lando said. "He *was* a cop. Back in Arizona. That's all I know. He either left or got bounced off. But he's mean. Watch out for him."

"I'll take it under advisement," I said. "You got something else to say, you'd better say it. You're the one called this meeting."

"You ever hear of the Doug Stone Theater?" Lando said.

I nodded. "Up on Vine," I said, "near Hollywood Boulevard."

"How'd you hear of it?" Lando asked. "I didn't even know who Doug Stone was."

"I'm older than you," I said. "Go on."

"Roger Fisk is planning to tape a television special there," Lando said. "A half-hour performance show."

"Okay." So that's what was going on. It explained the "Rogerwood" sign, the whole megillah. "Who's paying for it?"

"Fisk is," Lando said. "He couldn't get a deal with anyone, so he got fed up and bankrolled it all himself. Fisk's rented the theater, hired a crew, and he's taping this weekend. Five days from now."

"Saturday or Sunday?"

"Both," Lando said. "Two shows, wearing the same outfit. He's a rich kid from Arizona. His old man was some bigwig back home. He died and left Fisk and his sister a bundle. Roger came into town less than two months ago thinking he could buy his way into the clubs."

"Money doesn't open every door," I said.

"Yeah." Lando's beady eyes shot over my shoulder. In the dark, he looked like a cold rat. "Like this place."

"Was it your job to get Fisk material?" I asked.

"He had no act," Lando said. "He needed one quick. I met Fisk on the road in Arizona. He hired me to go out and start taping comics. Brought him the tapes and he paid me five hundred a night to start. I didn't have to worry about bookings. The clubs would be paid to put me onstage. His manager would set it all up for me."

"David Kelton," I said.

"Yeah," Lando said. "And you know what? I think Fisk is paying him straight cash. No commissions. Not that there've been any. I don't think the guy's had a legit paid gig yet."

So that's what Fisk was up to. Bankrolling a comedy career.

"I haven't met David Kelton," I said, "but I think I might have seen him. What's he look like?"

"Short guy," Lando said. "Blond, thinning hair. Wears a shirt and tie everywhere. Used to be a booker, then turned agent trainee. Was at one of the big agencies as a young Turk and they dumped him for a coke problem he has yet to get completely under control."

"How did he meet Fisk?" I asked.

"In rehab," Lando said.

"Guess it didn't take," I said.

"It was Kelton's third time, Roger's first," Lando said. "This was three months ago. In Arizona. Kelton saw this guy tossing the family cash around like a bunch of bad lottery tickets and convinced him he was ready for the big time. Kelton's been getting both Roger and me what stage time he could."

"So why are you telling me this?" I said. "You have a falling out with Fisk?"

"And Kelton. They reneged on my deal," Lando said, summoning up all of his considerable nastiness. "All along I told them I wanted to open up for Fisk," Lando said. "Maybe get on TV, too. I don't have any tape on myself. Who knows where this is going to end up? Roger's going to try to sell it to the major cable networks first. He let me think I had the gig. Promised me three thousand bucks for it. Used to call it 'our' show. But today Kelton told me Roger's not using a warm-up and cut me a check for the three grand. I took it to the bank and guess what? The account's closed." He scuffed a piece of gravel with his shoe. "I got ripped off because Roger doesn't want anyone to think he's afraid to go out solo in front of a thousand people."

"Where's he getting that size an audience?" I said. "Handing out flyers in front of Mann's Chinese?"

"No," Lando said. "A real audience might not laugh hard enough. He's renting one."

"What do you mean renting?" I said.

"He's hiring extras to come in and laugh at his act. Fifty bucks a head. At the end, they're supposed to give him a standing ovation. Kelton's having a casting director find people who can laugh good."

"Nothing's left to reality, is it?" I said. I remembered the name in the guest register at the security desk inside the Doug Stone Theater: Audiences Unlimited. "That all you came to say?"

"That's it," Lando said. "And . . . to give you this." He reached in his coat pocket.

I took a half step back.

He looked up and saw me move. "Relax, Kincaid." He smiled. On his face it was not a pleasant sight. "I just brought you a little present." He slowly drew his hand out of his pocket and put a small square black metal object in my palm. His fingers were cold.

I looked at it. It was the tape recorder he had plugged into the soundboard the night he had taped my act.

"A little souvenir," Lando said. "I'm out of the thieving business."

I pocketed the tape recorder and looked up at him. "Going back on the road?"

Lando shook his head. "I'm done with comedy, soon as Kelton pays me."

"Okay," I said.

"I just realized . . ." He shrugged. "I don't have what it takes yet. That's why I stole from people. I'm not a natural comedian. I have to work at it."

"You're just now figuring this out?" I said.

"Man, I can't get a break from you, can I, Kincaid?"

"No."

He laughed, a short, barking sound, and dug his hands deeper into his coat pockets. "I did some checking up on you," he said, "after our little tussle. You got quite a reputation in this business."

"It's been slightly tainted over the years with rumors of improper campaign fund-raising procedures," I said. "And then there was that scandal with the underage baby-sitter."

"You're a loner," Lando said matter-of-factly, like he was reciting a casting breakdown. "Nobody feels like they're your friend. You're in at all the clubs, but you've never broken through to the big time. No one knows where you live, where you come from, or if you have any family. You're always writing new material, and the ladies like you more than just a little bit."

"It's the strawberry blond hair," I said. "My piercing blue eyes."

"And I was advised to come clean with you," Lando said. "I didn't tell people what we were feuding over, but . . ." He looked down at his shoes. "I was told I should make it right between us. You don't start any fights, but you don't run away from 'em either."

"I like that," I said. "Can I put that in my press kit?"

"You can do whatever you want," Lando said. "I'm getting my money and getting out. I'll leave the noble battles to you, Kincaid. Do me a favor though."

"What?"

"Take this Roger Fisk down hard," Lando said. "That arrogant prick thinks he can do whatever he wants just because he's got money."

"Most people with money do."

He turned to go. "Maybe I'll see you again sometime," he said.

"Five-dollar cover," I said. "Two-drink minimum."

He left. I didn't say good-bye, I didn't wish him luck, and I didn't thank him. If it wasn't for him, Art Westcott would still be walking around and breathing.

I watched him get in his car and drive off. I didn't know it at the time, but this was the last time I'd see him, shortly before he'd have his throat cut open so he could bleed to death. I don't know if there was any way it could have gone differently for him. Maybe it was just his fate. He had backed the wrong horse, and it came back to trample him to death for no other reason than it just felt like the right thing to do at the time.

EIGHTEEN

I got in my car after meeting Ned Lando and drove south to where Kelly Malone was hosting the open mike at Chortles. I breezed past the doorman and walked into the showroom, where Kelly was onstage shticking it up between acts. There was a smattering of audience left. It was a quarter past eleven.

Kelly brought up the next auditioner and came to join me. She was dressed a tad more conservatively than last time, in a business suit that ended in a pair of shorts midthigh. She had her red hair piled up on top of her head, spilling off the sides and back in big curls. When she saw me she gave me a big kiss on the cheek and a long, rocking hug. "How are you, sailor?"

"I'm back in port," I said.

"Want to go on next?"

"Sure." I looked around the room. "How's it going? Find any bright, shining stars in the making?"

She made a face. "They all suck. We had almost a full house about an hour ago and they just couldn't take it anymore and walked." She looked over her shoulder, checking on the act onstage. It was an obese black woman who was doing a routine about how hard it was for men to have sex with her during her period. Now that's comedy.

She turned back to me. "What do you want me to say about you?"

"Just a special guest," I said.

"Can I mention your big shlong?"

"Only if I can say what you like to do with it."

She stood on tiptoe and leaned forward. Her red lips pressed against my ear as she whispered several suggestions in my ear, then eased away, looking at me with shining eyes.

"You should open a phone sex line," I said.

"Does that sound good later?" she asked.

"Actually, it sounds good right now," I said. "But we have to do a show."

"Oh, we can skip the show," she said.

"I never miss a show," I said. "I never go over my time. And I never steal."

"Oh, you," she said. "You are so serious about being funny."

"That's a good way to put it."

Kelly stepped to the back of the room and borrowed a flashlight from the ubiquitous Pluto. She flicked the beam at the woman onstage who had just walked another table out the door.

When the act onstage left to literally three hands clapping—one guy smacking the table with his palm—Kelly got onstage and threw out a one-liner and then told everyone they were in for a very special treat. She said this while two tables were reaching for their coats and settling their checks. Kelly started to tell them they were going to miss a great act if they left now and they'd be sorry. . . .

I made a motion to her. Cut the chatter. Bring me up. Let me do my stuff.

She saw me signaling to her and rushed through the rest of my intro: "So-here-he-is-Biff-Kincaid."

I took the stage and started by asking the two tables that were getting ready to leave to just "get the hell out." That got an instant laugh. "I'm serious," I said. "I've watched you people long enough; we're gonna have some fun so just get the hell out. They're undercover Mormons is what they are, sitting there and not laughing all night long . . ."

I got one table to stay that way. Then I turned on the other acts. "How about a hand for all of the open mikers you've seen here tonight?" I didn't get much applause. "It takes a lot of guts to get up here and perform when you have absolutely no material and no stage presence and no future in the business. I admire that."

A few guffaws from the real comics in the back of the room. Some glares from the tryouts who were hanging around. Hey, it's a tough business. You can't handle it, go back to Dad's furniture store.

I started hitting short and hard, one-liners, all of 'em. I managed to get a few laughs right up front, and I didn't slow down. These people had seen enough hemming and hawing. Time for some structured, road-tested comedy. Kelly said I could have twenty minutes, so I gave them my hit list and went straight for punch lines. I kept an eye on my watch as I paced the stage and speed-rapped through my best bits. I never went over my time. Wonder if Ned Lando had heard that about me, too.

I ended right on time and to my satisfaction and stepped offstage, but not before Kelly ran up to give me a juicy smooch. Then she dipped and curtsied and suggestively handled the microphone as she put it back in the stand. She was one sexy babe when she wanted to be.

I got offstage and stood in the back. Apparently I was the last one to go on, as Kelly wrapped up the show, thanking everyone and telling them to drive home safely. There were only two tables left anyway. Eight people. Open mikers and audience members trickled out as Pluto put some well-aged Aerosmith on the PA.

"Your place or mine?" she said as soon as she found me.

"My place is an hour away," I said.

"Mine's only ten minutes," she said.

"It's a done deal," I said. "In the morning, though, I've got some business to take care of."

"You going to keep playing detective?"

"I'm not playing." I tilted my head toward the stage where I'd just come from. "That's playing."

She nodded, then rocked forward on her toes to stand up and nip me on the chin with her shiny white teeth. She lost her balance and caught herself on my shoulders, pressing herself against me. I reached up with my arms and scooped them under hers. I could feel her curves against my straight lines.

"Whatever are we going to do to fill the time until then?" she asked innocently.

I leaned forward and dipped her down with a long, hard kiss, holding her just above the floor so her hair touched the carpet. I broke our mouths apart. She was flushing. Blood began to flow to other parts of my body as well, and I felt warm tinglings.

"We'll think of something," I said.

I headed back up to LA around noon. It would have been ten o'clock in the morning, but Kelly and I had started making love shortly after we woke up and that had lasted a nice long time. I was beginning to like her a lot. She was funny, she was sexy, she was great in bed, and she thought the same thing about me. Even Shadow, her cat, had started to warm up to me. He'd rubbed against my leg, purring, as Kelly and I made out in the kitchen right after breakfast.

Maybe I was onto something. Maybe we both were. It had been a while since I had settled down for any length of time with any particular woman. There were still the women I met after the shows in town and on the road, but they quickly tired of the late nights, the long absences out of town, and the loud friends. Sooner or later they met someone else, they wanted to know if I'd be interested in a job at their uncle's office, or maybe I could just do stand-up as a hobby.

That was usually when we parted company. Like I said, I never go over my time.

Kelly was new to comedy, but she seemed to understand its basics: the hunger, the waiting, the lights, the mike. She was as curious about it as I was when I was starting out, although that had been a long time ago. I'd endured countless question-and-answer sessions from newcomers, and I usually told them there wasn't any other solution than to just keep going up and trust the great gods of laughter a path would be opened to you. Kelly not only seemed to grasp the concept, she reveled in its explicit freedoms. At least that morning. I could see why she'd given up being a stockbroker.

I got in my RX-7 and headed north in the brilliant, clear morning that felt as though it was going to last all day. If I couldn't find Roger Fisk again, I could track him down Saturday at his show at the Doug Stone Theater. Maybe they were casting for the audience members now: Your name, please. And . . . could you laugh for us? Harder, like you just heard something hilarious. Okay . . . are you available this Saturday?

If I wanted to disrupt the taping Saturday, how should I go about it? How could I get to Roger Fisk? He would have a camera crew and security. I had barely gotten past them posing as a pizza guy. Was there really anything I could do about it?

I thought about Art Westcott and how I'd seen him left with half a head covered with flies in the room next to his kitchen. The night before he was killed, he was doing comedy at Chortles with Ned Lando, just as I had done the following night. What had he known that had proved so hazardous to his health? There was danger here, and I had to find it before it found me.

I got home and packed a bag. There was someone who might be able to help me figure this one out. I locked up my apartment and drove to the airport. I checked the Southwest Airlines counter first. The next flight to Phoenix was full. That was OK. The next one left in less than an hour. I could wait. On the road, you learn to get good at waiting. I had a latte and called ahead to Phoenix.

"Comedy Cabana," a female voice answered the phone. I asked for Everett Foster.

Then I held for Everett Foster.

"Everett Foster."

"Ev, it's Biff Kincaid."

"Kincaid! Where are you?"

"I'm at LAX, waiting for a flight."

"Where you headed?"

"Phoenix," I said. "I'm coming to see you, Everett."

"Oh, no." He dropped his voice. "I hope this has nothing to do with the Cabana's illustrious new owner, Roger Fisk."

"It has everything to do with Roger Fisk."

"Oh, no," he moaned.

"Oh, yes," I said. "Trust me: it won't take long. I just have a few things I want to clear up."

"Oh, good," Everett said. "For a minute there, I thought you were going to ask for stage time."

I arrived in Phoenix later that Tuesday, just around five o'clock. It wasn't summer, so the heat was only like an open oven door, not a closed one. I took a shuttle to a car rental counter and got myself a sporty little model with some solid air-conditioning. In less than an hour after I'd hit the tarmac, I was headed toward the Cabana.

The Comedy Cabana was set in a strip mall in a nondescript commercial area of Phoenix. When I got there it was a little after five-thirty in the afternoon. I'd played there enough to know to go to the delivery entrance in the back and ring.

Everett answered the door. He wasn't very tall, only about five five, with curly black hair and a full, cherubic face that lent itself easily to exaggeration. He dressed in loud, baggy clothes as a kind of costume to let even strangers know that he was in show business. He had started out as a clown, doing birthday parties and special occasions. Some of that had carried over to his wardrobe. Today he was wearing a Hawaiian shirt and bright blue parachute pants. He had the energy and expression of stage performance even in everyday conversation. For a short, slightly tubby guy he was quick in both word and deed.

"Kincaid!" He threw half an arm around me. Last time it was a whole hug. Things change.

He quickly let go, glancing over my shoulder to make sure no one was watching.

I followed his gaze. "I make someone's most-wanted list?"

"There're no rules against me talking to you," Everett said.

"Not yet there aren't."

"Come on in," he said, holding the door open even wider. "It's hot out."

"You sure you won't get in trouble?"

"Hey, you can't go onstage here, but no one said anything about you walking through the club in the daytime."

I stepped inside. The club was cool compared to the outside, the air-conditioning pumped up so high I could almost smell the Freon.

"Running the AC during the day?" I said. "That's a switch." We walked by the dark and deserted bar, the stage shrouded and empty. "Last time I was in here it was like a sauna."

"Roger Fisk has a lot of money," Everett said. "Anytime he walks in here, he wants to be comfortable."

"And when was the last time he walked inside his own club?"

"A few weeks ago," Everett said. He led me around to the ticket window, where a phone line was ringing on the reservation line. "My hour to work the booth. Jennie's at lunch." He punched a button. Jennie must have been the one who'd answered when I called from the airport. "Comedy Cabana."

As he took a reservation I looked around the offices. Pictures of comedians adorned the walls. Famous faces of the future mingled with anonymous acts of the past who had now gained notoriety. I noticed my picture was still up, high, toward the ceiling. A three-year-old headshot when my hair was longer and I weighed a little more, before I started going to the gym quite as much.

I lowered my eyes. Several shots of Roger Fisk were laid in a strip along the front wall. He wore the same clothes in every photo; they had all been taken on the same night. The prints were new, the frames shiny. He was furnishing his legacy, preparing for greatness.

Everett hung up the phone. "So . . ." He rubbed his hands together. "I can't put you onstage here: I had to cancel your next booking . . . did you just want to drop by to say thank you?" He grinned facetiously.

I pulled up a bent cane–back chair and sat in it backward. "How's the club?"

He dipped his head from side to side, in the universal gesture that roughly translated as so-so. "Comme çi, comme ça," he said.

"It's doing all right. The management is adjusting to the change in ownership."

"What needs adjusting to?"

Again, the glance around to make sure the walls weren't growing ears. "That Roger Fisk feels he can drop in here with no notice, no warning, bring in twenty people he met on the plane from LA, comp them dinner and drinks, while he yanks the headliner offstage so he can do twenty minutes. I mean, he literally will walk on that stage and stand there until the headliner notices him, then tell the guy to get lost, it's his club, he's doing the show, he'll let him know when he can come back up."

"There're no people like show people," I said. "If Fisk was looking to buy a club, why didn't he buy Gigglemeisters in Flagstaff? It's closer to where he's from, isn't it?"

"Gigglemeisters closed," Everett said, "last December."

"Oh," I said. Scratch that booking. "How's Roger's twenty minutes onstage?"

"As funny as a turd in a punch bowl." He lowered his voice. "A bunch of old jokes and then some original stuff. And look, just between you and me and the mike stand, I think he wrote most of it with a tape recorder. He has lifted from every act that's on the road from here to Philadelphia."

"Tell me about it," I said.

"He steal from you?"

I nodded.

"That why you're here?"

I nodded again.

"Uh-oh." Everett lifted his eyebrows and his open hands, slapping the palms down on his knees. "How'd that happen?"

"Fisk hired someone to steal for him on the road for the last several weeks," I said. "Has him tape acts and sell them to him." I looked around. "I wouldn't be surprised if he's got a tape system set up here for every act that comes through."

Everett blinked. "In two weeks, we're going to have a new booking system where we book one-nighters only. Roger says it's to get more repeat business."

"No, it's so he can steal more material," I said. "When you saw him, he had twenty minutes. He needs half an hour, and then he'll need more after that."

"Is that what he's doing?" Everett asked. "Out on the road, stealing material? We never know where he is or how to get in touch with him."

"He's in Hollywood right now," I said. "He's rented a theater near Hollywood and Vine and he's going to tape a special there, a half-hour concert of him performing stand-up in front of a crowd of at least a thousand people."

"A thousand people?" Everett's eyes narrowed. "How's he going to draw that kind of an audience in LA?"

"He's paying them," I said. "He's hiring extras."

"You're kidding."

"No," I said. "My jokes are a lot funnier."

"Wow." Everett looked over at the row of photos of Roger Fisk and then back at me. "You hopped on a plane just to come here and tell me this? Because I think long-distance rates are a little cheaper than a plane ticket."

I smiled. "I need some directions."

"To where?"

"You were the one who told me about Roger's father, Carter Fisk."

"Yeah," Everett said. "You couldn't live in Arizona for the last five years without hearing about Carter Fisk."

"You told me how he wanted to be governor and then president, how he started visiting D.C. all the time until he went down in a private plane with his wife and daughter less than a year ago. I got all that right?"

"Correct," Everett said. "Leaving the considerable family fortune to be split between Roger and his older sister."

"What's her name?"

"The older sister? Nancy, I think. Her office called recently, trying to find him."

"She have any interest in the club?"

"No. Never seen her in here; never heard her voice on the phone. Roger never talks about her, and no one's ever met her. She's tending the family construction or developing business or whatever."

"And that's up in northern Arizona," I said, "where Roger's from?"

"Yeah," Everett said. He shook his head. "You're the second comedian to ask me that question in the last week, but the first to make it all the way to Arizona."

"Who was the other one?"

"Art Westcott," Everett said. "You talk to him?"

"I saw him yesterday."

"Yeah? What's he up to?"

I took in a deep breath and let it out. "He's dead, Ev."

The shock hit him slowly, like he was smelling a gas leak. "Dead . . . ?"

I nodded. "Someone shot him in the head in the laundry room of his apartment. I was the one who found him."

"When did this happen?"

"I found him yesterday," I said. "The police think he was killed Saturday, right after he called me to take his place on the bill at Chortles. That's where I met Ned Lando, the guy who's stealing for Roger Fisk." I let the news sink in for another half a minute and then asked, "Ev, when exactly did Art ask you questions about Roger Fisk?"

"Just . . . Friday, I think." He looked at me, confused. "When was he killed—Saturday?"

I nodded.

"Friday. He called and wanted to talk to Roger. Left a message for him."

I leaned forward. "When did Roger get the message?"

"He didn't," Everett said. "I haven't spoken to Roger."

"Has anyone?"

"I don't think so. . . . Let me check." He tapped on a computer.

"We're supposed to log all of Roger's phone messages on computer so he can retrieve them from the road if he wants, but he never checks them." He shook his head. "He didn't get the message from Art Westcott or from his sister."

I'd gotten on a plane and flown here to ask my next question. "Everett," I said, "where can I find Nancy Fisk?"

An hour later I drove north out of Phoenix, through the mesas and the cactus. Every time I went to Arizona I always felt like I was driving through a Road Runner cartoon. I had a long drive ahead of me, three hours at least. More than once I pulled over to check my maps. Right on course.

As I drove north and east and into the mountains, the terrain began to change. Flat desert gave way to hills, sand became scrub, and eventually I found myself in the mountains, surrounded by pines and firs. Night was falling. I shut off the air-conditioning and rolled down the windows, breathing in the cool, clean mountain air. When you're from LA, you get to where you can taste clean air. I do a bit about it. When people in LA go on vacation, they don't plan much. Where are you going? Canada. And what are you going to do there? Breathe. I hear they have wonderful air there.

My destination was in the White Mountains of northern Arizona: the town of Show Low. It was almost nine o'clock in the evening and completely dark as I crossed the city limits. Show Low was one of a cluster of small towns in a resort and retirement area that depended heavily on the flux of out-of-staters in the summer and the ski trade in the winter. The two-lane highway was dotted with antique shops and vegetable stands. The houses were A-frames and trailers, surrounded by generous chunks of land. I'd gone from a Road Runner cartoon to an episode of *Lassie*.

The address I was looking for was a surprisingly urban-looking office building in the middle of town. Even at this hour there were lights on upstairs. There were pickup trucks caked with dried mud parked overnight in front, some bearing planks of lumber, right next to gleaming Cadillacs. Not too many foreign cars in sight. This wouldn't be a good time for me to walk in and announce myself. Not with what I had in mind. With the element of surprise, you always had to factor in the additional time and trouble you're going to cause people.

I parked across the street and watched for a few minutes. The sign above the door read FISK ENTERPRISES. In there somewhere was the domain of Nancy Fisk. I'd come all this way to find her and tell her what her brother was up to. I was gambling that he was the black sheep of the family who had inherited a fortune, and that she was the levelheaded older child who didn't want to see the business that bore her father's name start leaking red ink because of her kid brother's foolish dreams about show business.

I found a good motel for under fifty dollars and checked in. I ate some spectacular barbecue and scouted the local paper for a casino or a club where I could go up. No shows in sight. Looked like I was going to spend tonight offstage.

When I don't have a show to structure my evening around, I'm at a bit of a loss as to what to do. I went back to my motel and watched TV. At one point I went driving to try to find some local brews and have a pint. No luck there either. The micro-brewing fad had yet to catch on in Show Low. There was a liquor store that sold Newcastle Brown Ale, and I bought a large bottle of that. I brought it back to my room and quaffed it slowly, waiting for sleep to come. I needed my rest. Tomorrow was a big day.

NINETEEN

At approximately fifteen minutes past nine the next morning, I walked into the headquarters of Fisk Enterprises.

An office building in small-town northern Arizona three hours from Phoenix was not the same thing as an office building in Los Angeles. There was no security guard. There was a building directory that led me to the second floor, and I presented myself to the second-floor receptionist, a woman in her fifties with a modified beehive hairdo and cat's-eye glasses. She looked like a perfectly nice person. Another difference between here and LA. In LA the receptionists are all actresses who are mad at their agents.

"Can I help you, sir?"

"I'd like to speak with Nancy Fisk, please."

"Do you have an appointment?"

"No."

"May I ask what this is regarding?"

"It's about her brother, Roger."

That got her to pick up the phone. "Just a moment, sir. Let

me see if she's in." She dialed another number while I turned around and surveyed the second floor. Simple and modest. Meant to hide money as well as make it. Built by Carter Fisk, Roger and Nancy's father, was my guess. There were pictures of him on the wall. He was a tall, ruggedly handsome man, still lean in his fifties, prone to flannel shirts and jeans at photo ops celebrating the groundbreaking of some new development. Later pictures showed him in a suit shaking hands with a congressman and once in a group at the White House with the president.

There was a row of pictures that showed Fisk with a little girl as she grew up, from age five to adulthood. I assumed this was Nancy. Sometimes she was with another girl, a few years older. Around age seventeen, Nancy had blossomed from a gawky adolescent into a coltish young woman, with big blue eyes, a face-splitting smile like her father's, and a body that looked equally as good in blue jeans as it did in business suits. A beauty.

There were no pictures of Roger. Anywhere. Just Nancy and her father, or Nancy and her sister. The dead were remembered. She had no use for the living.

"Sir?"

I turned around.

The receptionist was no longer alone. There was a woman standing next to the desk holding a folder in her hand. She had a tanned, unlined face with startling blue eyes, like precious stones, and their gaze was focused on me. She was tall, as tall as I was, and dressed in black riding pants and a white blouse that fit her perfectly. Her brown hair was loose and hung around her face in curls with blonde highlights in them.

I looked over my shoulder at the pictures just to make sure. She was Nancy Fisk, a few years older than the last picture of her and her father, and not that much older than the last photo of her with her sister. She had been smiling in all of the pictures, and now she was not. She had soft lines at the corners of her mouth that made her lips seem more full. She was very, very pretty. I was impressed, and I'm from LA, where beauty is a form of agriculture.

"Who are you?" she said.

"My name's Kincaid," I said. "Biff Kincaid. I'm a comedian. I wanted to talk to you about your brother."

Nancy Fisk looked at me for a beat, then dropped her gaze to the receptionist. "It's all right, Doris." She turned to me again. "Shall we talk in my office, Mr. Kincaid?"

I nodded and tipped an invisible hat to Doris, who didn't know what to make of me. I followed Nancy Fisk out into a hallway with a brown carpet and white walls adorned with western art, most of it romantic visions of Native Americans in the time before the white man showed up to spoil everything with bullets and whiskey.

Nancy Fisk's office was at the opposite end of the hallway from the reception area. It was bigger than the living room in my apartment, with a view of the pine trees that spread just beyond the walls of glass that served as two sides to her office. Her desk was made of knotted planks. I sat in a chair with padded cattle horns for armrests.

Nancy sat behind her desk, framed by a large family portrait taken when she was about ten and already a remarkable-looking girl. It was the first picture of Roger I'd seen in her presence, and he looked to be about eight. The older sister was about thirteen. Their mother was still alive back then, and she had passed onto Nancy her height, her hair, and her eyes. Carter Fisk was smiling big. A family, in happiness, frozen in time at a point that was now too far back to reach.

Now there was sadness here, enough for a lifetime, and I had to use it to get what I wanted.

"What exactly did you want to tell me about my brother, Mr. Kincaid?"

"He's in trouble."

She nodded. This was nothing new to her. "What kind of trouble?"

"He may be involved in a murder."

I let that sit there on her desk like I'd served a summons, and that's how she looked at me. Time went by. I could hear the clock on her desk tick.

"Is he all right?"

"He's fine," I said.

"Then please elaborate."

"He's come to Los Angeles to try to make it as a stand-up comedian," I said. "But he's going about it all the wrong way. He's hired someone to tape other comedians' acts for him. He's using this material without the other comedians' permission. He's rented a theater in Hollywood to tape a half-hour concert special featuring him performing this stolen material. He's been paying clubs to put him onstage as well as to book the thieves he's hired to steal jokes for him. He's drinking and drugging his way around the comedy scene and rubbing the wrong people the wrong way."

"How does this tie in with a murder?" Nancy Fisk asked.

"One of the comedians your brother stole from is dead," I said. "A friend of mine by the name of Art Westcott. I got hired to replace him. That's how I got involved in this, and then someone your brother hired taped my act."

She nodded.

"How long have you known my brother, Mr. Kincaid?" she asked.

"Just a few days."

"Does he know you are here?"

"No."

"What exactly do you want me to do about this, Mr. Kincaid?"

"Get him to talk to the police," I said.

"Are they looking for him?"

I nodded.

"How did they get his name?"

"I gave it to them."

"Is he a suspect?"

"Not yet," I said. "Right now their only suspect is me. I was the one who found Art's body."

"What if it turns out my brother is not involved in your friend's death in any way?"

"Then bring him home," I said. "Check him into another rehab. Get him out of LA. It's too much for him right now. If he wants to get into comedy, he can do it the right way."

"And what way is that?"

"Get three minutes together. Go up at an open mike. Bomb. Go back again and bomb some more. Go up anywhere that'll take you. Go up at places where they don't have comedy, where you have to slip the deejay or doorman ten bucks to go on during the band break. Go up in steak houses, coffee shops, bowling alleys, any place with a mike and a crowd. Do that for a year. Then you'll have maybe five minutes. When you've got fifteen, hit the road as an opener. Move to another city if you have to, just for the stage time. But get on a stage every night for another year. Then you might have enough to be a middle. Go out on the road as a middle until you have enough to headline. That'll take two or three more years. Once you're headlining, stay out on the road until you're working every week from New Year's to Christmas. Hit the boats, the clubs, and the one-nighters. Forget where home is, how to cook a meal by yourself, or what your suitcase looks like empty. Five years of that, and then, maybe, just maybe, you'll be ready to hit LA. And that's starting a whole other obstacle course. You're in at this club. Then you're out. You try out here. Come back in six months. And that's if you're lucky enough to get on in the first place."

Nancy Fisk almost smiled. "Doesn't sound easy."

"After the first three thousand shows," I said, "it's a piece of cake."

She nodded slightly and moved a folder on her desk with her fingertips, as though its placement was critical to what she said next. "I doubt my brother is involved in a homicide," she said, "although he has committed some legally outrageous acts."

"Like when he was weatherman at your father's TV station?"

"KMCY. In Flagstaff," Nancy Fisk said. "The station manager had to fire Roger for being drunk on the air. Roger came to me and said the station manager should resign instead. Since I happened to be the station manager in question at the time, I disagreed. I stayed, he left, then I quit and then he put the station up for sale."

She leaned back two inches in her chair. "That was six months ago, and I think that's what started this whole mess."

"Why do you say that?"

"He went out and got arrested for drunk driving. Again. The court ordered Roger to go in another rehab. That's when he got it in his head to go to California and become a comedian."

"He never expressed any interest in it before then?" I said.

"Not that I'm aware of. He always thought he was funny. That's what he said when I found out he was drunk on the air. He said it was an act." She leaned forward slightly, folding her hands together. "The FCC didn't quite see it that way. We were fined rather heavily. I say we. All my father left the girl in the family was a lifetime job in Fisk Enterprises. Essentially, I'm working for my crazy brother. He somehow thinks I'm going to be able to make money as fast as he can spend it, but that's proven to be impossible."

"Your brother's ventures into show business must be getting rather expensive," I said.

Nancy lifted her eyebrows. "I had no idea how much."

"He didn't tell you what he was up to?"

"Since he left the TV station, we haven't spoken." She moved the folder again. "I've tried tracking him through private investigators, but Roger's behavior can be so erratic they've had trouble pinning him down. Your coming to see me is the first specific information I've had on his whereabouts in several days."

"There's more," I said.

She nodded. "Go on."

"He bought a comedy club in Phoenix. He uses it to rehearse his act. He—"

Nancy Fisk closed her eyes.

I stopped talking.

She opened them. "I'm sorry, I shouldn't be surprised. I knew he was trying to find a comedy club in Arizona to perform in, but I didn't know he was going to buy one. I called around until I found one that seemed to know him and I left a message for him there." She tried to smile and failed. "I didn't mean to indicate I wanted you to be quiet."

"No, that's all right," I said. "I know this must be painful for you."

"I've handled worse, Mr. Kincaid. Believe me." She looked at her watch. "And I want to hear what you have to say, but I must go meet with the contractor on my current obsession." Emphasis on the word *my*. She smiled slightly at her joke on herself. This time she succeeded. "Would you like to come with me?"

"Certainly."

We got up. She got a trim brown leather jacket out of a closet in her office and I followed her into the hallway and out a back entrance. Outside, we got into a well-used pickup truck she started and maneuvered adeptly. "We're just going about five miles," she said. "I'm building a retirement resort here on a portion of my family's property." We turned onto a main town road and headed into the sun. "A hundred and twenty-six ranch-style houses, all arrayed over five hundred acres. There's going to be a community center, a grocery store, a fitness club, and a stables. It should be finished by late next year. Half the fifty-three units we've already sold haven't even been built yet."

"Wow," I said. We were driving through town—what must have been downtown Show Low, if it had a downtown. There weren't many buildings over two stories high, and everywhere I looked there seemed to be plenty of parking.

I glanced over at the speedometer. We were doing fifty miles an hour and we weren't even on a freeway. I'd been in LA too long.

At an intersection I caught a street sign. "What is the Deuce of Clubs?" I asked.

"That's the street we're on," Nancy said. "Also known as just the Deuce. The whole town was won in a card game. Hence the name Show Low."

"What's this property you mentioned?" I asked.

"I'd been working on it with my father for the last two years." Her demeanor changed as she talked about her work. She became more animated. Her face relaxed. She didn't seem to need sunglasses as we drove into the slanting sunlight. We turned off on a side road lined with pine trees that two miles later ran out of pavement and became gravel. "The architect's pissed off at me right now because I ordered an addition to the community center after the contractor started building it." She looked at me and smiled. "Want to guess what it is?"

"A video game room?"

She shook her head. "A library. A fully stocked library containing all of my father's papers and books—he wrote three in the last ten years—as well as American and classic literature and an extensive reference and historical collection. Plus we'll have computers with Internet access and microfiche . . . I got the idea after I read a survey where most retirees said the one activity they looked forward to most in their golden years was reading. My father was a big reader. Averaged a book a week." Her face lit up when she talked about her father, as if she was talking about someone still alive. When she talked about her brother, it was as if he was already dead. "And I'm petitioning the local authorities to have the whole place declared a township. I'm calling it Carter."

"That's nice."

"That's just the beginning." As we drove, I saw the skeletons of scattered houses and a cluster of central buildings rise out of the hills and trees. "I'm going to add onto it in the years to come. Not just make it a retirement village. I want vacation homes, a resort, a conference center, even a youth camp for underprivileged kids . . . eventually turn a thousand acres of Fisk land into Carter, Arizona. City of the future. I just can't believe he didn't leave it to me. That must have been some kind of mistake."

I wondered if she was trying to be just a little bit funny. I looked at her sideways. She was smiling slightly, her eyes widening as she drew closer to the construction sight. Most people who are trying to be funny act deadpan or over the top. She wasn't. I guess she was serious. Most people who use the word *obsessed* about themselves are.

We parked at the construction site amidst a dozen other vehicles—paint trucks, flatbeds, and pickups—and she shut off the engine. "I'll be right back," she said. "You can get out and stretch your legs."

I nodded. This was her business time.

We both got out and I watched her walk across the construction site toward a trailer set up as an office next to the largest building: the soon-to-be community center. Several hard hats patrolled the area, hammering, sawing, and digging. Most of them stopped to look at their boss's ass in riding pants. Not that I could blame them.

True to my status as an out-of-town Angeleno, I breathed in the clean crisp mountain air. It had a cleanliness to it, like the difference between LA tap and what had come out of the faucet in my motel bathroom this morning. I remembered the altitude and decided I shouldn't start running wind sprints.

Instead, I thought about what I was going to ask Nancy Fisk to do as soon as she came out of that trailer. I reviewed what I'd said and heard that morning. There was an unsolved homicide in which I was a bigger suspect than her brother. Roger was going to tape a concert performance this weekend in Los Angeles, and she was overseeing a multimillion-dollar construction project here in the mountains of Arizona. Nancy and Roger Fisk hadn't spoken in months, and I had the feeling they didn't particularly care for each other. This would require a delicate touch.

Nancy came out of the trailer and walked over toward the shell of the community center, followed by two men, one in a hard hat and one in jeans and a flannel shirt. I took the hard hat to be the contractor. The flannel shirt must be the architect. He was carrying the blueprints. They seemed to be trying to convince Nancy of something she had already made up her mind about.

Then an argument broke out. I heard Nancy's voice rise to a near shriek and saw her fists clench as she began to shake at the shoulders and yell at the two men. One of them blinked and took a step back. The other one stood his ground. This was nothing new to him.

Nancy flung the plans to the ground and stomped her boot next to them as she continued her tirade. I couldn't make out words but she was almost screaming. Work slowed in other parts of the site. She turned her head to the side and I could see her features were discolored, turning red with anger.

And just as suddenly it was over. One of the two men began talking in a calming voice and Nancy listened, fuming at first. She began nodding her head and then she bent over to pick up the plans to look at them again, laughing to herself as if she had clumsily dropped them by mistake. She handed the drawings over to them.

They stood in the middle of the building yet to be and Nancy pointed while the two men consulted the drawings. After some discussion, the men broke off to the trailer while Nancy stayed on the site, looking around, filling it in with her imagination. No one spoke to her.

I was leaning against her truck. I eased myself off and picked my way through the muddy ground of the construction site. I was wearing sneakers when the terrain called for boots.

She had her back to me as I approached her, a big little girl playing in her dream house.

"What's the problem?" I asked.

"No problem," she said in a dreamy voice. It was as though the outburst had never happened.

I decided to make a joke to get her attention. "I think what this place really needs," I said, "is an Irish pub."

She came out of her reverie and looked at me, surprised to find me so close. "Ah. Yes." She picked up on the joke. She was in a good mood. "The pub I thought would go right over there." She pointed.

"I'd be glad to serve as a consultant on the project," I said. "I'm familiar with the subject."

She shaded her eyes from the sun. "Know some Irish pubs, do you?"

I nodded. "Some of them in Ireland."

"I've never been there."

"It's the most beautiful place on earth," I said.

"Then I'll have to go someday." She dropped her hand from her forehead. "Seen enough?"

"Have you?"

She laughed. "I can't get enough of this place," she said. "I'll probably have an office or a room out here where I can come and stay."

I looked around at the trees and mountains sloping away from the rise the community center sat on. As far as I could see, there was nothing but forest. We were on a choice bit of the planet. "It's something."

She started walking back toward the truck. "You want to ask me something, don't you?" We got in and she started the engine.

"It's about your brother."

"I'm not surprised."

"I want you to come to Los Angeles this Saturday," I said. "I want you to go to his show."

"To watch him perform?" She eased the truck into gear. We began the drive back into town. She seemed puzzled.

"No," I said. "I want you to shut him down."

She looked at me sideways.

"You're the only person who knows the family money as well as he does," I said. "Or even better. If you can somehow interfere with his cash flow so he can't pay his crew, I guarantee you the cameras won't roll. Then maybe he'll listen about going to the police."

She shook her head. "Roger withdrew a large sum of cash from the operating account of Fisk Enterprises before he disappeared—about five hundred thousand dollars. I've been able to make sure he can't do that again without me knowing about it, but if he spends it all and comes back for more there isn't really anything I can do."

"Oh," I said.

All the fun had gone out of her voice. She was no longer smiling. "I'll come to LA. I'll try to get him to talk to the police. But the only person who could ever control him to any degree was my father, and he's dead." She looked at me again. She let some road travel under the tires of her truck before she spoke again. "Have you ever known anyone who was bad?"

"Bad? Bad how?"

"A bad person," she said. "You try to see the good there, but you can't. If you show people like that kindness or trust, they think you're a sucker."

"Yes," I said. "I've known people like that."

"My brother is like that," she said. "I didn't want to believe it. Neither did my parents. I think my father left Roger his money as a final effort to get him to be more responsible. But Roger doesn't care about anything like that. He's like a jungle animal. He wants what he wants, and he takes it however he can. He does what he feels like. If you try to stop him, you're his enemy. When I fired him from his weatherman job he told me he hoped I committed suicide."

"Maybe this time you can get him to see the light."

"He's evil, Mr. Kincaid," she said. "That's what I'm trying to tell you."

"I believe you."

She lifted her eyebrows. "You're the first."

We arrived back at her office building and walked upstairs without saying anything. The receptionist glanced at me with new respect and handed her a sheaf of messages and faxes. Nancy turned and looked at me, shrugging with all the work she still had to do. I pulled out a business card, one that had my name, my headshot, and all my numbers on it. I gave it to her. She looked at it, puzzled. She'd never seen a business card with someone's picture on it before.

"You photograph well," she said.

"Thanks." I nodded at the pictures in the lobby. "So do you."

She gave me one of her business cards. No headshot on it. No rings on any of her fingers either. "I'll make arrangements to fly into Los Angeles Saturday morning," she said. "Do they have a Marriott there?"

"I only know of the one at the airport. But everything's there," I said. "It's LA."

"Then I'll stay at the Marriott."

"I'll call you Friday to make sure we're still on track."

She gave me a little smile. She was a major looker. I couldn't help noticing. "You just met me, Mr. Kincaid. When I say I'll do something, I do it. Saturday, noon, at the airport Marriott in LA."

The receptionist had run to the ladies' room. "I look forward to seeing you again," I said.

Nancy kept her smile on and extended her hand. "A pleasure to meet you. I never met a real comedian before."

I took her hand and held on to it. "You never got a call from Art Westcott, did you? He might have been on the same trail just before he was killed."

"No . . ." She tried to recall. "No, I don't believe I did. Last week I was here and I take it I'm not that hard to find, Mr. Kincaid."

"You know, most people call me Biff."

She didn't take her hand back right away and she didn't stop smiling. "Would you like for me to be like most people, then, Biff?"

"No," I said. "I don't think that's possible."

TWENTY

I had spent another night in Arizona at my fifty-dollar-a-night hotel and then driven to Phoenix and hopped a plane back to LA. That made it Thursday—two days before Roger Fisk was going to tape his concert special.

I stopped off at home to check my mail and my messages. Kelly had called. ("Biff, the police want to talk to me about you. They say it's about Art's murder.") I'd call her back later. I got back on the freeway toward the Valley and turned off at Studio City. I cruised along until I found the office building I'd staked out earlier in the week, hoping to get a glimpse of David Kelton. This time I didn't lurk across the street. I went right in.

I found his offices on the first floor, toward the end of the hallway. He shared a receptionist with an accountant and a company that specialized in cutting actors' demo reels.

The receptionist I'd spoken to over the phone wasn't in. Sitting in her place was a man in his thirties, too thin and too tall. He had dyed his hair green and had an earring in one ear and wore mascara. Somehow this didn't clash with his coat and tie. I was a long way from Arizona.

"Is David Kelton in?"

"Did you have an appointment?" he asked. His voice was higher than Kelly's.

"No."

He pulled out an appointment book. To look for what? An empty space? "And what's your name?"

"Call me Ishmael," I said. "Robert Ishmael." While he looked down, I scanned the offices. There were four closed doors, no one in the waiting room. The waiting room was decorated with a painting of the Sunset Strip. If I strained, I could find the sign for the Comedy Store. It was slightly blurred, the letters painted in red instead of black.

"He doesn't have you down for an appointment. . . ." The receptionist picked up the phone. "Let me see if he's in."

I listened carefully. The place was as quiet as a bank holiday. I heard a faint trill behind the door just to my right. A voice answered, but I couldn't make out any words.

"Yes, this is Jared at the front desk," the receptionist whispered. "Is David Kelton in today?"

Pause. I could barely hear someone speaking on the other side of the door to my right.

"Someone is here to see him," Jared said.

He listened, then put a hand over the phone to speak to me. "Do you have a messenger delivery?"

"Yes," I said. Whatever would get me inside.

"Okay. All right."

He hung up.

"You can just leave your delivery here at the front desk and when David Kelton gets in I'll see that he gets it," Jared said.

"Okay," I said, and turned and headed for the closed door on my right.

"Sir?" Jared said, his voice going higher and louder. "Sir, you can't—"

I opened the door.

Inside Kelton's office was a desk, a phone, a lamp, and a filing cabinet. There were two chairs for visitors. Sitting in one of the visitor's chairs was George, the ex-cop turned bodyguard for Roger Fisk. It took me a moment to recognize him because he had shaved his head, leaving the black goatee, and was wearing different clothes. Instead of a suit, now he was sporting a workout outfit. It fit snugly over his sturdy physique.

He was eating a fruit salad and drinking some ginseng tea from a wide-mouthed bottle. He looked like he'd been jogging in the neighborhood and had stopped in for a healthy snack.

I was still standing in the doorway when Jared stopped two inches away from my ear. "Sir, I can't—"

"It's okay," George said in his low, gravelly voice, his eyes not leaving mine.

"I'm sorry," Jared said to George, "I told him—"

"It's okay," George said. This time he looked at Jared instead of me, and this time Jared went away.

I stepped in and closed the door behind me. George took the time to wipe his hands on a sweat towel that was looped around his neck and sit back. He remained seated to show me he wasn't scared of me.

"What do you want?"

"Information."

"I look like the phone company to you, asshole?"

"No, you look like a thug who can't do any better than to get himself hired by a rich kid from Arizona who thinks he's a comedian," I said. "You know anything about Art Westcott?"

"I'm not good with names," George said.

"I'll keep it simple and try not to use any big words," I said. "Art Westcott is the comedian who performed with Ned Lando last Friday night down at Chortles. Saturday he called me to take his place. Right after he hung up the phone with me, someone blew his brains out."

"So?"

"So I learned later Richard Moftus has been paid to put Ned Lando onstage by David Kelton, Roger Fisk's so-called manager." I looked around for any sign of Kelton, a photo, a portrait. I had only seen the man from a distance, but I didn't want George to know that. "Lando was also being paid by Kelton, and Kelton's been getting his money from Fisk. Along with you, that's quite a payroll."

George nodded. He didn't want anyone to think his services came cheap.

"You think I blew away this Art Westcott?" George asked.

"Well, I look at it this way," I said. "I've found all this out in the time since Art was killed. I wonder what else Art knew that got his ticket punched. Right now the cops have me under suspicion. Besides, you've got to be doing something to earn your keep."

He held himself in check, but made a display of doing so. He could do better than that. There was only one reason pride had won over his temper; he'd seen me fight. He wasn't sure he could take me. Frankly, I wasn't that sure he couldn't. I just had to get him to make the first move so I could get him on the ground and knock the sass out of him.

"You know," he said, "I've kicked your ass a couple of times now, and I still can't remember your name."

"The name's Kincaid," I said. "And you never kicked my ass. You sapped me once from behind and the other time you had to help your boss get up off the floor."

George lowered his eyes. He had black eyebrows to go with his dark eyes and this was his snake look, meant to hypnotize his prey. "Maybe it's time I did the job right then," he said.

"That gushing sound you hear," I said, "is piss running down my leg."

George pushed his chair back and stood up slowly, taking his time to wipe his mouth and hands with his sweat towel and drop it on the desk. He pointed. "You're gonna need that," he said, "to wipe the blood out of your eyes."

"You ain't big enough," I said. "And you're too far away."

He went up in the air with a flying martial arts kick that would have surprised me if I hadn't seen it coming when he dropped into a stance and shifted his weight. I dove down, rolling on my shoulders and letting a leg of my own snap up and catch him right in the banana basket with my heel. He got his wings clipped midflight and crashed into the corner made by the wall and the door, his eyes popping open as he sank to the floor, clutching his stomach.

I got up and bent over him, patting him down for a piece. I found a knife and a can of pepper spray. He must have been afraid of dogs while he was running. I took them both and stepped back. He kicked weakly at me with one foot and I dosed him in the face with the pepper spray. His eyes and mouth tried to disappear.

Jared was knocking on the door with the flat of his hand. "What's going on in there?" he shrieked. "Open the door!"

I dragged George by the feet away from the door and around the desk, dropping him in front of the chair. I let him find it with his fingers. "Just play along," I said. "Tell me what I want to know, and I promise I won't hurt you anymore."

"Fuck you," he choked out.

Jared wasn't giving up. "I can call the police, you know!" he yelled through the door.

"Goddammit," I muttered, "George, now behave." I made it quick. I kicked the chair out of his feeble grasp and stepped on his clutching fingers. They didn't break, but they bent. I gave him two slaps across the face, same hand, both sides of it, palm side and knuckle side. It's not a lot of pain, but the surprise of it has a conciliatory effect. "Now let's put on a happy show for Jared, and he'll leave us alone to chat."

Then I went to the door and opened it. Jared almost fell into the room, his eyes growing even wider when he saw George slumped on the floor.

"Oh, my God," Jared said. "What did you do to him?"

"I didn't do anything to him," I said. "He just had a little accident."

"George," Jared said, "George, can you hear me?"

"Yeah," George managed to squeeze out.

"George, do you want me to call for some help?"

"No." George was trying not to cough.

"Everything is just fine," I said. "Isn't it, George?"

"Yeah."

I eased Jared out the door. "See? Everything's fine," I said. "We just had a little accident and in a few minutes all will be well in the Merry Old Land of Oz."

"But—"

I shut the door in his face and turned my attention back to George, who was trying to crawl away in search of more air and less pain. I knelt down beside him.

"I look at it this way," I said. "You're paid to do as you're told. If you clocked out Art Westcott, you don't know why."

He could barely breathe, much less talk. "I . . . I didn't kill him."

"No, I didn't think you did, George. Because getting Art to call another comedian to cover for him while a gun was held to his head was smart. And you're dumb."

"Never . . . met him."

"I'm looking for David Kelton," I said. "As Fisk's manager,

he's supposed to be the brains of this outfit. You know where he is?"

George shook his head and spit red globs out the side of his mouth. They ran into his goatee. "He quit," he rasped.

"When?"

"Today. This morning."

"Where's he live?" I asked.

George shook his head again. "Don't know. Somewhere in the Valley."

I sighed and got up and walked around behind the desk. I rifled through the drawers until I found what I was looking for: the part of a cable bill that was labeled FOR YOUR PERSONAL RECORDS. It had been left behind by accident. It listed David Kelton's name and address. Could be home; could be a mail drop. Only one way to find out. I put it in my pocket.

George had found a leg of one of the visitors' chairs and used it to crawl up from the floor. With one hand he blindly reached out for the desktop, landing his palm right in the middle of his fruit salad and knocking over his bottle of ginseng tea. He was desperately trying to open his eyes, coughing and spluttering.

I got up and walked around quietly, as George followed my exit, trying to get a bearing on my whereabouts. I stopped long enough for him to sight me against a wall and charge me from his squatting position on the floor.

Let the man have his pride. I stepped aside and he rammed his face into the white plaster, falling back, dazed, onto the floor.

"So long, George," I said, and turned to go. I stopped with my hand on the doorknob. "By the way," I said, "does this make the second or third time you've kicked my ass?"

I turned and left. Jared was sitting at his post, looking scared.

"That's my time," I said. "Tip your waitress and drive safely."

TWENTY-ONE

I drove to David Kelton's address. It wasn't a mail drop. It was a real apartment in Sherman Oaks, about five miles away. When I knocked on his door, he answered it.

When I'd seen him from afar, I saw a David Kelton slight of build, with thinning blond hair on top. Up close, he'd managed to lose even more weight and hair. He wore bulky clothes to disguise his lack of physical development. He had big eyes and a wide jaw. This made him look a little bit like Carol Channing.

When he answered the door, his large blue eyes were shot through with red. His lips were chapped and raw. His hair was tousled into blond tufts. He looked at me like he thought I might have come to kill him. I smelled a chemical vapor. Ether. I hoped they'd kept his room ready at the rehab center because it looked to me like he'd been hitting the coke smoke again.

"Are you Ray?" he asked.

"Who's Ray?"

He tried to close the door in my face. I stuck my foot in and gently forced it back as he strained with all his might. In order to put an end to this, I had to give the door a sharp shove. That knocked him back on to a couch. I stepped in and closed the door behind me. Forcible entry seemed to be the order of the day.

Although the sun was shining outside, all of the drapes and curtains were closed and very few lights had been turned on inside. Kelton rolled off the couch, grabbed a coffee cup caked with dried grounds, and held it above his head. "Get out," he said. "Get out or I'll use this."

"Go ahead and throw it," I said. "If it makes you feel any better. Get all the anger out."

He threw the coffee cup at me and I caught it one-handed, tossing it up and down in my hand like a softball. "You want to keep playing catch," I said, "or do you want to talk?"

He bolted from where we were standing in the living room and headed for one of the two bedrooms. For all I knew he had a gun in there and—worst of all—didn't know how to use it. I pitched the coffee cup at him overhanded and caught him right between the shoulder blades at the base of the neck just as he was rounding the corner in front of the bathroom. He changed trajectory and his forehead hit part of the bathroom door frame. He hung on to it to keep from falling to the floor. I walked over to where he was barely standing, moaning for breath. I picked up the coffee cup and tossed it up and down in my hand again.

"I forgot to ask," I said. "Did you want cream and sugar with that?"

"Who are you?" he said breathlessly.

I pinched him in the fleshy part of his chest just under the armpit and dragged him back out to the living room and tossed him on the couch as he yelped in pain. He bounced harmlessly against the cushions, coming up to a sitting position.

The living room was like the office: bare walls, only the most functional of furniture. It was the home of someone who didn't know how to live a normal life.

"My name's Kincaid," I said. "Biff Kincaid. I'm a comedian."

David Kelton touched his face and looked at his fingers to see if he was bleeding. He wasn't. "Yeah? And?"

"And this last weekend I worked with a comic named Ned Lando," I said.

"Oh, God." I could see his pulse beating in his throat.

"Lando taped my act and sold it to your client, Roger Fisk. I think Fisk plans to use it in the show he's taping Saturday."

"He's . . . ," Kelton tried to moisten his lips with his tongue but came up dry. "Roger Fisk is not my client anymore."

"What happened?"

"He fired me. I quit. Can I have a glass of water?"

I looked around the corner toward the kitchen. There were knives in the kitchen. "Yeah," I said. "From the bathroom."

He got up and walked past me into the bathroom. I watched him get a glass of water and bring it back to the couch. He swallowed it all in one draft.

"You were thirsty."

"Uh-huh."

He looked like a little boy waiting in the dentist's office, small and scared.

"Let me tell you why I'm here," I said.

"Okay."

"A friend of mine is dead," I said. "Another comedian. Art Westcott."

Kelton set the empty water glass beside him on the couch. It fell over soundlessly. He didn't care. "Oh, no."

"Oh, yes."

"How long?"

"A few days now," I said. "He was working with Ned Lando last week at Chortles in Hartford Beach. Art called me Saturday afternoon to sub for him, and then someone ventilated his skull with a three-fifty-seven Magnum."

"Oh, God." He brought his knees up to his chest. He was wearing dirty socks that had bunched at the soles.

"You know anyone that might want to kill Art Westcott?"

Kelton hugged his knees and rocked. "Roger."

"Roger Fisk?"

He nodded. "He's an evil man."

"I was getting that idea."

"He thinks people are out to get him when they aren't."

"Why did you quit?"

"I ran out of money," he said. "I had to make good on my threats to leave."

"That why you stopped Ned Lando's check?"

He nodded. "Roger said I'd spent too much."

"Why?"

"I had some unforeseen expenses." Kelton rocked some more on the couch and looked at me, pleading with his eyes.

"You bought drugs with the show money, didn't you?"

His eyes started to water. "I wanted to get back in the business," he said. "When I met Roger, I thought it would just be a step, something to get me on my feet. I didn't know he was going to hurt people. I didn't know he was going to hire someone like George." He let the implications speak for themselves. "I couldn't handle it."

I snorted. "I've met George," I said. "He can't hold his own in a fair fight."

"He doesn't specialize in fair fights," Kelton said. "He likes guns and knives. He's an assassin." He stopped rocking and put his feet on the floor, hugging himself at the elbows. "Roger said if I asked him for money again, he'd send George after me."

"How much does he owe you?"

"Thousands."

"What about the crew for the shoot Saturday?" I said. "The theater? The director? Have they been paid?"

Kelton nodded. "I fronted them a down payment out of my salary. The crew wouldn't take the job unless I gave them half up front."

"So this show is going through?" I said.

"It's what Roger wants," Kelton said. "He thinks"—he broke off in a light, feathery laugh—"he thinks it's going to make him a star." Without pausing, Kelton said, "Do you know how long he's been doing stand-up comedy?"

"No."

"Less than six months." Kelton smiled and showed me his grayish teeth. "He's been doing it for six months, and he thinks he's ready to get his own talk show or sitcom."

"From the show he's taping Saturday?"

"Yeah," Kelton said. "He wants to show it to the top agents, managers, and producers in town. He thinks they'll make him a star." More laughter. "Have you ever seen Roger perform?"

I shook my head.

"He's shit." Kelton was truly amusing himself now. "He's lousy. That's what I think he paid me for—to sit through his crummy, stinking act and pretend I saw something. I've got an eye for talent. Jesus, I was the first manager to sign Jimmy Paul."

"Jimmy Paul of *Saturday Night Live?*" I asked.

Kelton nodded.

"He's funny," I said.

"Of course he's funny," Kelton said. He was suddenly disdainful. "A blind man could see he had talent. He was what I had. That's where I was going. The movie deals, the cable specials. But then . . ." Another glance at the bedroom. He wanted to get back in there.

"You found a distraction," I said.

"Life," Kelton said, "is full of them."

I nodded. There was nothing I could do for him because there was nothing he could do for himself. He had opened a door he could never completely close again. Now I understood the decorating scheme of his apartment and office, or lack of one. Maybe he was trying to make his living and working space look like a rehab center. That was where he felt the most at home. That was where he felt the safest.

"I want your help with something," I said.

"What?"

"I want to get inside the show Saturday night," I said.

He snorted. He was starting to shiver. It wasn't cold. "Good luck."

"I know there was security around the Doug Stone Theater even while the set was being built," I said, "but I have an idea about Saturday night."

"What?"

"That," I said, "is where I need your help."

"I told you, I'm not in business with Roger Fisk anymore."

"One phone call," I said. "That's all I need."

"To who?"

I told him.

He stared at me. For a moment, his mind was off the drugs he had in the bedroom.

"Who do you think you are," he asked, "Batman?"

"Just get me inside," I said. "I'll handle the rest."

"How?"

"Haven't gotten that far yet."

I stayed while David Kelton dialed the phone. It was more than one call. He had to write another phone number down on a pad. At one point, he put his hand over the phone to ask me a question. "Do you want to use your real name?"

"Sure."

"If Roger or George finds out . . ."

"They might come after me?" I suggested.

Kelton nodded.

"Good."

Kelton stared at me again, then spoke into the phone. "Kincaid," he said. "Biff Kincaid. All right. I'll have him call you at home."

He hung up. "The man you want to talk to is Scott," he said. "I wrote his home phone number down for you." He got up from the couch and walked into the bedroom. I leaned over the couch and saw the phone number he had written on the pad. I picked it up and tore it off.

"This?" I asked him as he came out of the bedroom holding what looked like a modified water pipe, but there was no smoke coming out of it, just the smell of ether. His free-basing kit.

Kelton nodded. "Call him after six." He sat on the floor, using the couch as a back cushion, and proceeded to light up, smoking the last remnants of rock cocaine he had in the bowl. He inhaled deeply, closed his eyes, and let vapor drift out from between his lips.

Our business was done. He was no good to me or anyone else now. I put the phone number in my pocket and turned to go. "Thanks," I said.

I had my hand on the knob when I heard him say, "Biff."

I turned around.

He was standing up. He had risen to his feet noiselessly. His eyes were open wide, rimmed with red. He no longer looked meek and afraid. His lips were stretched in a mirthless grin. A chemical zombie.

"I got a great idea for a screenplay I'm working on," he said. "Want to hear my pitch?"

"I have to go," I said.

"You'll be sorry," he said. Then, as an afterthought: "Loser."

I opened the door and closed it behind me. Outside, the sun was shining. I could hear birds. I walked to my car. On my way I saw a dingy Cadillac pull up next to the curb and park, scraping a bumper. A guy my age got out, puffy in the face but lean around the ribs. Black tuxedo shirt over a black T-shirt, stained white pants, sandals with one thong loose, and silver rings on his fingers that had skulls and demons with their mouths open and screaming. His hair was buzz-cut and dyed white. He had shades on so dark I couldn't make out all the parts of his face.

I walked past him as he stood unsteadily on the curbside and studied the addresses on the apartment buildings, and I smelled whiskey and ether. Together, they made an odor like embalming fluid.

"Hey, uh . . . ," he said.

I turned.

"You know where one-two-eight-six-seven is?" he asked me.

I pointed to where I had just come from. "There."

"Thanks."

"You Ray?"

That confused him all over again. "Huh?"

"Are you Ray?"

"How'd you know that?"

I pointed again, this time to Kelton's door on the second floor. "He's in apartment number six," I said. "He's waiting for you."

Ray looked me over with his black lenses. "Who are you?"

I smiled. "The guy before Ray."

I turned my back on him. By the time I got in my car, Ray was already up the stairs and inside, closing the door on the outside world.

TWENTY-TWO

All I had was the name Scott and a phone number. It was a 310 area code; the exchange looked to be in Santa Monica. Call after six.

It was five o'clock now, and rush hour was in full throttle. I got in the traffic headed for the west side of Los Angeles, and it moved at the pace of sludge in a penitentiary sewer. I tried to distract myself with a little music, but it didn't work, so I tuned in to one of the all-news AM stations with their teeth-grinding, overcaffeinated chatter about the day's events and just bathed in hyperstimulation as I inched along the freeways.

Once I got to Brentwood, I pulled over and grabbed some broiled fish tacos at a Baja Mexican food place. I looked at attractive women as they walked past me on the sidewalk. I thought of Kelly Malone.

I finished dinner and found a phone. It was six, straight up.

Scott was home. He answered the phone like he was still at work: "This is Scott Dawson."

"Scott?" I said. "It's Biff Kincaid. David Kelton called on my behalf and—"

"Ah, yes, yes, yes," Scott said. "How is David Kelton these days?"

"The picture of health," I said.

Scott chuckled dryly. "You were lucky to grab him between rehabs."

I decided I didn't like Scott. "Anyway, I don't know what he told you—"

"Where are you?"

"At a pay phone."

"Where?"

"Brentwood."

"I'm in Venice."

"Okay. Where should we meet?"

"Do you know Main Street?" he asked. "In Santa Monica?"

"Yeah," I said. There was a theater there I'd done spots at.

"There's an Irish pub at Pier and Main," he said. "O'Brien's. Let's meet there."

"I'll see you at six-thirty," I said.

"Ah," he said, "better make it seven."

"How will I know you?"

"I'll be wearing an Audiences Unlimited sweatshirt. You?"

"Red hair, blue eyes. I look like Kenneth Brannagh." In profile. I like to think.

"The Shakespeare guy?"

"Yeah, him."

I hung up and drove.

Seven o'clock.

Giving some place an Irish name and serving Murphy's and Guinness and Harp all on tap and booking Celtic music acts in on the weekends doesn't automatically make a bar two blocks from the beach in Santa Monica an Irish pub, but it's a mighty good shove in the right direction.

I'd headed over as soon as I'd hung up the pay phone. I'd gotten to my rendezvous point at O'Brien's fifteen minutes early. I'd ordered a pint of Murphy's and was watching it slowly settle when Scott Dawson walked in.

Scott Dawson was a thin-waisted black man in his twenties with silver, wire-rim glasses, a lightly shaven head, and a single diamond earring. He scanned the room and I waved.

I was sitting in a booth. We shook and he sat down. He smelled of spicy cologne. His jeans were neat and pressed, his sneakers sparkling white. I don't trust anyone who sends their jeans out to the cleaners.

"Drink?" I asked.

"A glass of merlot," he said, "when the waitress comes by."

I looked around. No waitresses. I'd get it on my refill.

"What did David Kelton tell you about me?" Dawson asked.

I shook my head. "A phone number and a first name," I said. "I learned your last name when you answered the phone."

"Ah." He smiled, showing rows of polished enamel. "David remembers the rules." He paused. "When he remembers anything, you know."

I made a half nod. "What did he tell you about me?" I asked.

"A name," Dawson said. "And to expect a call."

My Murphy's was gone. I got up and replaced it with a Guinness and got Scott his merlot. He sipped it delicately, running a finger around the rim of the glass. "So what can I do for you, Biff Kincaid?"

"There's a show taping this Saturday night," I said.

He nodded.

"I think Audiences Unlimited is supplying the crowd."

"Which show is this?"

"It's a taping at the Doug Stone Theater at Hollywood and Vine," I said. "A comedian is taping a half-hour special there."

"Oh, yes," Scott said, "I'm working on that one. What's the comedian's name again? Roger . . . ?"

"Fisk."

"Roger Fisk, yes."

"Kelton said that extras were being hired as audience members," I said.

"Right."

"I want to be one of them."

"Okay." Dawson sipped his wine and ran a finger across his lower lip. "It's a hundred dollars."

"You mean, that's what it pays?" I asked.

"No, it pays forty," Dawson said. "It costs a hundred."

"You want *me* to pay *you* a hundred dollars?" I asked. "I don't get it."

Dawson was immediately impatient. "Look, we're hiring extras for this show, right? Now security's tight on this project. Each extra is to have a numbered badge they carry at all times but put in their pocket before taping so it doesn't show on camera. We cast extras out of our files, put a nice good-looking demographic up front, the best actors along the aisles, the shitheads in the middle. If you're up front or along the aisle, you're on camera more for audience reaction shots. We pay them forty bucks each.

"We do this all the time. We're not an audience research service. We don't stand out in front of Mann's Chinese with clipboards and ask people if they'd like to see a show. Look at your average infomercial. You think those people are sitting there applauding the new Miracle Muffin Maker for fucking free? No. Now for whatever reason, you want to be one of the audience members on this particular show. It's my side business. Sometimes there's a talk show taping someone wants to be in on, see their favorite singer, see their friend on TV. I can arrange it. The only audience coordinators who don't do it are the new ones. But it's a hundred dollars. Take it or leave it."

His mild tirade was over. He sipped his wine and looked somewhere else.

"There an ATM around here?" I said.

Dawson glanced at his watch. "There's one on the next corner," he said briskly.

"Be right back," I said.

I walked out the door and hit the ATM for a hundred bucks. I came back in with five twenties. I folded them in my palm and held the money under the table.

"I got it," I said. "It's in my hand, under the table."

He kept sipping his wine and looking somewhere else, but he took it. He pocketed it without counting it.

"Show's at 8:00 P.M. Saturday night," he said. "The extras are being asked to meet in front of the Doug Stone Theater at 7:00 P.M. That's when numbered badges will be handed out. Each number corresponds to a name. Yours will be one of them."

"That's it?"

He nodded. "We're done." He took another sip of wine and left the rest in the glass.

"I take it your silence comes with the price tag," I said.

He smiled. "Sure." He stood up. "Whatever you say."

I let him go. All there was left of him was half a glass of wine and the feeling that the temperature in the room had gone up half a degree, as if a cold draft had been stopped.

TWENTY-THREE

It's a long drive from the beach to the Hollywood Hills. On my way back into town I stopped in at the Comedy Store. I had a spot there at 8:30. When I checked in with the ticket booth, I learned the show had gotten a bit of a late start. I'd go on about 8:45.

I had a message waiting for me inside the ticket booth from Kelly Malone. I called her on the pay phone just outside the Original Room.

"Where are you?" she asked.

"The Comedy Store," I said. There was laughter behind me. I hoped she could hear it. "I have a spot."

"Where have you been?" she said.

"In and out of town," I said. I remembered I hadn't returned the call she'd left me at home.

"What's been going on?"

"It's a long story."

"I'd like to hear it."

"You want to hear it over the phone," I asked, "or in person?"

Pause.

"If you were to come down here," she asked, "how late would you be?"

"Not late, as long as I don't get bumped. We could watch the eleven o'clock news together."

"You remember where I live?"

"Of course," I said. "I have a built-in heat-seeking mechanism."

"Then I'll get the fireplace going," she said. "You bring the fuel." I hung up and got ready for my time onstage.

I killed, I destroyed, thank you, good night. I left 'em laughing and headed east on the Strip toward the I-5, stopping to pick up a bundle of pine logs at the market in Beachwood Canyon. As I passed my street I remembered something Kelly might need besides firewood. I keep an old suitcase under my bed that I save for times like these. I went and got that, pulling it out carefully, checking its contents, and loading it into the trunk of my car. Then I sped on down to Hartford Beach.

Kelly attacked me as I came through the door, tearing at my lips and hair as if they held nourishment. I reciprocated her ferocity, dropping my double load of suitcase and firewood bundle by the door as we wordlessly wrestled to the floor. She had put her cat in the bedroom and lit a fire in the fireplace, turning out all the lights. When she let me in, the living room was bathed in an orange glow. Heat-seeking mechanism was right. She had dressed for me, and she liked to shop at Victoria's Secret. An hour later we reached our climax together, her on her knees and elbows, me pumping inside her from behind, the amber light dancing across our alabaster skins.

By the time the eleven o'clock news came on, we were lying together in front of the fireplace, damp and pliant, the television off. The temperature had dropped outside to the sixties, and she hadn't turned on the heat. With a blaze crackling behind the screen, we were both cool and warm at the same time, turning sides under a cotton blanket stolen from the hall closet.

"What are you thinking?" she asked sometime before midnight.

It had been minutes since we had made any noise at all.

"A couple of things," I said.

"Like?" She threw a chunk of the real wood I'd brought on top of the starter log she'd lit. The wood hissed and popped, sending a shower of sparks against the black mesh of the screen.

"I'm wondering if there's anything to drink in the refrigerator," I said. She had a glass of wine sitting on a kitchen countertop she had not touched since I'd walked in. I seemed to be keeping company with grape drinkers lately.

"Go look," she said.

I got up, walked into the kitchen, opened the refrigerator door, and found a four-pack of Theakston's Old Peculiar.

"Nice," I said.

"I stopped by a liquor store," she said. "They didn't have any Guinness."

"This'll do," I said. I got a bottle out.

"You do that bit, you know," she said, "about British beers and ales and I thought . . ."

"Believe me, I'm not complaining," I said. "It's a fine Yorkshire ale." Using the light from the refrigerator, I looked around for a glass but it was too cold to stay away from the fire, so I came back, bringing her her unfinished wine.

"And?"

"And what?

"And what else are you thinking?"

"What a nice time I'm having," I said. I looked at her with a pleasant expression. "That's about it."

"How's the back of your head?"

"Just about healed up," I said.

She ran her fingertips over my thigh, touching a tender spot. "So how did you get this bruise right here?"

I looked. I hadn't felt it before, much less seen it—a saucer-sized leftover from my fight with George in David Kelton's old office. "Oh," I said. It was getting purple at the center, green around the edges. "That."

"Do you want some ice for it?"

"No," I said.

"How'd you get it?"

"I got in a fight."

"With whom?"

"Roger Fisk's bodyguard." I told her what I'd done that day and the day before that.

"Do the police have any suspects yet?" she asked.

"You mean *other* suspects," I said. "As far as I can tell it's still just me." I looked at her. "Don't worry. I didn't do it."

"Who do you think did?"

"I don't know," I said. "Pick a name out of the hopper: George the bodyguard, David Kelton, Ned Lando, Roger Fisk. Maybe even his sister."

"Biff, I think Art Westcott's murder is a matter best left to the police."

"I'm leaving it to them," I said. "I just want them to start realizing I'm the wrong guy to be asking questions about."

"So you're going to sneak into Roger Fisk's show Saturday night?"

"That's the plan."

"And what are you going to do once you get there?"

"Haven't finished the plan entirely," I said. "I think I'll wing it."

"What can I do to help?"

"I want you to stay down here in Orange County out of harm's way," I said. More silence. The fire burned. I turned over to toast my bruise.

"Can I see you before then?"

Tomorrow was Friday. I shook my head regretfully. "I've got two spots at the Store, and I want to be in town early Saturday for when Nancy Fisk flies in from Arizona."

"I'm scared," she said. "There are some dangerous people involved in this. They could go after you—or me, to find out where you are."

"That's why I brought this for you," I said. I got up and went over by the doorway, dragging the old suitcase I'd pulled out from under my bed. I opened the hasps and pulled out a weapon.

"This is a four-ten shotgun," I said. "Semiautomatic." The polished metal gleamed in the firelight. I held up a box of shells. "You load it like this." I showed her, keeping the barrel pointed at the fireplace. "Tomorrow morning we'll take it out and shoot it a couple of times." I ejected the shells and picked them up from where they'd rolled on the carpet.

I set the shotgun aside and reached back into the suitcase. Kelly was up on one elbow, the blanket draped over her hip. There was no expression on her face.

"This is a thirty-eight-caliber pistol," I said, pulling out a nickel-plated handgun. "Five shots. We'll do some target practice with this tomorrow, too."

I set the pistol aside.

"Pepper spray," I said, picking up a black cylinder that could fit on a key chain. In my other hand I picked up a device that looked like a TV remote control with two metal stubs that protruded like spider fangs. "And stun gun." I tested it once, to show it was fully charged. Blue crackling light arced across a space of less than two inches.

Kelly's eyes were still and large. "Where did you get those things?" she whispered.

I closed the suitcase, the armaments on the floor. "They're mine."

"Are those all the guns you have?"

"No," I said. "These are the ones I think you can handle on short notice."

"You expect me to shoot someone?"

"You're better off with them than without," I said. "Carry the stun gun and the pepper spray with you whenever you leave the house to go to the store or get gas. You can sleep with the shotgun next to the bed and keep the pistol handy around the house. Don't drive with them loaded in the car. They have to be unloaded and in the trunk. When we go shooting tomorrow—"

She shook her head. "I don't want you to leave any guns here," she said.

I took a beat before answering. "Kelly—"

"I've never had guns in my house," she said. "I won't start now."

"It's for your own protection," I said.

I looked at her. Her face was set. I wasn't going to change her mind. Not tonight. I packed up the thirty-eight and the four-ten and zipped the suitcase closed. "I'll leave the pepper spray and the stun gun," I said. "Okay?"

She took a moment to weigh her objections. She didn't have any objections to nonlethal forms of self-defense. "Okay," she said.

I put the spray and the stun gun on the kitchen counter and the suitcase by the door where I'd left it when I walked in, then I went back to join her in front of the fireplace, throwing another log on the fire.

"I don't think I could ever shoot another human being," she said.

"Wait until one tries to shoot you," I said.

She sat up. She didn't want our bodies to touch for some new reason. She looked at me with an expression leftover from her bad days working the stock market. "Have you?" she asked. "Has someone tried to shoot you?"

I nodded.

"What did you do?"

"I shot back."

"And what happened?"

"He missed," I said. "I didn't."

She looked at me for a long time. Her lips were pressed together firmly. "Did you kill him?"

"No."

"Who was this person?"

"I never found out," I said. "I was on the road in Florida, finishing up a week headlining at a hotel lounge. Someone must have sat through the show and seen me get paid behind the bar. Eight hundred bucks in cash. I went to my room, packed my bags, and was walking them out to my car at about one in the morning when some guy and his buddy stepped out from behind a pickup truck, called me by name, and told me to hand over the money. One of them had a gun in his hand."

Kelly was both fascinated and horrified. "What did you do?"

"I gave it to them," I said. "I know better than to resist an armed robber. I took the cash out slow and tossed it aside while I ducked behind another car." I'd gotten that advice from a cop: You go one way, the money goes another. "The unarmed one took the money and ran; the other fired under the car at me. I was wearing my thirty-eight on an ankle strap." I nodded in the direction of the suitcase. "I unskinned it and shot back. I tagged the shooter in the fleshy part of his thigh and he ran off, yelling. Police came. A bartender had seen it while he was taking out the trash. They never caught the guys. I never got my money back either." I looked at her. "End of story."

She looked down in the bottom of her glass of wine as though the dregs were telling her fortune. She swirled it once and finished it all off in three swallows. She put the glass on the hearth and gathered most of the blanket around her.

"I didn't know comedy was like that," she said.

"Sometimes it is," I said.

"And I didn't know you were like that," she said, "a man who carried guns and shot people."

"Sometimes I am."

"That is, when you're not getting into fistfights. Or finding dead bodies." She shifted the blanket around her until she was wearing it like a tent. Only her head and hair showed as she arranged herself in a lotus position.

"Kelly, I don't go around asking for trouble," I said. "I deal with it as best I can."

"I'm just not used to it," she said.

"I don't know anyone who is. But I'm sure there are people who are."

She didn't look at me. "I don't know that I want to—get used to it, that is."

I didn't know what to say after that. Enough minutes passed to bring us close to midnight, and when the fire started to die down I didn't stoke it up anymore but instead went into the bedroom and moved Shadow out of the way to turn back the covers on the double bed. Kelly made a dash for the bed, diving under the covers even though the sheets were cold, and we made a show of shivering and making funny sounds like brrrr. We were freezing solid and holding each other for warmth and that got us laughing together. We each took a turn running into the bathroom and yelling eeeeowww, the toilet seat was cold, and yumyumyum how the water tasted better than up in LA. When we were both under the covers again, I warmed her hands and feet against me and started kissing my way up her arms and legs; and we started making a fire of our own, like we were in a little cabin in the woods, away from all the harm and trouble in the world.

TWENTY-FOUR

It was Friday midday when I headed into LA, the traffic unusually light. Most people are anxious to get out of town, and I was headed in. I took freeways all the way back home. The Hollywood freeway northbound has a neat little exit that empties out to the base of Beachwood Canyon right at the intersection with Franklin, just a few blocks from my apartment. I landed at home just in time for lunch. Kelly and I had had each other for breakfast before she went into work at Chortles.

I had some time to kill so I walked down to the strip on Franklin, which is a collection of restaurants, bars, a bookstore, a coffee house, a theater, and other miscellaneous shops, none of which belongs to a chain. I wandered in and out, eating lunch and scanning the Friday entertainment trades. Nothing about Roger Fisk or his upcoming special.

After lunch I cruised by the Doug Stone Theater and saw huge equipment trucks parked outside, the kind that usually meant location shooting of some kind was going on. I watched as a Betacam and tripod were being lugged inside. If Fisk was bankrolling all of this, he had a lot of green to burn and the smoke was getting thick.

After I got back I hit the gym, working out to the point of pain, punching the heavy bag until my hands were numb. I walked home to shower. When I got there, my message light was blinking.

"Hello, Biff?" A female voice gave my name a teasing twist. "You didn't say your name on your outgoing message so I hope I have the right number."

Nancy Fisk.

"I couldn't get a plane out tomorrow, and the only flights from Phoenix today that weren't booked solid were the earlier ones, so I'm here in LA ahead of schedule." She gave a little laugh. "I'm at the airport Marriott, in case you don't remember. If I don't hear from you today, I'll just hope to talk to you tomorrow. I'm not going anywhere. Good-bye."

She hung up.

So she was here early. It was an unexpected development, a last-minute change, the kind I'd learned to roll with and be suspicious of all in the same life. Like I'd told Kelly, I had no solid idea who was behind Art's murder.

I called her back, still in my gym clothes. It was three o'clock in the afternoon.

"How was your flight?" I asked.

"Much more crowded than the last time I flew," she said. "But that was three years ago to Albuquerque. I don't travel a lot."

"This your first time to LA?" I kept the questions gentle, innocuous, letting her lead me somewhere.

"No," she said. "But . . ." She had developed a self-deprecating laugh outside of the office. "I don't seem to remember much. I have no idea where I am. Near the airport, that's all."

I saw an opening and I had an idea. "You're actually not far from the beach."

"Really?" she said. "I want to go there. Eat some real sea-food."

"I know just the place," I said. "The Enterprise Fish Company in Santa Monica."

"Is the fish fresh?"

"Still flopping."

"Do I need a reservation?"

"They don't take them," I said. "So on a Friday night you'd want to get there a little early." I deliberately let it sound like she was going by herself.

"Oh, here . . . I found their number in the phone book," she said. "I can call them and ask for directions. You know what? I'll just take a cab there and back. Unless, of course, you'd care to join me. Do you have plans for dinner?"

Bingo. I was in. "No. Sounds fun."

"My treat of course. I insist."

"I'll handle the after-dinner entertainment then," I said. I'd invite her to my shows at the Comedy Store. "I just got back from the gym so let me clean up and I'll pick you up around five."

"It's a date," she said.

I hung up. She had gotten into LA early. She was so unfamiliar with Southern California she didn't know which way the water was. Most likely she hadn't been here almost a week ago to put the cap on poor Art Westcott, but I thought I might drive her by the apartment where he had been killed and see if she started sweating.

An hour later I was flying along the freeways, looping my way to the airport exits. I stashed my car in valet parking and called Nancy Fisk from the lobby. She said she'd be right down.

The elevator doors opened and Nancy Fisk walked into the lobby, this time wearing a little black linen dress with black pumps and gold, hoop earrings. She looked stunning.

"Is this okay?" she said. "This place isn't too dressy, is it?"

"No," I said. "Very casual. Like everywhere in California."

I got my car from the valet and opened the door for her, trying not to stare too long when the hem of her skirt rode up on her tanned, smooth thigh. She wore no stockings. She had great legs. She didn't look much like a murder suspect, but neither did I and some folks thought I was guilty as hell.

I got in on my side and headed out for the beach. I turned to her when I heard her chuckle. "What?" I asked.

"Oh"—she said, waving a thought away—"here I am, heading out to the beach in a little red sports car with someone in show business." She giggled again. "I feel so Californian."

"Later we can go to a yoga class and read each other's auras," I said.

"Sounds mellow," she said.

This time I laughed.

"You haven't been here in how long?" I asked.

"Since I was a kid."

I looked at my watch. Time enough to enact my clever plan. "We've got a few minutes before the crush hits at the Fish Company," I said. "Let me give you the nickel tour."

"Okay."

"You'll need your sunglasses." I hit the 10 freeway and headed straight for the coast, right into the sun.

"What . . . ?" Nancy sniffed the air and rolled down her window, her fingers splayed to feel the wind. "What's happening to the air?" She masked her eyes with a pair of large, round, shaded spectacles. Movie star glasses.

"It's cooling down," I said.

"Why's that?" she asked, looking overhead for clouds. "Is there a storm?"

"No," I said. "We're headed for the beach. It's cooler there. In more ways than one."

We passed the turnoff for the restaurant and I drove us into the last tunnel before hitting the beach, the magical spot where the 10 freeway turns into the Pacific Coast Highway and the sea and sun and sky are opened up all before you.

She took in a breath and let it out with a moan. "Oh, my God," she said. "It's so pretty."

She looked out at the sand and water, with the rollerbladers and cyclers cruising along under their own power, tanned bodies gleaming in the sun. There were hours of light left in the day. Lifeguard towers stood watch over the pounding waves. Seagulls spun and dove. She turned and looked at the cliffs up on the other side. "Are those homes up there?" she asked.

I nodded.

I took us up to Sunset, then turned in and brought us back inland, weaving my way through the Palisades, our drive punctuated by, "Oh, my God," and, "How lovely," from the passenger's side.

Soon enough we found ourselves puttering along Main Street, lined with galleries, boutiques, and all kinds of places I never go into. We were less than half a mile from where Art Westcott had died.

"I'd always thought LA was just a bunch of smog and traffic," Nancy said. "I had no idea it was so pretty."

"We're in Santa Monica," I said. "A different animal."

"Why don't you live here?" she asked.

"I have."

"Why did you leave?"

"They did away with rent control in my building," I said. I looked at her. "Let me show you my old apartment."

"Is it in Santa Monica?"

"It's in another town just up here called Ocean Park."

I took the turns to Art Westcott's apartment, watching her out of the corner of my eye.

"You ever going to move back to the beach?"

"Sure," I said. "Soon as I get my own sitcom."

"Let me know when you do," she said. "I'll come visit you."

"Deal."

I made the last turn off of Anchor and onto Fourth, the street Art had lived and died on. She seemed to be innocently interested in her surroundings, one hand out the window, feeling the air. Either she had never been there or she was in the running for a Golden Globe.

On Fourth Street, I slowed and pointed to Art's apartment building. "There," I said.

"Ah." It was a square block of apartments and didn't look like much. The end apartment had a good view of the water. "How is it on the inside?"

"Nice," I said, as we passed it. I was ad-libbing. "Roomy. And in the summer it doesn't get too hot. The ocean air cools it off." I looked at her as she looked at it. Not a crack, not a waver, not a sign that this place had any significance to her other than a casual sight. I headed toward the corner.

"So what happened there?"

"What?"

She pointed. "There's yellow tape up," she said. "It looks like the police have been there." I slowed to turn and looked over my shoulder. Hirsch and Chavez had marked Art's apartment as a crime scene. I felt a cold burning in the pit of my stomach. I should have checked this out before I'd brought her here. If Hirsch and Chavez eventually talked to her, I'd have a hard time explaining this.

"I don't know," I said. "Maybe somebody got robbed."

"Guess you're not sorry you don't live there now," she said.

"No."

I turned off Fourth and headed back to Santa Monica and

Main Street. My experiment was over. Now I could relax, at least for tonight.

I checked my car in a lot a block away and we walked along Main to the Enterprise Fish Company. The restaurant was the size of a barn, with high ceilings and decorated with fishing gear. Specials were marked on a chalkboard. California youth in white polo shirts and navy blue skirts and pants carried trays of food and drinks to and fro. There was low music, high chatter, and the smell of the giant U-shaped mesquite grill in the back, broiling filets of salmon, swordfish, and snapper.

We got a table for two by an aquarium. As we walked to it, other men looked up from their meals and away from their wives and scanned Nancy with a healthy appreciation. I walked behind her and watched the way her brown-and-gold hair fell about her neck.

"Biff, this is wonderful," Nancy said. "If the food is as good as it smells . . . ?"

"It is," I said. A busboy brought water. I lifted it in a toast. "Cheers."

"To what?"

"You started calling me Biff," I said.

She smiled at that. She liked that. "To our first-name basis." Clink.

We ordered. Her brother's name had yet to be mentioned. I didn't mind. We engaged in the kind of small talk people do when they are on a first-date basis, never mind the names.

When the check came, she caught me looking at my watch. "Am I keeping you from something?" she asked.

"No," I said. "I have time. I have a spot at the Store. Two, actually."

"At what store?"

"The Comedy Store," I said. "On Sunset."

221

She was immediately interested. "You're doing comedy tonight?"

"Yes," I said. "At about nine o'clock. Don't worry. I've got plenty of time."

"Can I come see you?"

"Sure."

"You don't mind?"

"Not at all."

She smiled big. "Oh, this is great. I've never been to a comedy club before."

"Never?"

"No."

"Another first then."

She smiled and showed teeth, perfectly white. Her hazel eyes were glittering. She looked at nothing else but me. "Yes."

We got to the Comedy Store by show time: eight o'clock. I snuck Nancy in the back, and we took a table in the far corner. Since she'd paid for dinner, I insisted on buying her drinks. I remember her telling me she was a teetotaler and neither of us had drunk anything at dinner, but she felt "even more Californian" by drinking Perrier.

The lineup was solid: Bobby Lee, Argus Hamilton, Johnny Sanchez, then me. I'd have to come out swinging to follow Sanchez. There was no emcee. It was tag team: Each act brought up the next one. Nancy grew even more excited as my slot grew nearer, and when I got up to go onstage, she squeezed my hand and wished me good luck.

I killed. I slammed home my setups with punch-line delivery and improvised a few bits out of current events. I directed a lot of my attention toward the tourists in the audience, beginning with the phrase "for those of you visiting us in LA, perhaps for the first time . . . ," and when I said it I looked back at Nancy. Big smile. White teeth. Very pretty.

It was wham-bam-thank-you-good-night-ma'am-drive-safely-and-tip-your-waitress-and-bartender. I got off to great applause and brought up the next act, making my way through the tables, stopping to shake a few hands along the way. Playing the Comedy Store on a weekend night, the crowd packed to the door . . . it was times like these I felt sorry for people who'd never done stand-up.

When I sat back down next to Nancy, she scooted her chair closer and squeezed my hand again, leaning in close. "Oh, you were great!" she said.

I'm always parched when I get offstage. "They're a good crowd," I said, reaching for some water.

She held on to my hand. "No, but you were *really* good," she said. "I mean, I've talked to you some and I thought you were funny, but I didn't know you had a . . . a . . ."

"An act?"

"Exactly!" She rocked back and laughed and held my one hand in both of hers. "I didn't know you had an act. Are those all of your jokes, or do you have more?"

"There're more," I said. "I have another spot in the second show. I can either run you back to your hotel or you can hang out for . . ." I looked at my watch. "Another two hours."

She looked at me with her eyes shining and that big smile of hers and said, "I'm not going anywhere."

"Okay then," I said. "Sit back and enjoy the show."

I was on early in the second show and I switched up my act, dropping the tourist stuff and concentrating on the locals. Funny how a crowd can determine your choice of material. At least that's what I told myself. I knew I was showing off for Nancy, letting her know I could do two spots back-to-back and not repeat any bits. Always glad to make a new fan.

I did just as well the second time. Two for two. I got offstage and this time Nancy hugged me. "You are so funny," she said. "I am having such a good time."

"Me, too," I said. "Believe me." I looked back at the stage. "Spent plenty of nights looking at my shoes."

"Don't tell me you don't always do this well?"

"Sometimes I hit a rough patch."

"Hard to believe," she said.

"It happens." I looked at my watch. It was an hour from midnight. "Ready to go?" I said. "We both have a big day tomorrow."

She nodded wordlessly. It was the closest we'd come to discussing her brother all night. We'd successfully distracted each other from the subject.

I had parked in the lot right behind the Comedy Store, and she waited while I maneuvered my RX-7 out of its spot. On the way back she kept up a steady flow of questions: How did I come up with material? How long had I been doing it? What was the road like? Had I ever been on television? Did I know any famous people? I felt like I was being interviewed by the prettiest reporter in town.

I pulled up in front of the Marriott and handed the keys over to the valet, asking Nancy if I could walk her up to her room. "Of course," she said.

We got in the elevator. "Well, I had a great time," she said. "This was the most fun I've had in I don't know how long. Good food, good entertainment, and good company." She put her hand on my back. "And here I was dreading this trip—" She stopped.

I took her elbow. "It was my pleasure, Miss Fisk."

I was touching her and she was touching me. She looked into my eyes and then broke her gaze to look down at my mouth, then back up again. I turned to where I was facing her, not just standing side by side. I don't know what would have happened if the elevator doors hadn't opened on her floor. Actually, I do know what would have happened. We would have started making out like we were at the drive-in movies.

"Here we are," I said, leading her off.

I walked her to her room. She fished out her key, unlocked her door, and turned to me again. "When will I see you tomorrow?"

"Why don't I call you around five," I said. "We'll make arrangements then."

She brightened. "Maybe another dinner?"

"Maybe," I said.

"Deal," she said. She breathed in once and let it out, looking down at her purse. "You're very funny, Biff. I think you're going to go far in this business."

"Come quite a ways already," I said.

"Yes, it seems you have."

She paused. I hesitated. The moment of truth.

"Well . . . ," she said, looking over her shoulder at the door.

I touched her neck with my fingertips. "I don't believe I said this yet," I said, "but you look absolutely beautiful tonight."

"Thank you," she whispered. "No, you hadn't said that." Her eyes lowered. "It's nice to hear. I've had my mind so much on the family business lately . . ."

I drew her close and she moved with me. I kissed her first on her cheek then moved to her mouth. She slid her arm up and around my shoulder, squeezing it with her hand, arching herself up on one toe. Her mouth opened and our tastes met, her hand sliding up to caress the nape of my neck, and I looped my arms around her back.

We broke.

"Wow," she whispered. "Been a while since that happened, too."

I kissed her again, and this time her hand slid off my shoulder and started stroking my rib cage. She stopped and put her head over my shoulder to whisper in my ear. "Oh, God," she murmured, "now is not the right time for this."

"Do you want me to stop?"

"Not right now," she said, and put her face in front of mine. "Not just yet." She leaned her forehead forward to touch mine while she reached out with one hand to open her hotel room door. It swung open, revealing an inviting darkness. She took my hand and stepped back, leading me forward like we were slow dancing. Her eyes were lidded and her mouth open and shiny as the shadows slid over her face and body.

"I have to warn you," she said, "because it's been a while. I may get too excited. I may get . . . wild."

I closed the door behind us with my foot. "You bet you will," I said.

TWENTY-FIVE

Nancy Fisk woke up half an hour after I did, when I was sneaking out of bed to go to the bathroom.

"Morning, cowboy," she murmured hazily. She ran a hand through her hair as she sat up, letting the covers fall away from her. A charming lack of modesty.

"Good morning." I sat down on her side of the bed. The bathroom could wait. "How'd you sleep?"

"Ah." She chuckled. "Like a rock. A dead rock." She looked at me with eyes lidded by sleep. "I wish I'd known about you Irish guys earlier," she said. "You are something."

"God invented whiskey so the Irish wouldn't rule the world."

"You sure make up for it in other ways." She rubbed her hands over her face and peeked at me through the fingers. "Was I naughty? Was I a bad girl?"

"Yes, you were."

She put a hand on my naked thigh. "Do you have to go somewhere?"

"You mean right now?"

She nodded.

"I was going to the bathroom."

Her hand moved. "And after that?"

"I was coming back to bed with you."

She took her hand away. "Okay." She smiled again, showing her phosphorous teeth. "I thought you might have been trying to sneak away."

I stood. "Now why would I do a thing like that?"

When I came out of the bathroom, she had burrowed under the covers and was peeking out like a little kid. "I got cold," she said. Her eyes traveled down my body. "And so did you." She laughed.

"No fair." I walked around to my side of the bed and crawled in. "I can't find the thermostat in this place."

With both of us under the covers, she rolled on top of me, holding her body above mine, just barely touching. "Would you like me to warm you up?"

"That'd be nice."

She lowered her head to my neck, nuzzling it with kisses, moving her way up to my ear. Her body was firm and athletic and tan. "I've got an idea," she whispered.

"What's that?"

"You ever been to the wine country?"

"Yes," I said. "But not in a while."

"I never have," she said. "Is it nice?"

"It's great," I said. "Especially this time of year when it's not too hot."

"Well . . ." She started on the other side of my neck. "Why don't we get in your little red sports car and head up there?" She pulled back and looked at me impishly. "I'm not due back at the office until Monday morning."

I looked at her for a second and put my hands on her shoulders. "Nancy," I said gently, "we can't. Not tonight."

234

She looked puzzled until first memory and then understanding seeped into her face. She rolled herself off me, putting a hand to her head. "I . . . I . . . completely forgot about all that."

"I'm sorry I had to remind you," I said.

She sat up, this time holding the covers close. "Today's the day, isn't it? When my brother's going to do that show."

I nodded.

The sensual playfulness was gone from her features. In its place was a weary purpose. "Like I said, I'd forgotten." She looked at me. "You hadn't, though, had you?"

"No."

"Well, this is weird, isn't it? Here I am in bed with the man who is plotting against my brother."

"Nancy, your brother needs help. You said that yourself."

"That's why I'm here," she said, a touch angrily. "That's why I've always been there." She hit the covers with her fist. I remembered the tantrum she'd thrown at the construction site up in Show Low. Her face was reddening. "I'll probably be dealing with him and his problems for the rest of my life. And after all the pain he put my parents through . . ." Her words ended in a furious growl.

I didn't argue with her. She was working herself into a fit of some kind, the inner rage feeding on itself, revving like an engine in overdrive. "Nancy . . . ," I said.

"But you," she said, her eyes glaring at me, "all you care about is getting your jokes back." Her hands clenched the bedsheets.

"That's not all I care about," I said. "A friend of mine has been murdered."

"But it's the main thing, right?" She spat the words out as she stood up. "Getting famous so you can look down on the rest of us." She looked as though she might attack me.

I had to calm this woman down. I stood up on the other side

of the bed, letting the mattress separate us. "Your brother is wanted for questioning by the police in an ongoing homicide investigation," I said. "Until he talks to them, I'm under suspicion. That may be fine with him, but not with me. As for him stealing my act, that is some of the same material you saw me perform onstage last night," I said. "It's mine. I wrote it. I worked on it. I perfected it. You saw what I can do with it. I'm not letting it go."

Her face softened. The anger left her. She sat back down on the bed. "I'm sorry," she said. "This isn't easy for me."

"No, I don't imagine it is." I sat down next to her.

"He doesn't have the right to interfere with people's lives like this," she said. "My brother, that is."

"I'll be there with you," was what I said.

She reached for my hand. I let her take it.

"Let's do what we have to do," she said.

There were tears in her eyes.

After breakfast downstairs I left the Marriott and went back home. The Nancy Fisk I had first met—serious and dour—was back, and the frisky lover had gone into hiding. It was just as well. I had to concentrate on the day's preparation for the night's events. No time for the wine country.

When I unlocked my front door and stepped into my apartment I saw I had an unexpected visitor.

"Hey, Irish," Richard Moftus said. He was sitting on my futon couch, which he had dragged to the middle of the room, and holding a gun in his hand. I recognized the gun. It was mine. A .38 special. Soft-nosed bullets. One would take me out. For good. "What's your trouble? Ain't you glad to see me?"

I left the front door open behind me. I had left Richard Moftus off my truncated murder suspect list. I'd just scratched Nancy's name off. Maybe it was time to add another. "What are you doing here, Richard?"

"No 'Hello?' No 'How-are-you?' Just 'What-are-you-doing?' What a lousy host you are." He pronounced it *awe*. "You come on my boat, I serve you a Murphy's Stout and play you jazz." He looked down at the gun in his hand. "Is it this?" He gestured with it. "This I got out in case it wasn't you that was walking through your own front door. I found it under the bed with that arsenal-in-a-suitcase you got stashed there." With a one-handed flip he popped out the chamber and emptied the bullets on the couch, then closed the gun back up again and set it next to the loose ammo. "That make you feel any better?"

I closed the door behind me. "A little." I looked over at my phone answering machine. It was blinking. I had two messages.

"One of those calls is from Kelly," he said. "And one of them is from me." He had left his toupee off that morning and was wearing a baseball cap that said "Chortles" in its place. "Kelly told me about how you been playing detective," he said. "How you was packing heat like a movie tough guy."

"In the process I met some guys who do it for real," I said. I sat down in my TV chair across from him.

"Yeah, the Ocean Park cops came to see me yesterday," Moftus said. "Sorry to hear about Art Westcott. He was a funny guy."

"Yeah."

"You found him dead, huh?"

I nodded. "But I didn't make him that way."

"That's what I told the cops," Moftus said. "But by the time they finished with their Mutt and Jeff routine they got me thinking maybe *I* did it."

"What'd you tell them?"

Moftus grinned. Those stained teeth again. "That if I'd done him, they wouldn't have found the body yet."

I nodded and smiled in spite of myself. "Good one."

"They wanted to know all about your fight with Ned Lando," Richard said.

"Ned Lando told the cops he didn't know anything about a fight or Roger Fisk or whatever the hell I was talking about," I said.

"I'll bet that went over big."

"Yeah, maybe I can do him a favor sometime."

"Well, I told 'em you were telling the truth," Moftus said.

"Thanks."

He loooked around my apartment some more, while staying seated. "Nice cozy little place you got here, up in the Hollywood Hills."

"Thanks again," I said. "How'd you get in?"

He grinned. "Kincaid, I got a checkered past. Locks don't keep me out."

"Doesn't surprise me."

"And that's why Kelly asked me to come up and check in on you," he said. "She's worried about what you're doing tonight."

"What'd she tell you?"

"She says Roger Fisk's putting on some comedy show at a theater in Hollywood, and you're thinking of riding in there like the Lone Ranger."

"And she told you she's worried about me?"

"She asked me to look in on you. You got the slightest idea what the hell you're doing?"

"I'm going to take Roger Fisk's sister to the show, and then get backstage somehow. I'm hoping afterward she can talk some sense into him."

Moftus had a neutral expression. "Uh-huh."

"I flew to Phoenix earlier in the week to convince her to shut down her brother's operation," I said. "Roger inherited the family purse and he's robbing it to highroll it in Hollywood. I'm going to try to get her to convince him to cool down. She says he's throwing away the family fortune."

"What if he don't listen?"

"Then she's going to try to have him proven incompetent."

Moftus nodded slowly. "When's she coming in?"

"She's already here."

"What's she look like?"

"Like her brother," I said. "Good-looking and rich."

"She the reason why you didn't get my message?"

"I was out," I said. "Late."

"That where you were last night?" he said. "With her?"

"I had two spots at the Comedy Store," I said.

"I know," he said. "I called there looking for you."

"And?"

"And Dennis Cameron who was working the door says you were there with some hot broad," Moftus said.

"That was her," I said. Next time I saw Cameron I'd have to tell him to mind his own business. "Nancy Fisk. She flew in from Phoenix to be at tonight's show. All of today's flights were sold out so she came in yesterday. Early."

"So you were showing her a good time?"

"I was showing her the material her brother stole from me," I said.

"Don't explain why you didn't have the time to call me back," he said. "Nor Kelly neither."

"What are you, her dad?"

"No, shitbird, I ain't," Moftus said. The tone of his voice shifted a gear lower. "But in the entire time I known her she's never been as interested in another guy as much as you. I seen her pass on every other comic that come through Chortles. But you, with your golden hair and blue eyes and cocky attitude, you got her attention. I'm telling you that she ain't no doll to keep on a string along with three or four other skirts at the same time. She's serious about you. Now either reel her in or cut her loose. Let her find someone worthwhile. Let her be happy. She deserves it."

I wanted to say something about the woman I saw on the way to his boat. I wanted to lash out at Moftus with all my powers of retaliation. I wanted to treat him like a drunk heckler, cutting him down to size so fast he was sorry he ever opened his mouth.

There was a long pause before I thought of just the right response.

"I'll treat her right, Richard," I said. "Whatever happens, I'll be fair."

"Man to man?"

"Man to man," I said. "I'm—"

"Save it," Moftus said. "Now about tonight."

"Yeah?"

He started picking the bullets out of the folds of the couch. "You ever walked into hard action like this before?"

I nodded.

"Then I was wondering if you needed any backup."

"Well, I'm not going to turn it down."

"Good." He reloaded the handgun, leaving the first chamber empty. "What else you got besides the popgun here?"

"A twenty-two derringer," I said. "A nine-millimeter pistol. A four-ten shotgun. A thirty-odd-six rifle."

He frowned. "Not all of that was in your suitcase under the bed."

"You think I'm stupid enough to keep all my guns in one place?" I asked. "What have you got?"

"An AK-forty-seven," he said. He held a finger to his lips. "Shh. Don't tell nobody. A forty-four, just like Dirty Harry. A three fifty-seven. Couple shotguns. Couple deer rifles. A few little popguns. Kevlar vest."

"Where are they?"

He nodded toward the street. "In the trunk of my car," he said. "You tell me what I should do with them."

I caught him up on all the details of tonight's show. "Let's have you outside in the parking lot of the Doug Stone Theater. I'm going in as an extra. We'll rent a couple of cellular phones, the kind that double as pagers. Let's have each other's numbers on speed dial. I'll page you every ten minutes as a signal. I miss one, you come in the back door loaded for bear."

Moftus nodded. "Got it."

"Don't start shooting until you find me," I said. "Look out for Fisk or his bodyguard, George. You know George?"

Moftus nodded. "Seen him."

"He's shaved his head now," I said. "Still got the goatee."

"Okay," he said. "You want to bring the cops in on this?"

"Not yet. The cops only want whoever killed Art Westcott," I said. "So do I, but I want Roger Fisk out of the comedy business, too."

"What if one's related to the other?"

"They're definitely related," I said. "My bet is Art Westcott's killer will be there, too."

TWENTY-SIX

Moftus and I drove separately to a U-Haul and rented a pair of cellular phones. We tested our connection a few times, and he said the next time I would hear from him would be when he got to his vantage point at six-thirty that evening. He was going to head south to check on the club. Kelly was running it tonight by herself.

I killed the next two hours at the gym, not working myself hard, just getting strong and loose and limber. I dressed in jeans, a loose pullover, a logoless baseball cap, and sunglasses. I looked like I was ready to bomb a federal building.

It was five o'clock when I got back to Guiseppe's Pizzeria, my old stakeout, at the corner of Hollywood and Vine, across the street from the Doug Stone Theater. I stretched two slices, a salad, a diet soda, and a cappuccino out over the next hour and a half, reading through the local papers while keeping an eye out on the equipment trucks and crew that came and went through the front and back entrances of the theater.

At six o'clock, searchlights were rolled into place. What?

Signs were put up in front of the glass doorways. Private party. Closed to the public.

Red velvet ropes were put in place, hung from brass stanchions. Wait a minute. Three huge bouncers with headsets, in a uniform of black pants and red shirts, began to patrol the area. A field camera crew showed up and began to take b-roll shots of the preparations. Someone got a ladder and started hanging letters on the marquee: THE ROGER FISK SHOW. When they climbed down, a switch was thrown and it lit up in a huge suspended block of white light.

At six-thirty, the first of the extras began to show up.

The cell phone rang on my hip.

"Kincaid, it's me," Richard Moftus said.

"Where are you?" I asked.

"On the 101 freeway," he said. "It's all jammed up. I'm gonna be late."

"Okay," I said. "They've just started setting up. The marquee's lit, there are searchlights in place, a camera crew is taping the whole thing. . . . "

"You're kidding, right?"

"Nope. He's making it look like a real cable special."

"I'll drive by once when I get there just to see it," Moftus said. "Call you when I'm in place."

I hung up and squared my check, dropping two bucks into the tip jar. When I turned around for one last look out the window, I saw Nancy Fisk had shown up early.

I crossed the street and found her, wandering in front of the empty ticket booth. She was wearing a black pantsuit with black boots, her hair up and sunglasses of her own. I guess she thought she was in disguise. I recognized her in three seconds. It would take her brother maybe two.

I crossed the street and found her, taking her by the arm. "We need to keep you out of sight," I said, by way of greeting. "We

244

don't want to spook your brother by letting him know that you're here just yet." I guided her to a spot just by the now-abandoned ticket booth, in a corner that was lined with old newspapers and smelled of stale piss.

She nervously touched her hair. "I wasn't sure what to wear," she said, looking around her. "I took a cab here and the guy didn't speak English very well so we got lost a couple of times." She looked at the noisy crush of traffic on Vine, even on a Saturday. Hollywood was filling up with all kinds of action. "This sure is a big city."

"I'll get you back to Arizona soon enough," I said.

"That wasn't what I meant."

I looked around. A crowd of a hundred or so extras had gathered in front, actors of differing shapes and sizes. The kind of people you'd see walking the street every day, provided the street was somewhere on television. In half an hour there'd be a thousand, and they'd provide enough cover for us, but in the meantime . . .

"We have to get you a pass," I said.

"Pass? What pass? You didn't say anything about a pass."

"At seven o'clock, the audience wranglers are going to start calling out names and handing out blue-colored passes with numbers on them," I said. "It marks you as an extra. Then you can get in and sit next to me for the show. Your brother has plenty of security working this event."

"What for?"

"He thinks some people may be out to get him," I said. "And guess what? He's right."

"What if Roger sees me in the audience while he's performing?" Nancy asked.

"He'll have the stage lights in his eyes," I said. "Trust me, he won't be able to see past the front row. You haven't met his bodyguard, George, so he probably wouldn't recognize you ei-

245

ther. As for getting you a pass, the coordinators who control these events are open to a little baksheesh."

"What's that?"

I rubbed my thumb against my first two fingers in a universal gesture. "Bribery."

I scanned the crowd for whoever from Audiences Unlimited was going to start calling names and handing out passes in the next few minutes, and that was when I saw Scott Dawson.

"Oh my God," I said.

"What?" Nancy asked. She followed my gaze. "Who is it?"

"Just who I needed to see," I said. "Stay here."

"Biff, what—?"

I left her and walked straight over to where Scott Dawson was standing. I called his name when I was within arm's length of him. His expression told me he had no memory of who I was or our previous encounter. This happens a lot in Hollywood.

"David Kelton referred me to you."

The name didn't register on Scott's delicate ebony features. All he said was, "Okay."

"And you promised me a pass for tonight.

He looked at me. "Yeah."

"Now I need another one."

His thin, shaped eyebrows lifted. "Another one?"

I nodded.

"Here? Tonight?"

"Yes."

He looked away from me, letting my request process through the cool, flowing mercury of his brain. I wondered what the price would be this time.

"Did you hear about David?" he asked me.

"No."

"He's dead."

"Dead how?"

"Someone broke into his apartment and, uh, beat him to death with a chair," Scott Dawson said. He spoke very precisely, his diction as clean and neat as his wardrobe. The words were hung on hangers. "The police think it's a drug deal that went bad."

"Could be."

He looked at me. "You think it's something else?"

"Could be."

"David and I had another conversation after he referred you to me," he said. "You'll forgive my memory. I'm not good with faces. Or names."

"What are you good with?"

"Numbers."

"What did David tell you?"

"He asked if you had gotten the pass to the show and I said yes. He said he doubted you would live to use it. Yet you are here and he is gone. Why?"

"When I find out, I'll let you know."

"I liked David," Scott said. "I knew he had problems, but we were interns together back in college. And I don't like many people. Even less of them like me."

He pulled two passes out of his back pocket. They were marked ALL ACCESS. "Here," he said. "Knock yourself out."

"Thanks," I said.

He tried to smile and realized he'd forgotten how.

A voice behind us yelled: "All right—everyone listen up!"

I turned. There was a heavyset young woman with a shag blonde haircut, wearing a white blouse and a navy skirt, and standing on the bed of a truck parked in the driveway next to the theater. She had a clipboard and a pen and a jaw like Kirk Douglas. Next to her by the truck was an olive-skinned college-aged kid with thin shoulders. His large ears stuck out from beneath his black hair, which was cut into a skullcap. He held a fistful of passes.

"I am Cindy from Audiences Unlimited," she said, her voice a toneless bellow. "This is Greg. When I call your name, last name only unless there's two of you—be quiet!" She glared at a group of talkers. "I will say this once. I will call your names in alphabetical order. Come forward and claim your numbered pass. You have to listen carefully for your name because I will call your name only one time. If you don't claim it, we move on and you don't get paid.

"At seven-thirty we open the doors," Cindy continued, her tone reflecting a long-held belief that most people were stupider than she was. Someone else was talking and she made a big show of rolling her eyes. "If you don't shut up, not everyone can hear me and some of you came all this way for nothing! I repeat: At seven-thirty we open the doors. Your pass lets you in. Take your seats like you would in a movie theater, except we've marked which section you are to sit in. We shut the doors at eight and they are locked from the outside. Now." She looked at her clipboard. "Adams!"

As the names were called, extras were shuffling forward to Greg, getting their passes, and drifting away. "Adelson! Anderson! Ansalone!" Scott Dawson had gone somewhere. I worked my way back under the marquee. "Anson! Antone! Asner!" I turned to find Nancy Fisk in the crowd, but there were too many people. Cindy moved on. "Baker! Barker! Bartell!"

Nancy was cringing in the corner where I had left her, surrounded by crumpled newspapers and stained sidewalk, afraid to let any part of her surroundings touch her except through the soles of her shoes.

"I got you something," I said, and held the pass out for her.

"Do I put this around my neck?"

"Here," I said, and looped it over her head. "This will get you in. Now all I have to do is claim my pass and then we go inside at seven-thirty and find a seat."

She nodded, unsmiling. "Toward the back. I don't want any-one to see me."

"We should be okay."

There wasn't much more to talk about. She wore her discom-fort like a wool blanket. Cindy called names until she got to the Ks. I left Nancy's side, claimed my pass, and went back to her.

Except she wasn't where I'd left her, in the corner with the old newspapers and aroma of aged urine. I looked around and didn't see her anywhere in the immediate crowd. I retraced my steps, forcing my way through the herd of extras until I was all the way to the sidewalk, practically standing in the gutter. I went up on tiptoe, scanning the heads. There were hundreds of people gathered to get in. It was seven-fifteen by my watch.

I worked my way back to our meeting place, but still no sign of Nancy Fisk.

She was gone.

TWENTY-SEVEN

I stayed where I was for the next five minutes, intently searching the milling throng, but found no Nancy Fisk.

The phone on my hip went off. I flipped it open.

"Hello?"

"Kincaid, it's me," a tinny voice said. "Moftus."

"Richard!" I said. At least one person wasn't letting me down. "Where are you?"

"I'm in the parking garage about a half block west of Vine on Hollywood Boulevard, next to a gyros place," he said. "They got a bathroom here and everything. Maybe I'll start booking comics in."

"Uh-huh," I said, still looking for any sign of Nancy.

"Hey, what's wrong?" he said. "You got a smart remark for everything and now you're all serious-like."

"I'm in front of the Doug Stone Theater," I said. "I got my pass to get inside. There must be a thousand people here. I got another pass for Fisk's sister, but I seem to have lost her."

"She was there and now she's not?"

"That's right," I said. "I don't know what happened to her."

"Maybe she went to warn her brother."

"She could have done that a long time ago."

"But maybe she didn't want to until now," Moftus said. "People get all funny when they got to turn on their family."

"Yeah," I said. "Yeah. Dammit."

"Kincaid, you ought to not be that surprised," he said. "What did you think—you bang a broad and she's your slave, like a zombie?"

"No," I said, through gritted teeth. "I . . . I don't know what she's thinking."

"I'd keep an eye out for her on the Boulevard if I knew what she looked like," he said. "We're burning batteries here. Every ten minutes, give me a ring. I got a little screen here tells me who's calling, so just ring once or twice so I know it's you. I don't hear from you, at fifteen minutes I call you. At twenty I send in the cavalry."

"Got it," I said, and hung up.

"All right, everyone!" Cindy the Bellower was now up front by the doors. Greg was still at her side. He had a single pass left, and he looped it around his own neck. They were flanked by two of the security posse. Standing by was the beta camera crew. "We're going to open the doors now! Security guards will be checking passes! There is a camera crew here! There are camera crews inside! As of now, you can expect to be on camera! So act happy, like you're having fun! I'll talk to you again inside, but until then, look alive!" She turned and nodded to one of the security people. He unlocked both sets of glass doors and propped them open. "Let's go!"

The searchlights fired up and began swinging back and forth in front of the theater. Traffic immediately began to slow. The extras began chatting and smiling, the betacam crew took shots, and I put a half smile on my face as I hung by the doors to see if Nancy Fisk was anywhere in this crowd. One of the security musclemen saw me hanging around. "You going in?" he asked.

"I lost someone," I said.

"Haven't we all?" he said.

I looked at his deadpan expression for a second. "That's funny," I said.

"Thanks."

"There another way into this place?" I asked. "Besides this way?"

He shook his head. "There's the artist's entrance in the back," he said, "but you have to have an all-access pass."

"Like this?" I said, showing my pass with Roger's face on it.

"Yeah, like that." He kept his eye on the flow of human traffic. "You better get in. I hear they overbooked the extras. You can wait for your friend inside."

"Thanks," I said, and moved past him into the lobby.

I waited in the lobby for another five minutes. I didn't see her. Up on easels in the lobby there were posters of Roger Fisk on-stage with a microphone in his hand. Below the posters were banners that read ROGER FISK: THE NEXT COMEDY SUPERSTAR!

It was stupid of me to bring Nancy Fisk here, to involve her in trying to curtail her brother's ambitions. She most likely had gone to the rear entrance of the theater to warn her brother. Legally, he was the one controlling the family money. She didn't stand a snowball's chance in Hell of overturning her father's will. Her best bet was to get back on Roger's good side. How was she going to do that? By turning me in. Now he knew I was here and would be on the lookout for me. That would make what I had to do all the harder.

After five minutes I dialed Moftus's number, let it ring twice, and hung up. All was clear. From now on all I had to do was press the redial button and keep an eye on the time.

I joined the crowd squeezing into the theater. The stage set was now completely built, with the ROGERWOOD sign in place, and plywood palm trees and a fake lifeguard tower to one side. It was a tourist's vision of LA. In the center of the stage was a cordless mike in a stand. There were transparent TelePrompTer panels on both sides of the stage, and a camera on a crane to capture the crowd's reaction. A production crew of at least a dozen walked around purposefully, testing monitors, lights, and cameras. It was a real show.

A portion of the center aisle seats had been removed to make room for a studio camera mounted on a pedestal. The red light at the top was off. The monitor was on. The operator had a headset and was sitting in a folding chair, sipping coffee.

A black rectangle was mounted above the stage, hanging in space by guide wires: an applause sign.

I was in the left aisle of the center section. I began looking for a seat. I wanted to hang back where I wouldn't attract too much attention and wouldn't end up on camera.

I watched as Cindy lumbered down the aisle and clambered up onstage, her bulk shifting underneath her blouse. She went to the mike in the stand and tapped on it.

"ALL RIGHT EVERYONE LISTEN UP!!" The sound boomed out over the heads of the front row. Everyone immediately hushed. Some down front groaned in pain. Cindy turned to someone offstage and made a motion to turn the mike down.

There was a shriek of feedback that made me wince, another moan from the crowd, and then Cindy tried the mike again: "Okay, is this better?"

A thankful "yes" from the crowd.

"Okay, welcome to . . ." She glanced at her clipboard. "The Roger Fisk Show." Another look at the clipboard. "Now, who's Roger Fisk, you might ask." She gave a little chuckle. "I'm supposed to read this to you. It's from his publicist: 'Roger Fisk is best described as Hollywood's hottest undiscovered talent. His skill at stand-up comedy will amaze you and the sharpness of his wit will bring you to tears. Entertainment insiders are already comparing him to the likes of Richard Pryor, Robin Williams, and Jim Carrey.'" Cindy managed to keep a straight face. "Okay," she said, with a big nod. "Guess that clears that up."

A slight wave of chuckles went through the crowd. Some people were still being seated. I overheard two extras behind me talking about how they were right, this was a vanity production. They had worked another job a few months ago where a dentist from New Jersey had hired a crowd to watch him sing an evening of Sinatra songs at a Hollywood nightclub. Terrible.

"Let me give you the lowdown here," Cindy said into the mike. "We're taping a special for cable or broadcast—don't know which network, hasn't been sold yet. But this came together on such short notice we needed to hire you guys to make sure we had a full house for the cameras, of which there are five." She pointed out the camera mounted on the crane and the one in the center section. "Those two there, two more onstage, and then we have a hand-held—where's the hand-held?" A camera operator down in front of the stage raised his hand, then lifted up his camera. "There's the hand-held." She turned back to the crowd. "Now the important thing is to remember not to look into the camera lens, especially the hand-held camera roaming the aisles. Other cameras onstage may be focusing in on your re-actions from time to time." She slowed down her words to give them emphasis. "Do. Not. Look. Into. The. Camera. Lens. That's the surest way to be cut out. Now."

She shuffled some papers on her clipboard. "Just a minute ... where is that? ... okay. When Roger comes out, which should be in about ten minutes or so, he's going to need a stand-ing ovation, like he's already a big star. So let's run through that once, okay?" She brought a beefy hand up to her forehead to shield the lights from her eyes. "Is everyone about seated? Okay. Let's give it a run-through." She cleared her throat. "Ladies and gentlemen, Roger Fisk!"

The audience of extras got to their feet, clapping and cheering. Cindy let it go on for about ten to fifteen seconds then cut it off with a wave of her arm. We sat back down. "Okay, that was . . ." She held a hand out parallel to the ground, palm down, and made a slow seesawing motion with it: so-so. "Okay. We're going to try it again. But first, I wanted to introduce you to our little performer's friend here." She raised her arm to point to the applause sign. "Phil, can we—there we go." The applause sign began to flash the word APPLAUSE in brightly lit letters. The extras began automatically to applaud. Cindy smiled sardonically. "Yeah, you all know that one, don't you? Okay, stop." The sign flashing quit and so did the hand clapping. "We've added something else, a little extra, just for tonight . . . if we could . . ."

The sign began to flash a second word: LAUGHTER.

"And when that happens," Cindy said, "you, of course, will laugh." The sign shut off. "So let's try it. Roger tells a joke, we come to the punch line, it's the funniest thing you ever heard in your life, and—" She made a sweeping motion with her arm.

The LAUGHTER sign began to flash and a wave of genuine-sounding amusement went through the crowd. Me, I've never been a good fake laugher. I never would have gotten hired for this job.

"Okay," Cindy said, "now the longer it stays lit, the louder and longer your laughter is to be, and don't be surprised if you see this combination."

The sign flashed LAUGHTER then APPLAUSE.

There was some intermittent laughter and applause but Cindy cut it off. "So let's run that one all by itself. Roger Fisk says something absolutely hilarious, yet so truthful and meaningful you can't help but applaud but first you have to laugh so . . ."

The sign flashed LAUGHTER. The extras laughed. As the sign kept flashing, the laughter kept building. The extras took direction well, like the professionals they were.

Cindy said: "And then . . ."

The sign switched to APPLAUSE, and the crowd made a graceful transition from hilarity to hero worship. This was making me ill.

"Okay," Cindy said. She swung her arms back and forth like an aerobics instructor. The effect on someone so short of stature yet wide of girth was somewhat comical, and she played to it. "Everyone feeling warmed up?" A pleasant rumbling from the assembled masses. "Ready to try that standing ovation again?" The sound of mass affirmation followed.

"Alllll righty then," Cindy said. "You're going to have to do this twice—once at the beginning, and once at the end when he leaves. So, get ready. Okay, the lights dim, the spot hits the stage, and ladies and gentlemen, the biggest star in the world, Roger Fisk!"

The audience erupted. People got to their feet in an amazing simulation of a spontaneous standing ovation, clapping, whistling, and making a joyful noise. I stood up with them, trying to blend in. Cindy cut off the ovation with a wave of her hand.

"Very nice," Cindy said. "Very nice indeed. Okay." She turned another page on her clipboard. "I think that's about it." She turned in response to a voice from the wings. "What?" She listened. "Okay."

I kept looking over the crowd. No Nancy Fisk.

"I now want to introduce you to Phil, the stage manager." Cindy held a hand out to her side and Phil stepped out. He was the bearded guy I met at the theater when I was posing as a pizza delivery man. He was in a polo shirt and jeans, one hand on his transceiver, which he used to click into the PA system like a football referee.

There was some mild applause. I guess the extras were just

following their training. "Thank you, folks," Phil said. "How about a hand for Cindy?"

A little clapping. Cindy made a mock curtsy and got off the stage.

"Okay, we're going to start the show here in just a little bit," Phil said. "I wanted to let you know that this is a live show and we are going to shoot it as a continuous live performance. However, we may have to stop and start again due to a technical problem or some other unforeseen circumstance. Now, if that happens, you'll hear someone—most likely me—say 'Cut.' Just stay in your seats and wait until we get whatever problem we have straightened out and then we'll start again. Okay." He clicked off and spoke into his headset once more, listening for a response that caused him to nod. "Okay, let's roll tape," he said over the PA to the crowd: "We're starting, folks."

He walked offstage as I heard someone call out: "Rolling!"

Another voice: "Speed!"

Phil's voice again, over the PA, but now he was standing out of sight in the wings. "And three . . . two . . . one . . . action!"

Taped music rumbled through the theater speakers, a peppy mixture of jazz and rock, an anthem to show business hype. Then, over the PA system, a professional-sounding voice giving a Letterman-style introduction: "From Hollywood! Sort of kinda live! It's the next big name in comedy! The best-looking man in show business . . . Ladies and gentlemen, Roger Fisk!"

The show was starting.

TWENTY-EIGHT

Roger Fisk walked on stage, basking in the light of twin follow spots as the crowd pummeled him with applause at the tail end of his standing ovation. The sign above him was flashing like crazy. Roger's pose was casual and confident, as if this was something he was used to. Finally he waved it off, taking his hands out of the pockets of his teal silk suit and making a gesture like okay, that's enough, settle down.

He was dressed to the nines, I'd give him that. The spotlight shone off his freshly pressed suit and he had a yellow dress shirt underneath it with a flashy tie. He was wearing a thousand dollars at least, down to his shiny loafers.

He looked the part. He had successfully created the illusion that he was a stand-up comedian of no small repute, with an act honed, from years on the road, and now he was going to break it down one more time on tape for the audiences watching at home.

Then he stepped to the mike and opened his mouth.

"So, how many of you assholes are getting laid tonight?"

The laughter sign flashed. The audience responded in turn.

Roger grinned. "Because if you are, I've got a few tips for you." He took the mike out of the stand. It was an awkward gesture. He wasn't used to working with a microphone. I could tell. It didn't fit in his hand right.

"First, buy your condoms before," he said. Two flashes of the LAUGHTER sign. "It's so awkward when you're with a girl that's ready to go, and you gotta get your condoms on the way home." Three flashes. I guess Roger had gone through the script and coded which jokes he thought were one flash, two flashes, three flashes . . .

"Because whatever convenience store you duck into, it's gonna be the one where the guy behind the counter arrived from Pakistan two days before."

It was Kelly's bit. She had done a routine about women buying condoms, and stumbling across a guy who didn't speak English well. Roger had listened to the tape Lando had made of her act and had rewritten it to be from a guy's point of view. And he was opening with it.

He did a bad parody of a foreign accent: "Hello, can I help you please? You wish to buy the what? The comic books?" Then he switched back to the character of the frustrated customer. "No, condoms." Clerk: "Cartons? Cartons of Marlboros?" Customer: "No, condoms, you stupid fucking greaseball!"

He'd changed that part of it, too. Kelly's response had been to point out how even in different cultures, men never think to buy birth control.

Instead, Fisk had made it a racial slur, and used that as a transition into a tirade against immigrants. "God, I'm sick of all these people coming into our country. People from countries I never heard of! I think they just start a country, teach 'em to drive cabs, and then send everybody here!"

And so it went for the next five minutes. Fisk's delivery was crude and unpolished. He was jumping from bit to bit. He had no central theme or point of view. He had just chosen what routines had gotten the biggest laughs and strung them together. As a result, what had seemed harmless and playful with other comedians was now ugly and biting. His targets were women, foreigners, minorities, and the elderly. He chose society's oppressed and stomped on them some more. His attitude was that of the sneering dominator, who punished the weak for being so downtrodden and unfortunate they couldn't defend themselves. He couldn't even fake sympathy or compassion.

Fisk didn't understand what the comedian's role could be in a free society: the railer against authority, the social satirist who celebrated the individual over the autonomous monolithic corporations trying to mold us into one consumerist mass, the thoughtful clown who caroms against brick walls that will never come down, and a warrior poet who liberated inner truth—even if that inner truth was how much you didn't like the way toilet paper was packaged, or what was pocket lint and where did it come from.

Comedy was the little man made big, the big man made small, the pompous taking a pratfall, and the pathetic made proud. As Charlie Chaplin once said, "All I need to make a comedy is a park, a policeman, and a pretty girl."

Fisk didn't want to be funny. He just wanted to be famous.

I was mesmerized by this spectacle of comedy one step removed, stripped of its indefinable essence. Fisk's sense of stagecraft was clumsy and inept. He lacked likeability. He had anticharisma. It was like listening to jazz programmed by computer.

Then the phone on my hip rang.

The phone trilled again before I was able to get it out and answer the call. My seat neighbor turned to look at me. I ducked down to talk.

"Hello?"

"Kincaid?" It was Richard Moftus.

"Richard, hi."

"What the hell is going on?"

"The show's started," I said. I was whispering, both hands cupped around the phone.

"Well, I ain't heard from you for the last quarter hour, so I was getting worried."

"I'm okay," I said. "I'm watching the show now, so I'll call you in ten minutes."

"Then that means I got time to go pee," Moftus said, "if I take the phone with me."

"Go for it."

We hung up.

I put the phone back on my hip and noted the time. I'd have to remember to call Moftus back, no matter where I was. I couldn't have the noise of the phone ringing give me away.

At one point in the show Roger stopped tape by abruptly yelling, "Cut! Cut! Cut!" into the mike. Phil walked out onstage with a headset on. Roger made no effort to kill the mike or cover it up as he complained that "the bitch running the TelePrompTer isn't waiting for me to finish before she moves on to the next fucking joke." Phil nodded and said he would attend to it. Then Roger turned to the audience and told us to laugh a little louder, please. "You're all just sitting there like you're dead," he said disdainfully. "Act like it's funnier."

There was an uncomfortable silence until Phil's voice was heard counting down to restart the tape. "Three . . . two . . . one . . ."

I took the time to put in an "I'm okay" call to Moftus: two rings and I hung up. Roger picked up where he had left off. The audience's laughter was louder, but more forced.

I had to call Moftus once more during the show, and it was

just as Roger finished up his act. He had been onstage for a little over thirty minutes and he had used five bits of mine, plus those I recognized from at least two dozen other comedians. He wrapped up with his closing bit, said thank you and good night, and then I heard him stop tape again.

I froze. I'd wanted to use the closing ovation as cover noise while I called Moftus. I had the phone out and in my hand when Roger stopped the show.

"Cut! Cut! Cut!" he screamed at the audience. "You fuckers are supposed to stand up! Goddammit! How many times do you have to be told?"

A lone voice spoke up: "Are you going to have an encore or—?"

"Shut up!" Roger was standing at the front of the stage, his fists clenched at his side, his handsome bronzed face turning crimson, the veins in his neck bulging. Just like when I got into the fight with him at Paradise Isle. "You shut your fucking mouth! You give me a standing ovation as soon as I say good night or I'll clear this place out and bring in a whole new audience! If I have to pay them a hundred dollars a head I will, but you assholes will never get a dime!" He stepped back from the mike, his lips pressed together, his eyes popping. "Now, let's take it from my last line, and when I say good night you better be on your feet!" His vision shifted slightly to the left, and then he stepped forward and grabbed the microphone, pointing his finger and yelling to someone in the audience: "Where are you going? Where the fuck do you think you are going?"

"I quit," came the reply from an upper aisle. Someone was leaving.

"YOU CAN'T FUCKING QUIT ON ME!!" Roger's voice was so shrill it went into a higher register. "I DIDN'T GIVE YOU PERMISSION TO QUIT!!"

No response from the departing extra.

"SECURITY! GRAB THAT MAN! GRAB HIM AND BRING HIM BACK TO HIS SEAT!" Roger was shrieking into the microphone so loudly it was painful to my ears.

From my seat, I could see George waiting patiently in the wings. Phil was whispering in his ear and George nodded. Security didn't do as they were told, probably because they knew they would be charged with kidnapping if they did.

"WHY DIDN'T YOU GRAB HIM?!" Roger screamed. "YOU—YOU'RE ALL FUCKING FIRED!! ALL OF YOU!!"

George and Phil stepped onstage. George distracted Roger while Phil switched his headset back into the PA system.

"Folks," Phil said, "sorry about the confusion, but I think we're going to take it again here from the 'thank-you-good-night.' Just give us a minute to straighten out a few details and then we can wrap it up, okay? Thanks for your patience."

He looked over his shoulder at George, who was calmly listening to Roger as Roger let loose with a stream of invective, gesticulating wildly with his arms. Now would be a good time for me to slip out to the lobby and head backstage.

I took the opportunity to make one more call to Moftus. I let his phone ring once to let him know I was okay, then I shut my phone off and folded it back up, and as I was putting it back in my pocket I dropped it.

It slid under the seats and away from me. I couldn't tell where it had gone. No one seemed to have noticed. Roger had calmed down some, and now George was doing the talking. Phil was talking on a headset to the side of the stage, keeping an eye on George. George turned and gave Phil a single uplifted index finger. One minute.

The crowd was starting to buzz in little pockets, talking amongst themselves. I saw someone reach for a jacket. They were thinking of making a run for it.

I could either wait until the theater was clear and find my phone, or I could head out now.

To hell with the phone. I'd find it later.

I got up out of my seat and walked quickly and quietly to the nearest lobby door. No one said anything. All eyes were on the stage. There was a lone security guy in the lobby, but when he looked at me I flashed my all-access pass and he nodded me on.

I walked out the front door and out into the night air. Vine was still thick with cars. This being Saturday night, the inflowing traffic to Hollywood Boulevard was only going to get worse. I rounded the theater to the alley. The truck Cindy had been standing on had moved. Next door was a parking lot. It was full.

I found a pay phone and called Moftus to tell him I'd lost my phone and I'd call him again in fifteen minutes.

I headed down the alley. Along the side of the theater there were four exits, but only one of them had a small tin canopy and a single rusted lightshade beaming down. I walked toward it. On the scratched metal door was a faded plastic sign: ARTIST'S EN-TRANCE.

Outside was another security goon in a red shirt and black pants, wearing a headset. I walked up to him, my pass cupped in the palm of my hand.

He opened the door for me. "How's the show going?"

"Great," I said. "He's hilarious."

I walked in. Where I found myself was in a corner of the backstage area, beside a series of curtain pulleys. The ropes ran up in the air, disappearing into darkness.

The show was still stopped. I was hidden from the view of anyone in the wings, and I wanted to keep it that way. I saw a metal circular staircase leading to a second story, and I went up it, making sure my shoes didn't ring a rung.

The staircase ended at a wooden doorway, left slightly ajar. I pressed it halfway open with my fingertips. The door opened out onto a hallway lined with dressing rooms. I waited for someone to yell or walk by or do something, but there was no response. I opened the door wider and stepped through, just as I heard Phil count down tape again and Roger say into the microphone, "Now where was I?"

Roger started into his closing bit again, but his words were muffled as I stepped from the metal staircase landing into the hallway and closed the door behind me. The hallway was lit by just a few bare yellowed bulbs. I counted six dressing rooms, all along one side, painted white a long time ago, the doors sitting open or closed to various degrees like a mouth full of dog's teeth. They'd be a good place to hide out—or to ambush someone.

At the end of the hallway there was another door that was the twin of the one I had just come through. It had been left open and through it I could see the top of another metal staircase. This one must have led to the other side of the stage.

I wanted to find Roger's dressing room first. I started with the room nearest the staircase entrance. The door was closed, the paint on it worn and peeled. I opened it up and turned on the lights. There was a mirror set flat against the wall. A steel pipe on wheels for a clothes rack. Bent wire hangers hung from it. A sink. A bathroom with a tub-and-shower combo.

There were five more dressing rooms left. I could hear Roger calling to stop tape again, before the audience applauded. No screaming this time. He had forgotten something. "Could we do it again?" he asked into the mike, and prompted the only real laughter I'd heard from the audience all night long. Roger chuckled at his own unknowing witticism. "Please?" he asked.

Phil's voice came over the PA: "Sure, Rog."

Another round of mild laughter. I didn't have much more time. The second dressing room was the same as the first one. The third one I checked was Roger's.

Roger's dressing room had been cleaned up considerably, and it was double the size of the other two I had seen. There was a bouquet of fresh flowers. I didn't read the card to see who it was from. Maybe he'd sent it to himself. There were blowups of the same photos I'd seen in the lobby, mounted on poster board and hung on the walls. A new couch had been brought in. The bathroom smelled of cologne and fine soap. Thick plush cotton towels hung off the shower curtain rod, still damp from when Roger had used them. Jeans and a T-shirt hung on wooden hangers, next to a garment bag. There was an open bottle of whiskey, a drinking glass with mostly melted ice in it, and a short cut straw powdered with white residue in front of the makeup mirror. Looked as though Roger had needed a little cocaine therapy to help with his stage fright.

I thought the best plan was to wait until Roger was alone, when he was changing clothes, and then surprise him. If George walked in, at least I would have the advantage of having the drop on his boss. I checked Roger's clothes and his hanging bag for weapons. There were none.

I went back out into the hallway. I could use the dressing room next door, but that might be used as a guest bathroom after the show. I checked the remaining two dressing rooms. They were unused, with no signs of habitation. The last one, closest to the door opening onto the second stairway, was butted up against a painted brick wall. It had a light on under the door. I put my ear to it to listen for signs of occupancy but there were none.

I opened the door slowly. No one was inside.

I stepped in and looked around. This might be a good hiding place, if no one else had found it yet. I turned around to close the door and that was when I saw George standing behind me, a gun in his hand.

His head tilted back in pleasant surprise when he saw me.

"Well, well, well," George said, "look who we have here."

I ducked and moved as he spoke but he arced the gun through the air between us and it connected on the side of my head. I stumbled backward and fell against the wall, but by the time I got my feet underneath me he had a forearm under my chin and the gun pressing into my belly button.

"Couldn't stay away, could you?" George whispered, eyes and teeth gleaming in a smile. "Had to come back for one last ass-kicking."

I heard a roar from downstairs, echoing upward from the other side of the hallway, as the crowd rose to its feet and gave Roger Fisk a standing ovation.

The show was over.

TWENTY-NINE

There were loud voices and heavy footsteps coming upstairs. Roger was in a good mood. His laughter echoed in the hallway. A door opened and closed not too far away.

"Roger!" George called. "In here! Looks like I was right!"

"You knew I was coming?" I asked. I wondered if Nancy hadn't waited until tonight to betray me.

George let me go but kept the gun pointed at me. "Hands on your head," he said. I raised them and he patted me down. "No weapons," he said, more to himself than to me, and then with my hands still on my head George punched me in the throat with his fist and planted a second fist in my stomach.

I went back against the wall, falling hard on the wood floor, and sawed air through my throat until I was strong enough to get on my hands and knees. Hearing and vision returned just in time for George to say, "I owe you something, Kincaid." And then he kicked me in the side.

The point of his shoe felt like the blunt end of a pickax. I rolled over on my back, lying like an upturned crab at George's feet. George was entertaining himself with my agony. He looked down at me with all the compassion of an eagle feeding a mouse to her nestlings.

A second figure loomed overhead. Roger Fisk had changed out of his suit and back into his T-shirt and jeans, a towel looped around his neck, his hair spiked from a rubdown. His chiseled features registered genuine surprise.

"Kincaid," Roger said. "What the hell are you doing here?"

"He can't talk so good right now, boss," George said.

"Get him on his feet," Roger said.

George took one side and Roger took the other and they dragged me upright. I managed to lock my wobbling knees as they leaned me against a wall.

Roger leaned out and casually slapped me across the face. "I asked you a question, big boy," he said. "What do you want?"

My voice had lost a lot in transmission. I was as hoarse as a whore in confession. "Same thing as last time," I rasped.

Roger grinned. "Still think I stole your act, huh?"

"I . . . I know you did."

He shook his head slowly. "No, I bought it, asshole," he said. "Fair and square. Product of a free economy."

"Lando . . . sold it to you."

His eyebrows arched like Jack Nicholson. "Who?" He turned to George. "Ned Lando? You know a Ned Lando?"

George shrugged and made a show of looking confused.

Roger looked back at me. "Never heard of him."

My voice was coming back by degrees. "He's dead, isn't he?" I said. "You killed him just like you killed Art Westcott."

"No," Roger said, drawing the *o* sound out, making it go up and down like a roller coaster, the way John Belushi did. "David Kelton killed Lando and . . . who was that other guy?"

"Art Westcott, you son of a bitch."

Roger struck a pose like Steve Martin. "Well, excuuuuuuuuuse *me!* I have a shitty memory for names. Was that why you've been such a pain in the ass?"

"He was my friend," I said. "I found his body."

"You should have just let it go, Kincaid," Roger said. "Now you know too much to go on living."

"You should have stayed in Arizona," I said, "doing the weekend weather drunk off your ass."

Roger's mouth went into an O of mock surprise. "Oh-ho-ho-ho," he chortled, giving George a reaction before ramming his fist under my chin. My head snapped back and connected with the wall behind me. Ouch.

He brought up another forearm across my throat. It was getting tender there. He got in my face so close I could feel his breath.

"You're like all the other comedians I met," Roger said. "You think you all know everything about everybody." He changed his voice to a mocking tone. " 'Gotta start out at the bottom, gotta write your own stuff, takes ten years to get anywhere.' " He gritted his teeth. "And you know what? It gets none of you losers anywhere. You're like rats at the bottom of a barrel, fighting over the last piece of a cheese, while I'm king of the mountain."

He pressed against me harder. I tucked my chin down and was able to keep importing air. "I came out here to make it big, and if you saw tonight's show I already have. So what if I took your act? Who cares? I didn't want to wait ten years while I figured out how to write my own stuff. I hired Lando. I told him what I wanted and he got it for me. Half an hour. Of killer material."

He reached behind him and George put the same butterfly knife in Roger's hand that I'd seen at Paradise Isle. "So you saw Art Westcott, huh?" His lips were pulled back from his teeth. I could see the color of his gums. "You know what? I was there when he got his brains blown out. Think he looked pretty? You wait until I get through with you." He put the knife blade under my nose, lifting it up by millimeters. I started to straighten up. I could feel the blade's sharpness. It was like a poultry knife. I went up on tiptoe. "You won't believe what you see in the mirror. You'll be holding pieces of your face in your hands, and that's before we kill you."

"Let him go, Roger," said a new voice.

Roger's eyes went wide with surprise. The pressure on the knife blade relaxed. He didn't need to turn around. He had known that voice all his life. It belonged to his sister.

Nancy Fisk stood in the doorway, unarmed.

"Where've you been?" I rasped.

"Shut up," Roger said to me mildly.

"I chickened out," Nancy said to me. "Then I came back."

George turned toward Nancy, pulling the gun from his jacket, and Roger said, "Stay, George."

George stayed.

Roger held me against the wall with one hand. "Nancy," he said as he faced his sister. "You shouldn't have come here."

"Roger," Nancy said, "let Biff go." She stepped into the dressing room and closed the door behind her.

Roger shoved himself away from me with a palm to my chest. I eased back against the wall. Neither Roger nor George were looking at me now. I felt something warm under my nose and touched it. Blood.

"How did you find me this time, Nancy?" Roger said. He'd been surprised by his sister before. It was in his tone.

"Biff brought me," Nancy said. "I'm here to take you home, Roger."

"But I don't want to go home, Nancy." He sounded like a child who'd been caught experimenting on the family dog with his chemistry set.

"You need help," she said. "I'm your sister and I'm here to help you."

Roger chuckled mirthlessly. "You know who you sound like?" he said. "You sound just like Mom."

"Mom would have dragged you out of LA by your ear weeks ago," she said.

"And then I would have gone to Dad and Dad would have let me do whatever the hell I wanted," Roger said. "Because I was Dad's favorite."

"Shut up," Nancy said. Her face had gone pale. Her lips lost their blush.

"Girls can't come to the office with Daddy," he said in a child-like voice. "Girls need to stay home and play house."

George looked at Roger. I looked at George. Neither of us knew what to make of this.

"Father and I were working on the latest development project for years," Nancy said. "He wanted me to finish it. He wanted me to pick up where he left off."

"I got news for you, Sis," Roger said. Roger toyed with the knife, as though it was a plaything. "I was Dad's favorite project. Dad didn't give a shit what the girls in the family did. You know why? Because you were just going to get married and pump out babies, none of whom were going to bear the family name." He shook his head. "You and sister Lizzie both. See, I was the only boy. I had the name. I had the seed." He grabbed his crotch and shook it. "And that's why you work for me, not the other way around."

"A mistake," Nancy said. "You being left in charge was a mistake."

"No, the mistake was when you fired me from the TV station," Roger said. His childish demeanor was gone. He stopped playing with the knife. "See, that's when I knew you thought you knew better. You always did. Now I'm making it big in Hollywood and you can't stand it."

"Stealing other comedians' jokes and hiring an audience of

actors to laugh at you isn't making it big," Nancy said.

"Who told you that? Biffy Boy here?" He pointed the knife at me. "Well, he's not going to be around much longer to cause anyone any more trouble, but if you ask me I don't think Biff knows the first thing about making it in Hollywood. He hasn't done it. He's not a big star. See, this cable special's just the beginning. I haven't even told you about Phase Two."

"What's Phase Two?" Nancy asked.

"My own feature film," Roger said, grinning broadly. "Shot right here in Hollywood. Lights, cameras, action. Hey, a good script, the right budget, I'll be the next big thing this time next year."

"What kind of budget are we talking about, Roger?"

"I'd say ten or twenty million ought to do it," Roger said.

"We don't have that kind of money to make a movie, Roger," Nancy said. "Certainly not to make a movie and finish the Carter township project, which is what Dad wanted."

"Yeah, *we* don't have twenty million," Roger said. "*I* do. Of course, that's just to shoot the damn thing. Then there's prints, marketing, distribution, advertising, the premiere parties . . . you wait and see. It's going to be something."

He cackled, an audience of one.

Nancy looked down at the floor, angry and weary at the same time. "Roger, people are dead."

He shrugged, tossing the knife in the air again. "I didn't kill 'em."

"But you hired the people who did."

"So?"

"So Dad is not around to clean up after you anymore," she said, her voice rising. "And I refuse to do it. I will not be the one to sweep your misdeeds under the rug anymore."

"Misdeeds?" Roger guffawed. "Oh, you don't know the half of it," he laughed. "We're not talking parking fines here. We're talking men, on their knees . . ." He clasped his hands in front of him in mock prayer, giggling. "Begging for their lives. If that doesn't get me the high-roller's suite in Hell, I don't know what will."

She kept talking. "I want you to walk out of here, with me, tonight. Alone. If you owe anyone any money, I'll pay it. If you have any loose ends, I'll take care of them. But this has to stop now."

Roger stopped being amused. He tossed the knife in the air and caught it by the handle. "No fucking way, Sis," he said, as if she'd asked him to borrow the keys to his car. "I ain't going with you nowhere, no time, nohow."

She raised her eyes and looked at him. Moisture streamed down her cheeks in twin trails. "I'm so sorry to hear that," she said.

He tossed the knife again. "You don't know how sorry," he said. He nodded at me. "We're going to pin all our troubles here on old Biffy-poo: three bodies so far, plus his own suicide." He held the knife in an underhanded posture, facing his sister. "But if I were to throw you into the batch, then how much trouble do you think I would save myself, huh, Nance?" He took a step toward her and grabbed a handful of her hair, suddenly yanking her head back. Nancy grimaced in pain. "I am so very tired," Roger said through clenched teeth as he raised the knife to her neck, "of you fucking with my life."

"George," Nancy said, her voice strained.

"Yes, Miss Fisk?" George said.

"Now," Nancy said.

"Yes, Miss Fisk."

Roger looked from Nancy to George to Nancy again. George's gun had been on me. Now it went to Roger. The balance of power had shifted.

Roger relaxed his grip in Nancy's hair, the knife loose in his hand. "Hey," Roger said, "George, what the—?"

And then George raised his gun and shot Roger Fisk in the face.

THIRTY

The gunshot wrenched Roger's head back on his shoulders minus an eye. In its place was a dark splayed mess the size, shape, and color of a wet rose. He fell against the wall, but since his brain was no longer operating his arms and shoulders he lurched backward and plummeted to the floor like a dummy made from pillow stuffing, still clutching the knife.

George's gun was very quiet, the shot not loud enough to make my ears ring. I was standing against a wall, and I stayed there.

I looked from Roger's dead body oozing oily red fluid from the head over to George, ready to claim the kill, and then to Nancy, her tear-lined face turned away from her dead brother. She didn't want to have to see.

George saw she wasn't looking. He stepped over and probed Roger's throat with his whole hand, feeling for a pulse. "Fuck, I think I broke his neck," he said softly to no one in particular. He straightened and looked at Nancy, waiting for his next orders. She lifted her face to look into mine. Her grief was old. Her brother had died a long time ago. This was just the messy inevitable conclusion, like putting to sleep a beloved pet gone mad.

"Biff . . . ," she said.

I waited.

She spread her hands, gesturing at the dead body on the floor. As if there was anything she could say.

"How long," I said, "has he been working for you?" I nodded at George when I said "he." George didn't mind. His face had as much expression as an executioner's hood. His gun was still out and ready.

"All along," George answered. "Before we left Arizona."

"George came to me and told me what Roger was up to, like you did," Nancy said. "He said he wanted to help the family."

"You mean the family fortune," I said.

"Biff, you have to understand," Nancy said. "Roger was going to spend it all. Millions. Everything my father worked for. I couldn't let that happen."

"So this was all a setup," I said. "My act getting stolen, the show, everything."

She shook her head. "Roger did what he wanted to do. George did as Roger told him. I just wanted to know where he was and what he was doing. I truly thought his crazy schemes would run their course and I could get him back to Arizona. But . . ." She tried not to look at her brother's corpse, but she couldn't help herself. Maybe she had never seen a dead body before. "Something went wrong."

"What?"

"You, asshole," George said. His gun was looking at me like a next meal.

"Sorry," I said.

"Shut up," George replied.

Nancy took a step forward and I felt myself press against the wall behind me. She saw me recoil and stopped. "Biff, it doesn't have to be this way," she said. "If you want, you can have it all back. Your act. Everything. I'll even give you money. More than you've ever had in your life."

"If . . . ?" I said.

"If you just . . . help me," Nancy said.

"How?"

"Say it was you who did all this," she said. Fresh tears coursed down her cheeks. "Roger and Ned Lando and Art Westcott."

"Confess to triple murder?" I said. "I don't think so."

"When I'm through with you, you'll say you killed OJ's wife," George said.

Nancy took another step toward me, her voice pleading. "Biff, I have lawyers. They can help you. You might not even have to spend a day in jail. Ever. I promise. And when it's all over, I'll set you up with enough money for the rest of your life. Maybe . . . someday . . . it's hard to imagine right now . . . but we can even be together again."

I looked at her, then at George, then at Roger's dead body.

"Your brother's not the only one who's bad," I said to Nancy. "Killing must run in the family."

Nancy Fisk looked at me for a long, quiet minute. "Then I'm sorry you feel that way, Biff," she said.

I'd heard that tone before, just a few minutes ago. Before she'd ordered her brother shot in the head.

"You going to kill me?" I said. The back of my mouth had the same taste and consistency as a roll of pennies.

Nancy backed away from me. Blood from her brother's brain was leaking across the floor, and she looked down to make sure she wasn't stepping in it. She didn't say anything.

"To answer your question," George said, as if he was being asked if he wanted parmesan cheese on his spaghetti, "I think so. Yeah." He reached forward with his foot and dragged the knife out of Roger's lifeless grasp and along the floor toward him, fishing a leather glove out of his pocket. "But it's got to look good. A struggle to the end, you know?" He pulled the glove onto one hand with his teeth and picked the knife up off the floor, thinking out loud. "So if you have a gun and I have a knife, then I would have to mortally wound you before you killed me. Then you'd bleed to death on the floor before help can arrive." He shifted to a bad imitation of Jon Lovitz. "Yeah, that's it. That's the ticket." He chuckled to himself. "I loved that liar guy, didn't you?"

"You won't get away with this," I said.

"You know how many times I heard that right before I snuffed a guy's candle?" George said. He hefted the knife and stepped forward. "So for it to look convincing, I'm gonna have to slit open your belly and let your guts ooze out. That's gonna take some time. About ten minutes. I've done it before. A slow way for you to die, and I get to watch." He cocked his head and his eyes traveled over my face and upper body. "Maybe a few more struggle wounds—like missing an ear or a stab all the way through the hand." He turned to Nancy. "You probably should wait outside."

Nancy nodded, looked at me in farewell, and opened the door to the dressing room.

"Hi, Kincaid," Richard Moftus said, standing in the hallway dressed in a duster and a flat-brimmed fedora and holding a double-barreled shotgun. "Sorry I'm late."

Nancy screamed and dropped to the floor. If it was her instinct, it was a good one, because Richard held the shotgun at waist level and would have cut her in half with the blast if she had been standing in the way.

George turned around with the knife in one hand and his handgun in the other and fired once at the doorway. Moftus staggered back into the hall with a look of surprise on his face as the slug hit him in the chest.

Nancy scrambled out into the hallway, literally over Moftus's body. Moftus yelled in pain as her knee dug into his groin. George stepped forward, standing in the doorway, and aimed a shot directly into Moftus's open mouth. He would have blown Richard's head off except I leaped on him from behind, looping an arm around his neck and jerking his head back.

The bullet went into the wall above Richard's head and George dropped his gun. It fell to the floor.

George and I staggered backward into the dressing room. I couldn't bring him down, just change his direction. He whipped around, trying to shake me off. I lifted my legs off the ground and wrapped them around his waist. My shoulder knocked against the dressing room door and it slammed shut on the hallway just as another load from Moftus's shotgun blew a hole in the baseboard.

We were now stuck in the dressing room together. George roared like a wounded gorilla and we went down as one onto the floor, hard.

I shoved myself away from him and got to my feet. Some of Moftus's shot had caught George in the foot. He rolled over on all fours with the knife in his hand and he was ready for me. We were both already bleeding.

I lunged for him and he whipped the blade through the air in an arc that sliced me across the forearm less than an inch deep. I yelled and threw myself against him as his arm completed its semicircle and rammed both of us up against the wall, driving a rusty coat hook deep into his back so hard he grunted.

Someone tried the lock on the door to the dressing room. Moftus. The doorknob was stuck. He put the weight of his body against it and it held. Again. That was a lot of weight. The door was jammed solid.

I tried to move George around on the metal hook already in his body to work it in deeper but he dropped the knife into his other hand and jabbed up at me from below, sticking me on my right, just below the right side of my rib cage. I jumped back and he came at me, my blood on the blade.

Another shotgun blast roared through the room and the lock and surrounding wood disintegrated. A mirror on the wall shattered. I couldn't see what happened next because I fell backward and tripped over Roger Fisk's dead outstretched legs. I lost my balance and twisted in midair to land on the floor, my palms full of glass shards and wooden splinters.

I had a second's mercy, and then felt George impact on top of me, driving me face first into the floor. The knife ripped into my side, cutting me open just below my right armpit. It was a glancing cut, long and shallow, piercing only skin and fat. The next one would count.

Pressing against the pain, I shoved with my left hand while dropping my right, rolling George onto the floor and using his own weight to pin his knife arm. I still had my back to him. I could either escape or attack.

The door to the dressing room was kicked open and Richard Moftus stood there, shotgun in hand, like a Brahma bull.

This time George was not so slow with the knife. From behind me he threw it so it whipped through the air and sank into Richard's bicep on the arm that held the shotgun.

Richard sputtered and dropped the shotgun. It clattered to the floor. I scrambled to get the gun as Richard pulled the knife from his shoulder and held it ready, leaning against the wall.

I got my hands on the shotgun. Moftus was leaning against the door frame, his arm soaked in blood. I pumped a shell into the chamber as George bent down to pick something up off the floor. He'd found his handgun.

Moftus said, "Kincaid."

George wheeled around, bringing his sights to bear.

I fired.

The shotgun blast filled the room with smoke and sound. I yelled.

It looked as though someone had dumped a bucket of spaghetti sauce into George's lap while he was still standing up. The impact shoved him back against the wall. The gun slowly fell out of George's hand onto the floor. As his butt slid down the wall, he groped for the gun again, but this time like a blind man.

I stepped through the doorway and tried to pump another shell into the shotgun chamber. Empty. Now that's luck.

I used the end of the barrel to scoot George's gun away from his hands and he looked up at me, blood bubbling from the corners of his mouth, soaking his goatee. For a second, it seemed as if he wasn't sure who I was or what he was doing there dying on the floor of a dressing room at the Doug Stone Theater.

I heard Moftus fumble out his cellular phone and call for an ambulance. I bent down to look George in the eyes.

"We're getting help," I said to him.

"If they were here now," George muttered, "it'd be too late."

He slowly slumped over on the floor, his ear coming to rest on a piece of broken wood. It was becoming difficult for him to keep his eyes open.

I couldn't think of anything to say. My side burned from his knife wound. Roger Fisk was cooling down. Kelton and Lando were dead. Our friend George had just stacked up too much bad karma in one night and gotten gutshot.

"Never thought I'd be done in by a comedian," he whispered.

I still couldn't think of anything to say. He coughed. More blood came out his nose and mouth, and his eyes stopped moving in midblink. Life slid out of him and went somewhere else, if it ever goes anywhere after you're through with it.

I heard Moftus walk in the room behind me. I stood. I pumped the shotgun once more to make sure it was empty. It, too, was dead.

I handed it over to Moftus, who leaned it against the wall with his good arm. "The sister got away," he said.

"She won't get far," I said. "She's not an experienced traveler."

Moftus sat himself down on the floor, wincing. He opened his coat to reveal a Kevlar vest, damaged by the round George had fired at him. "Damn bulletproof vests," he said. "If the shot don't kill you, you feel like you busted a rib."

Sirens in the background, faint. Growing louder. I couldn't stop looking at George's half-closed eyes.

"Your first one, huh, kid?" Moftus said.

I nodded numbly. "I don't even know his last name," I said.

"You won't sleep," he said. "Not tonight."

The sirens found what they were looking for. Us.

"And after that?" I asked.

"You'll need my boat."

THIRTY-ONE

I hung up the cellular phone and went topside on the *Trifecta*, carrying a Perrier still in the bottle for Kelly and a Murphy's in a pint glass for me. As I climbed out of the galley, the boat rocked slightly against a wave and I stopped so I wouldn't spill anything. The balancing act caused me to lean on the side that still had stitches. They pinched, but didn't pull.

It was a clear day on the ocean, with just enough breeze to get us to Catalina. Kelly was the captain, standing at the wheel, keeping an eye on the sail trim. Every now and then she'd have me adjust something, but right now we were on course, the harbor and Avalon dead ahead. The air smelled sweet and salty, the only sound of traffic that of the waves beneath us. No motors, no people.

It was Thursday. It had been five days.

I handed Kelly the Perrier and offered a toast. "Torpedos away."

She swigged. She was wearing a one-piece black racing swimsuit, scooped low in the back and cut high over her shapely thighs. She was letting her red hair fly in the breeze and looked at me through a pair of reflective lenses. "Now what exactly do you mean by that?"

"You'll find out when we moor at Catalina," I said, fitting myself just behind her.

"If I can wait that long," she said. She moaned and arched her back as I kissed her on the neck. "Might need you to swab the deck."

"Sounds kinky," I said. I felt her move as she helmed the boat and I stepped back and sat down. "Sure you don't want anything stronger than that water?"

She shook her head. "Not while I'm driving."

I nodded. "Good idea."

"How was Richard?" she asked. "You were on the phone with him awhile."

"He's better," I said. "Turns out he did break a few ribs, but it was when he was fighting his way through the security guard outside the artist's entrance at the theater." I chuckled. "One of them had to be treated for a concussion. A six-foot, two-inch bodybuilder and Richard Moftus takes him down like a flyweight."

"He's tough, our Richard," she said.

"Oh, he's got his soft spots."

No comment. Just wind and sails and sea. We'd been sailing for more than an hour. The breeze made my T-shirt flap.

Richard had been right. I hadn't slept the first night after I'd shot George. The cops told me his last name was Selia. No known family. The cops had plenty of questions for me that same night, so I didn't have much time to think about it. When I got home, by myself, it had hit me. I found myself looking up at the Hollywood sign at night, watching the sun come up as the coyotes went to bed.

"What about Roger's sister Nancy?" Kelly asked. She dipped

her head to look at me over her mirrored sunglasses. She was a very pretty lady. "The one that hired that guy."

I took a draft of my Murphy's. Someday I was going to go to Ireland and drink it out of a tap right at the brewery in Cork.

"She's dead."

Nancy Fisk had escaped the dragnet the cops had placed for her at LAX. She had changed hotels before coming to the theater, and went there to grab her belongings, which included a suitcase full of cash. She traded some of it for a car off a lot on Century Boulevard and drove back to Arizona in the night. When she got back to Show Low she got her father's pistol and went to the construction site for the Carter, Arizona, Community Center and shot herself there.

She had stayed on life support for three days before she died.

"How well did you know her?" Kelly asked.

"It turns out not at all," I said.

I heard a low whoosh and looked to see. There were dolphins racing the boat in its bow wave.

"And what about you?" Kelly asked. "Where did you go?"

I looked up at her, squinting. My sunglasses were looped around my neck. I put them on but didn't say anything.

"We've been together since eight o'clock last night and you've said maybe twenty sentences, not one of them a joke," Kelly said. "I think you talked to Richard more on the phone just now than you have to me. I called him to find out what happened, since you didn't want to talk about it. You must have gotten up a dozen times last night to do God knows what. Walk around in the dark, I think."

"I killed a man," I said.

"And you never have before?"

"No," I said.

"He sounded like a bad character to me," she said. "Maybe he had it coming."

I shook my head. "I've shot people before, but they didn't die."

"Then maybe you had this coming, too."

I looked at her without my sunglasses.

"What I mean," she said as she glanced over her shoulder, "is you play rough. You get in fights, you carry guns, you don't back down. For a comedian, that's a little extreme."

"You'd be surprised," I said.

"That's why it put me off at first, when you told me those stories and showed me those firearms," she said. "I thought: someday, he's going to kill someone or get himself killed." She brought us alongside a mooring buoy just within the harbor. She crawled over the boat like a monkey to tie us off but kept talking. "So now that happened, and you're tormented by it. Could you have not killed him? Maybe. But he was a professional, hired to do a job. He would have killed you with no more thought than you would have shot a rat." She went to the bow and dropped anchor. Then she came back and sat by me, so close her knee touched mine. "It's the path both of you chose. This was a possible outcome. You both thought you would survive. You were right. He was wrong. That's all. You're obsessing over a given risk. You think it was a momentary quirk of fate, when it was there all the time."

I switched hands on the Murphy's and put my fingers in hers. She took them. I could fall in love with this woman.

"Biff, you haven't performed in almost a week, have you?"

I shook my head. "How did you know that?"

"I called the clubs," she said. "I was trying to get hold of you. You unplugged your phone. I had to call Richard. He was the only one you were talking to." She took my one hand in both of hers. "You have to go up right away. You have to do comedy again. Soon. Never mind George Selia and Roger Fisk and Nancy

Fisk and Ned Lando and David Kelton. They're all dead. Don't let your sense of humor die with them."

"I'm not ready yet," I said, "to get back onstage."

"If there's one thing I learned from getting into comedy," she said, "it's don't wait until you feel ready. Just jump on in."

I tried to smile.

"You told me there was a gig on Catalina," she said, tilting her head towards the island. "Runs Wednesday through Saturday."

"I know," I said. "I've played it."

"I called the manager," Kelly said. "He said he'd give you some stage time. A ten-minute guest spot. Every night we're here, including both shows Friday and Saturday."

I looked down at my shoes. "You take it," I said.

"I would," she said, "but I'm quitting."

I looked up. At her. "You're quitting comedy?"

She nodded. "I'm going to go back to being a stockbroker," she said. "My old firm has an opening." She took a deep breath and let it out. "I start Monday."

"But what about Chortles?" I said. "Richard said—"

"Richard's going to sell the club," Kelly said. "He wants me to invest the money. It's not much after the mortgage, but I'll do what I can. He's moving aboard this thing and booking road gigs." She patted the boat on a cushion. "Soon as he heals up."

We were sitting in the water, just outside of Avalon, gently bobbing on the waves. A water taxi came by to take us onshore but I waved him off.

"I'll be getting up at four in the morning," she said, "to be at the office by the time the market opens. That means going to bed at eight. It's like I'm hosting a morning show or something." She sighed. "I'm going to have to buy a second alarm clock. You've seen how quickly I wake up."

I nodded.

"But . . . maybe on the weekends . . . unless you have a spot at the Store . . . you could come down . . . or we'd meet for dinner . . ."

"It won't work," I said.

She fell silent.

"I've tried it before," I said. "I'm up until midnight every night, at least. I sleep until ten. I don't choose that schedule, that's just the way it is. And that's when I'm in town. In ten days I'm supposed to go on the road."

"Where are you going?"

"Florida."

"How long are you gone for?" she asked.

"A month."

More silence. Waves lapped and sucked at the side of Moftus's boat. Catalina Harbor is a great place for long pauses in conversation. They don't seem so quiet.

"So what do we do?" she said. She was looking at a distant point on the horizon and seemed to be blinking a lot.

"We go into Avalon," I said. "And I'll do the first show tomorrow night. You do the second. Saturday night we switch."

She smiled with half her mouth. "I told you I quit," she said.

"One last show," I said. "One last gig."

She reached a finger under her sunglasses and rubbed at the corner of one eye. I squeezed her hands harder. I didn't mean to make her cry.

"You know," she said, "I've never done a road gig."

"You haven't?"

She shook her head. "This would be my first."

"You ever been to this club?"

"No."

"It's great," I said. "About a hundred seats. Tables set in a semicircle. Great sound system. It's the weekend and it's close to summer so it'll be packed."

"I didn't bring any stage clothes," she said.

"Neither did I," I said. "Wear what you got on."

"This?" She pulled at the black elastic fabric of her swimsuit.

"Yeah," I said. "Put a skirt around it if you have to."

"I . . . I . . . left my notebook . . . with all my material . . ."

"Didn't you say something about not waiting until you're ready?" I said. "Jumping right in?"

She looked at me from behind her sunglasses, the smile going from a half to a full, and then she leaned forward and kissed me and I kissed her back. We had not made love in a week. Now I could feel the pent-up lust in all its force, hooves beating at the stalls, ready to bolt.

My hands raced up the sides of her swimsuit, gently molding her flesh. Her mouth opened wide and I wrapped her up in my arms. For just a second, I felt like I was in the end of a James Bond movie.

A loud air horn interrupted us and we both turned to look. It was a ferryboat carrying tourists just leaving Catalina. Some were wearing shorts, loud hats, and cameras, clicking away at us, yelling encouragement.

I waved back. Kelly hid her face against my shoulder, laughing. "Now when you become famous those'll turn up in the tabloids," she said to me. "I'll be married and have two kids and my daughter will come to me and say, 'Mommy, when did you know that Kincaid man?' "

I whispered, "And your husband will want to ask, 'What did you do after that?' "

"And I'll tell him," she said. "I'll tell him every filthy erotic detail of the whole weekend."

I stood up and looked at the sun's position. Hours to go before it set, over the island's hills.

I took her hand and brought her to her feet. "He'll lie awake that night," I said, "wondering what kind of woman he married."

"A tart," she said, leaning against me. "A hot, horny, red-headed floozy who once screwed a comedian because he was cute and funny and had a big boy downstairs."

The boats moored nearby were empty. I picked Kelly up. She liked it so much she let out a whoop. My stitches didn't feel so great when I did that, but what the hell. I turned to the open companionway and the doors that led to the cabin and the bedroom below.

"The poor bastard," I said.

"He doesn't know what he's in for," Kelly said.

"I don't even know him," I said, "and already I feel sorry for him."

She laughed, all the way down.

ABOUT THE AUTHOR

Dan Barton is a professional stand-up comedian.